THE GIRL
WHO WASN'T CHOSEN

THE GIRL
WHO WASN'T CHOSEN

A.y. Johlin

Copyright © 2022 by A.y. Johlin

All rights reserved. No part of this publication may be reproduced, stored or transmitted in any form or by any means, electronic, mechanical, photocopying, recording, scanning, or otherwise without written permission from the publisher. It is illegal to copy this book, post it to a website, or distribute it by any other means without permission.

This novel is entirely a work of fiction. The names, characters and incidents portrayed in it are the work of the author's imagination. Any resemblance to actual persons, living or dead, events or localities is entirely coincidental.

A.y. Johlin asserts the moral right to be identified as the author of this work.

First edition

ISBN: 978-0-578-36542-8

This book was professionally typeset on Reedsy. Find out more at reedsy.com

To Natalie—
For being the best little sister I could ever ask for

Chapter 1: An Old Man Ruins My Life

Jumping out of windows is harder than it looks. Sneaking away from my dad? Even harder. This time he grabs me in midair with his meaty hands. They sink into my shoulders like falcon claws, plopping me onto the floor. Its mossy floorboards scratch up my knees. I glance at the sunny window behind me, packed with bright banners and whispering crowds. I was so close to joining them. So close to meeting him. But instead, I get another lecture. Great.

"Leda, what'd I say about jumping out of windows?" he demands. He's a tall man with a slick bald head, furry brown beard, and big belly. The combination makes him resemble a fuzzy bear, which usually causes me to hug him. But not today. Today I don't have time for hugs.

"Not to do it until I've put my shoes on so I look nice for the ceremony?" I squeak. Curse my high-pitched ten-year-old voice! It always makes me sound like I'm nervous. For the record, I am never nervous. That's probably why my parents want to install boards on our windows.

"Daddy! Daddy!" Two kids burst into the bedroom. Mack and Nella. My annoying little siblings. They each have a fistful of shaggy hazel hair and grubby fingers. Grubby fingers which latch onto my dad's legs, yanking him away from me. He sighs, pinching my nose. "Just go prepare with everybody else. I don't want my coolest daughter looking bad for today's ceremony." He turns his back to me, addressing my siblings instead. I hang my head as he laughs with them. Fine. I guess I'll do what he says since sneaking past him is impossible. Then I drag myself into my family's glass shop, which is attached to our house's front.

The stench of moss whams into me first. Then the clink of tiny glass statues, the stuffy cobblestone walls, and the chilly windows which normally mark the entrance to my family's shop. Today, people cluster inside it. I mean, it's always stuffed with people since there's nine of us, counting Mom and Dad. But now we've invited the neighbors too. The noise alone nearly drives me to jump out the window again. Kids argue over which fingerless leather gloves to wear while women braid seaflowers into their hair and men smash berries in wooden buckets. The commotion is in preparation for today's choosing ceremony, but why work this hard if we arrive so late that the Skycharter misses us? How can he pick the best Sun if he can't see all the candidates?

I sigh. The least I can do is put my sandals on so I look good for the Skycharter. Then maybe try another escape plan. I trudge over to the kids wrestling over gloves. The sandals should be on the other side, wedged right underneath the fighting kids.

"I want the dark ones!" one girl screeches.

"But they're mine, my grandma bought them for me!" a boy argues.

"Excuse me," I say.

"Well, she said I could have them."

CHAPTER 1: AN OLD MAN RUINS MY LIFE

"She said I could have them too!" a different girl says.

"Hey, let me through!" I yell. Finally, a few eyes turn towards me and some kids shift, creating an opening in their thick crowd. The hum of sweaty bodies presses against my shoulders. I reach in between them, onto the back shelf where one pair of leather sandals rest. Only for a short boy with chubby cheeks to snatch them before I can. Gabriel. My second little brother. He giggles at me, then races off to play with a few friends. Ugh. I roll my eyes, searching for another pair under the shelves. That's when the whispers start.

"Who is that girl again? The one who yelled?" a tall girl asks. My face burns as my body stiffens. I thought Mira would've remembered my name. We talked yesterday.

The boy beside Mira shrugs. "Dunno. But I'm guessing one of the Roubis kids. I kinda remember Alec saying he had two little sisters." Bare wood scratches against my palms. There are no sandals left.

"Really? Another sister?" She tilts her head. "There's so many Roubis kids, I only remember the interesting ones." Interesting ones? My lip quivers as I leave the crowd. It doesn't matter. A bunch of older kids won't make me sad for today's ceremony.

My shoulders droop anyways as I trudge over to a jar decorated with painted blue flowers. There's nothing inside the foggy glass piece. Oh great. If I'm the only girl without seaflowers braided in my hair, I'll be the laughing stock of Walend! There's no way the Skycharter'll pick me then.

I twist my body around the counter to face a lady surrounded by a flock of other women. She braids the hair of a younger girl, her laughter bouncing off the various glass statues, pots, and cups.

"Mom!" I call. "Do you have any extra—"

"And then I told him he needed to—" she continues. I stomp my foot. The women finally glance at me. But their hazy eyes latch onto the screaming kids and rowdy men behind me instead.

"Do you have any seaflowers left?"

"Oh, I thought I already braided flowers into your hair, Nella?" My mom stares at Irene, my older sister, continuing to weave glowing flower petals into her inky hair.

"I'm not Nella, Mom," I grumble. I don't even look like my youngest sister. She's six!

"Oh, I'm sorry sweetie. We don't have any left." She returns to chatting with her friends.

I sigh, tiptoeing towards the door. Then I open it, glancing back at Dad. He's busy chatting too. Well, at least I can leave early now!

The smell of seawater and a ring of eerie black mountains greet me as I leave. My house borders our village's edges near the Aurorian Mountains, the mountain range that grew out of the sea and trapped our country from the world. I wiggle my toes in the pine-green grass. Then smile. Because today's going to change my life. Today I'm going to be—

"How long are you going to wiggle your toes in the grass?" A boy my age glances up from his book. I don't talk to him often but I'd recognize those black curls anywhere. Jorge Makos. The farmer boy who taught himself to read.

"As long as it takes to cheer me up." I cross my arms, wiggling my toes even harder. He narrows his eyes. "Hey, at least I don't spend my time reading!"

Jorge flips a page. "I'm reading because I actually have a dream. Someday, I'm going to be accepted into Evin's

CHAPTER 1: AN OLD MAN RUINS MY LIFE

Academy for Special Children. You probably don't even understand what it's like to dream."

"I do too!"

He raises an eyebrow. My dream is even better than going to our capital's best boarding school. I mean, who wants to go to school?

"I'm going to be the next Sun." Just the thought of being Solia's next hero sends tingles down my spine. Crowds cheering for me as I fight monsters. People screaming in joy when I finally destroy the Aurorian Mountains. I can't wait! "I've been training for years now. Practicing sword fighting with a broom and doing push-ups every morning. It's pretty serious."

Jorge snorts. "You want the Skycharter to choose you? That's even crazier than getting accepted into an Evin Academy."

"The crazier the dream, the better it is." I brush off my dress. "Anyways, I've gotta get to the ceremony early to get in front of the crowd. Seeya later!" I skip off to the center of our village. Grassy fields morph into dirt roads peppered with wildflowers.

"Hey, wait!" Jorge jogs behind me, dodging a lanky woman. His mouth twists into a sneer. Oh great. He's going to mock me again. Surprisingly, it then twitches into a smile. "I want to see the look on everyone's faces when the Skycharter picks a girl from Walend as our next Sun."

I grin. Maybe he's not so bad after all. I'll just have to convince him that school is not worth it. Mom still tells me horror stories about the time she accidentally got stuck in one when trading glass pieces in Evin. Well, when she has time to talk to me. Six other kids and a shop to run doesn't leave lots of time.

"Plus, you're forgetting this." He reaches into his pocket and pulls out a glowing blue flower. Its petals curl like fish fins and it reeks of sea water (like basically everyone in my village does). At the flower's base is a twisted, moon-white stem.

"A-a seaflower," I stammer, then clear my throat. "Thank you! Where'd you get it?"

"I pulled it off a cliff for my mom. She doesn't need it, though. She has a bunch of them already." He tosses it to me and I tuck it behind my ear. "I had to fight a few Ocean Eaters to get it."

I touch my ear. "You had to fight monsters and climb a cliff to get this? That's so cool!" I cheer then rush further into Walend's center.

There, masses of people with brown hair and eyes like my own await the ceremony. Dark purple banners swing, their silky surfaces brushing my shoulders. Walls belonging to rocky houses trap the crowd in the village's narrow streets, causing the nervous whispering and trampling of feet to echo across the streets. The strong aroma of trampled wildflowers wafts through the crowd, while the blur of leather and sweaty backs swarms my vision. Jorge and I still manage to emerge at the crowd's front, where a few children fidget with their thick clothing and kick up dirt.

"Ladies and gentlemen, welcome the magnificent Skycharter!" Walend's Lord booms overhead. He rests on a wooden makeshift stage, which is riddled with holes and smells like an odd mixture of rats and body odor. Not exactly the best first impression you can give a visitor. Or the eager crowd watching the ceremony. I try not to let the stitched-together curtains, creaky old boards, and foul stench bother me.

What I focus on is the wiry man standing at the stage's

CHAPTER 1: AN OLD MAN RUINS MY LIFE

podium. The Skycharter. The only living man I've met who knows what's beyond the Aurorian Mountains. If that isn't awesome, I don't know what is.

He wears a purple and blue robe, embroidered in silver with maps of the sky. The thin cloth looks as smooth as a baby's cheek. Then there's his warm brown eyes and long, stormy gray beard. It has to be the biggest beard that's ever existed! That settles it. He's officially the coolest guy ever.

"I'm pleased to finally be here, in, ah..." he pauses, checking the slip of paper in front of him. Of course he forgot the name of my village. Walend is never on any Solian map. "Walend, such an adorable little village." The Skycharter clears his throat, surveying the crowd with sharp eyes. Villagers flood the small roads. Some even sit on grassy patches in the shade. Others lean out the windows of their houses, peering at the man through slitted eyes.

"For hundreds of years, one man from my world, the glorious world outside Solia, has made the treacherous journey of crossing the Aurorian Mountains which trap you all in a land filled with dangerous monsters and little food. Our hope is that our superior knowledge can save you from these terrors," the Skycharter declares. His voice sounds like the chiming of bells mixed with the crackling of a cozy fire. The crowd and I lean forward as his warm words swarm our ears.

"Today, I will use that knowledge to pick your new Sun." I beam, bouncing on the soles of my feet. The afternoon sun and my smile warm my cheeks. "This child will grow up to become Solia's savior, protecting you from murderous monsters and conniving criminals. At least until the next Skycharter returns to choose a new Sun in fifty years. This very child will try, like the twenty-four Suns before them, and may even succeed in destroying the Aurorian Mountains and freeing Solia, reestablishing its former glory."

Giddy whispers arise from the crowd. Jorge cracks a smile. Just the thought of leaving the clenches of the Aurorian Mountains melts any Solian's heart.

The Skycharter clears his throat again. Dozens of eyes latch back onto him. "Now, to determine if this person is among us today, if Solia's next hero will come from Walend, I will use the same method my people have used for an eternity: consulting the sky." The crowd murmurs, nudging each other. We're all wondering the same question. What does he mean? What sort of magic will he use to choose our Sun?

Gasps erupt as the Skycharter twists his body upwards, cranking his neck so that his head directly faces the sky. His body goes slack while his fingers twitch in the humid air. Then, in a fit of sudden madness, he bellows, "Oh dear sky, tell me if our new Sun is here!" I follow his gaze upwards to the stone-like clouds.

A raindrop slaps my forehead, spreading its icy touch across my face. Seconds later thunder crackles. Gasps erupt.

"Our Sun is here!" The Skycharter's voice lowers. Puffy, amazed breaths trail his words.

He scans the crowd and suddenly his gaze meets mine. I jump up. This is it! The moment I've been waiting for! But there's something hazy about his dark brown eyes. I've seen those glossy eyes before. That look before. It's the look people give you when they're too busy changing diapers or sweeping the shop to talk to you. The look people have when you're trying to pick out leather sandals and they can't remember your name. My mouth dries.

He looks away.

CHAPTER 1: AN OLD MAN RUINS MY LIFE

My legs nearly crumple and my vision blurs as he meets the nervous eyes of another little girl. He whisks through the crowd, straight towards her. "Young girl, what is your name?"

"Kore," she squeaks, twirling her stringy black hair. A small jet of blue emerges from the back, a slightly deeper shade than the flowers nestled in her hair. My eyes widen. I've known Kore for years, but I've never seen that strand before. She must've hidden it. Freckles dot her round face, resting underneath her onyx-colored eyes, while in her right hand is a book, despite every other kid in Walend (except Jorge) being illiterate. She's extraordinary. Someone fit to be a Sun. My gut churns. The humid air threatens to suffocate my lungs.

The Skycharter grips her shoulder. "You, my girl, are destined to do great things for this country."

She nods, pale from shock. He clutches her little hand and leads her through the crowd. People part ways, excited whispering replacing nervous chatter, while Jorge yanks me backwards so I don't bump into the duo. My hand grazes the Skycharter's long robe. It feels like gold, smooth and soft. I stare at my dirty hands, which are covered with fingerless leather gloves. They don't look fit to touch gold.

The Skycharter returns to the stage, where he retrieves a wooden bowl crammed with yellow liquid. He dips a flaky brush in the liquid and, with a sweeping gesture, paints a yellow circle on Kore's face. Even from afar it's easy to tell that the golden marking mirrors a sun. Cheers erupt. The sound jams into my skull like elk antlers.

"People of Walend!" the Skycharter shouts. "Citizens of Solia! This girl is your twenty-fifth Sun! Your next savior!"

The screaming intensifies as people jump and clap. They scramble around, retrieving buckets filled with the same blue liquid. With shouts of glee, they pour the liquid on their faces. Their markings form smudged handprints, all identical to each other.

Mira and her friend do the same. Bits of berry juice from their wooden buckets spill onto my ankles. It smells like sour milk.

"Did you see Kore's blue strand of hair?" the girl gushes. "It was gorgeous, I've never seen anything like it!"

Her friend bobs his head. "And the book she was reading too. I can't believe nobody realized she was going to be our Sun earlier. Between that book and her hair, she's the most interesting person in Walend. Maybe even Solia!"

Salt stings my mouth. It takes me a minute to realize it comes from my own tears. This was supposed to be my day. They were supposed to be cheering for me. Calling me interesting. Painting a pretty sun on my face. Not some Kore girl, who sits in her grandma's house and reads all day. Who didn't memorize every story about our Suns. Who didn't spend hours using anything she could find (brooms and twigs mostly) to teach herself sword fighting. This isn't fair!

I bolt, running past the fallen banners and worn-down houses. All the way back to my family's little shop, in this little village everybody forgets. Finally, I race inside a stone-rimmed shop and hide behind a wooden table that is littered with glass items. Directly in front of me is a row of pristine glass statues, which also happen to be modeled off previous Suns. They glint in gold, green, and red, winking at me in between fighting a monster or lifting a boulder. You know there's something wrong when even statues' lives are more interesting than yours.

Under their scrutiny, I sob. Then burrow my teary face into

CHAPTER 1: AN OLD MAN RUINS MY LIFE

scratched-up knees, only to glance up after a rustling sound pierces the air. My dad enters the shop, spilling sunlight onto all of the statues. Now practically glowing, their colors fill the room, painting our faces in glistening shades of red and orange. Dad locks eyes with me and strolls over.

"Leda," he murmurs, crouching down to my level. His sandals squeak with the movement.

"Leave me alone!" I shout, pressing my face back into my knees. The tears sting my skin, finding their way into the dozens of tiny scratches peppering my legs.

"Why are you crying? Aren't you happy we have a new Sun?"

I say nothing. He should know why. He's my dad. He's supposed to pay attention to these things.

"Come on, did a leafer catch your tongue?" Dad tickles my knees.

I giggle. It's enough for me to stop hiding. I sigh. "It's just not fair! What does Kore have that I don't?"

"Leda, sometimes life can be unfair." Dad sits down, furrowing his bushy brows. "Do you remember the heroes from your mother's stories? The ones who were our previous Suns?"

"Yeah." I sniffle.

"What were they always like?"

"Brave, kind, and selfless."

"Yes, but there's more to being a Sun than that, Leda. Our heroes have to be different." He drums his fingers across the wooden planks.

I tilt my head. "Different?"

"Exactly. Something has to be unique about them. They can't be like everybody else because no ordinary person can do what they do. That's why they have to be extraordinary." Dad exhales, then continues, "And Kore is a very extraordinary girl. Do you know why part of her hair is blue and she lives with her grandmother in the woods?"

"No." I narrow my eyes.

"You really need to spend more time talking to our customers," he mutters. "Well, it's because Kore was born with the gift of controlling water."

"So, I could never be chosen, b-because I was born normal?"

"That's the way it has been since our first Sun was chosen," Dad says in a weary voice. "But listen to me, that doesn't mean you can't be happy."

"Huh?"

"What I'm trying to say"—he rests a firm hand on my shoulder—"is that you haven't been given as much as Kore has, but you just need to..." He grits his teeth. "Make do with what you have."

I try repeating his words, but my throat remains dry. So instead, I stare at the moldy floorboards we sit on. Multiple knocks rap on our door. My siblings. They're probably looking for Dad's bucket.

Dad pats my shoulder, half-heartedly grinning, then stands up, grabbing our bucket. Blue liquid, which was made from grinding up wild berries, swirls around in it.

"Come on." He takes my hand and leads me outside, to where the rest of the village cheers. Finally, we return to a grassy spot away from the pathway packed with my family and friends. Only three of my siblings don't have the markings painted on them. Dad sets the bucket down and dips his hand in it, smearing Nella's face. Alec and Gabriel are next. That leaves me.

My hands shake. I know what this means. If I put that liquid

CHAPTER 1: AN OLD MAN RUINS MY LIFE

on, I'm showing the rest of the world that I'm ordinary. That I'm just a regular village girl, stuck living in a boring village, looking after cows for the rest of her life. Another blob of blue in the sky the Sun lives in. Another blob of blue the Sun needs to save.

"Remember what I said." Dad nudges the bucket towards me.

"Make do with what I have," I whisper and smear the cold liquid on my face.

Chapter 2: Cows Suck

Two Years Later

I hate cows. And I'm pretty sure they hate me too. "Ione!" I tug on the rope I tied to the black cow. "Stop. Eating." She moos, crunching on some grass. "Come on!" I pull again. She yanks her head and I lose my grip on the rope, slamming into the ground. Rocks rattle against my back while grass tickles my arms. I groan, closing my eyes.

"Need some help?" I open them to a rough, calloused hand. I take it.

"Thanks," I say to Jorge, narrowing my eyes at Ione. "Your cows are jerks."

Twelve-year-old Jorge Makos is still a bookworm and mocks me even more than before, but now he's my best friend. Turns out we got along pretty well despite our vastly different opinions on cows.

Today Jorge wears his usual: sandals, dark brown pants, a light brown shirt, and a short-sleeved leather jacket, all of which are not actively falling apart (unlike my dress). His thick black hair is somehow neat, the large curls framing his face like a painting. Plus, he wards off the sweat and stench that accompanies everyone else working at his family farm. Instead, his warm brown skin is practically spotless.

CHAPTER 2: COWS SUCK

"Sure." He picks up Ione's rope, guiding her away from the field. "My cows are definitely the problem." The cow peacefully follows him, mooing happily. That's just rude. Jorge narrows his dark brown eyes, watching the rocky terrain ahead of us. "This should be all of them."

"Finally, the cow watching is over." I open my arms with a gentle sigh. The evening's red sun dances across them like flames. "You know what that means." I grin. "Time to go on an adventure!"

When I first became friends with Jorge, he hated working at his family farm. So, I volunteered to help him. My family already had more than enough help at our shop. But Jorge also hates favors and he only accepted my help when I asked him to explore the woods with me in exchange. Now it's tradition that after finishing our chores, we trudge into the woods and hunt monsters. Well, Jorge shoots them with his bow and then forces me to listen to his rants about books for hours.

Jorge raises an eyebrow as Ione follows him dutifully. Stupid cow. "And abandon Ione?"

Tiny rocks crunch underneath our leather sandals. They're long and dark, snaking up our calves and stopping just underneath our knees. "Fine, we'll put her back," I grumble. "But we've gotta do it quickly. The woods are too dangerous to go into at night." If Jorge takes too long again and we end up skipping another training session, I think I'll go crazy. Between the stinky cows and my screaming siblings, I need those fun adventures with my best friend.

Jorge nods then travels down the rocky side of the field. It marks the edges of Walend, resting on top of the cliff separating our village from a stony shore. It's a long fall down so we're always extra careful when retrieving the cows.

I glance at the shore beneath us, which consists of a beach with gray sand, tumbling dark water, and, of course, mountains. The Aurorian Mountains, to be specific. The same mountains which surround the entirety of Solia, isolating it from the outside world. They're huge, at least three times the cliffs' height, and stuffed shoulder to shoulder with nothing but a hair's distance separating them. Each is made of an unnamed stone that even Evin doesn't understand. It's hard, black, and shiny, so thick that no weapon or tool can pierce it. Together, they form a wall of black stone that blocks out the evening sun.

"At least this view makes all the hassle worth it." I gesture to the stony mountains.

Jorge smiles. "Only you would be crazy enough to call those mountains beautiful."

"Well, someday we'll destroy them, so we might as well enjoy them while we can."

"You're a lot more optimistic about Kore than I am." Jorge tiptoes around a ledge to ensure Ione doesn't fall.

"Oh, Kore, right," I grumble. "What do you have against her?"

"Nothing against her. Just…" He gestures to the shore. "See that man down there?"

I narrow my eyes, finally noticing a lean figure standing on the dull sand. "Barely."

"Well, I always see him when we take the cows back to the barn. Waiting to train her."

"How do you know he's waiting for her?" I hone in on the man, trying to uncover what Jorge sees. He's short and cloaked in leather. Looks like a normal dude to me.

"Because half the time she shows up and they train. Half the

CHAPTER 2: COWS SUCK

time she doesn't and he waits there, frowning."

"So what you're saying is that our Sun skips her training."

Kore not attending her training. That would be like Jorge's parents refusing to farm for us. If that's true...

He shrugs. "Those are only my observations. Hopefully, there's a better explanation."

The wind kicks up as we descend down the cliff, flapping my frizzy braid. My family calls it elk hair because it's so thick.

"Do you think the Skycharter will come back, and choose somebody else?" The question sounds more like a squeak than a statement.

"Probably not. They only visit every fifty years."

"Right, of course, that makes sense." I pinch my eyes shut for a moment. *Make do with what you have, Leda. You're not supposed to be chosen. You're ordinary. How could you forget that?*

"Are you okay?" Jorge asks, studying me with alert eyes.

"Yeah, I'm fine." The brittle wind whips past my ears. "It's just that your cow is really irking me."

He laughs. "Oh, I can't wait for you to milk them tomorrow."

"Jorge!" I holler as he snickers all the way back to his farm. He stops when we reach it solely because he knows his parents are around. They don't like him picking on girls.

Jorge and I stroll over to the barn. It's a large building with sturdy wooden planks for walls and a thatched roof. I open the door. Then I bristle as I'm greeted by the usual moos, powdery dirt, and shadowy barn.

Jorge lugs Ione off to our last empty stall while I find myself wandering to the barn's back. Dozens of items hang on its wall. Most are simple farm tools, pitchforks and shovels, the stuff my eyes glaze over. But one of them stands out among the rest. Jorge's bow. I stroke its wooden arc, which is engraved with pictures of wolves and elks.

One of my favorite things about Solian weapons is the images engraved on them. Sometimes they're of villages, other times they depict past Suns. And sometimes, as in Jorge's case, they illustrate the wildlife found in the thick forest engulfing the majority of our country. Either way they're beautiful. After all, they're supposed to remind you of what you're fighting for when in battle. Not that I've ever been in a battle before.

"Hey Jorge, you ready?" I call.

He ducks out of a stall, keeping his back turned away from me. "Actually, I think we should stop doing those adventures."

"W-what?" My voice cracks.

He rubs his head, fidgeting with a curl. "I-I have more duties at the farm now that I'm older, and it's not like we're ever leaving here. Training to fight monsters isn't that important anymore. You get it, right?"

My fists clench. I don't get it at all! "Whatever. Have fun with your stinky cows." I storm out of the barn before he can reply.

The wind screeches as I leave Jorge's farm, passing by dark buildings and wild berry bushes. I can't believe Jorge said that. I can't believe he actually believes we'll never leave Walend. My heart tightens. Is he right? A wet pine needle bristles against my wrist, breaking my train of thought. I'm here. In the forest Jorge and I usually fight monsters in. Looks like tonight I'm going home through them alone.

Walend has one main rule—"don't disturb the peace"—which mostly means don't change nature. Ever. So, all our houses are spaced apart, in areas where there weren't too many trees or animals living there because no one wanted to cut down

CHAPTER 2: COWS SUCK

forests. The exception is the main village, where my house is, since there was already an open grassy plain there when our nature-loving founder, Walend, first arrived. Unfortunately for me, this rule means I have to walk through the woods alone to get from Jorge's farm to my house.

I teeter on the wood's edges. Long trees with dark wood jag out like crooked teeth while the hissing of animals makes me jump. Normally, I'm fine exploring them with Jorge but at night, alone, the woods are terrifying. Plus, because of wind and lack of sunlight, it's freezing and dark. Not fun conditions to walk home in.

Goosebumps bristle across my tan skin. I can do this. I can walk home alone in a tiny forest without Jorge. It's easy— I stiffen as bushes rustle beside me. Then inhale. It's nothing. I'm fine. Everything's fine. I continue only for them to rustle again. A blur of blue darts out from behind them. A blue blur I recognize. Wait a minute. Peeking out from behind a tree, I notice Kore, her hands full of books, scrambling through the woods. A single dark blue strand of hair rests near the edge of her face, sharpening her soft jawline.

Didn't Jorge say she'd been skipping all her lessons? I narrow my eyes. Maybe I can find out why. There's got to be a good reason, right? After all, the Skycharter chose her. I'll just follow her, find out what she's been doing, and then Jorge and I can be at ease. No more neverending fantasies about the Skycharter coming back to choose m— choose someone else. And anything's better than walking through these creepy woods alone, worrying about Jorge the whole time. I nod, that settles it. I'm following her.

Chapter 3: Don't Follow Girls with Blue Hair into the Woods

Kore is difficult to follow. She's lean and darts about the woods as if she's traveled through it a million times. Honestly, she probably has. Nevertheless, I follow her, hopping from tree to tree. For a moment she stops, glancing backward. I duck behind a tree. Its damp wood scratches against my fingers, sending chills through my spine. Then Kore continues scrambling through the woods.

Finally, we reach a small cottage with a chimney, little yellow roof, and rosy glass windows (which I recognize as my dad's design). Kore stiffens then exhales, drumming her fingers across her books' covers.

Her white dress blows in the wind as she approaches the cottage. The door swings open, revealing a towering woman with silver hair trapped in a tight bun, shriveled skin, and cold, dark eyes. Kore's grandmother. I've seen her before in my dad's shop. Kore shrieks as her grandmother yanks her inside the cottage. My eyes widen. Is she okay?

Without the worry of Kore spotting me, I leave the scratchy tree I'd hidden behind. On the cottage's right side is a stained glass window depicting a sun (which was also made by Dad). I glance at the wild berry bushes underneath it. Maybe if I

CHAPTER 3: DON'T FOLLOW GIRLS WITH BLUE HAIR INTO THE WOODS

hide in them, I can watch through the window. I dive into the bushes. Thorns cut my skin and berry juice splatters my clothes, but I can see through the window.

Inside is a hallway filled with gifts from Solians. Exotic frogs croak in wooden cages while complex tapestries hug the wooden floor. People from all across the country visit Kore's house, giving her those lavish gifts to honor the Sun. If there's one plus to Kore getting chosen, it's finally putting Walend on the map. Stern paintings of previous Suns glower at Kore and her grandmother, who stand near the window, bickering.

"Kore!" Kore's grandmother shrieks, shaking the girl's shoulders. "Where have you been!? Asher waited for four hours!" Kore quivers at her grandmother's sharp tone. She doesn't meet the older woman's eyes as the candlelight's warm light flickers across her black hair. "Well!"

"I was reading," she murmurs.

The grandmother snorts. "You were reading. You skipped out on training— training which will help you save our entire country— because you were reading!"

"I'm sorry," Kore whispers, backing away from her grandmother. The woman towers over her. Her twisted face and bulging eyes strike fear into me, even though I'm cowering in the bushes.

"You're sorry. Just saying sorry isn't acceptable. Kore, you are our Sun! You have the ability to finally free our country from these mountains. To end everyone's suffering! You have a duty to be better."

"Well, maybe I don't want to be the Sun!" Kore snaps. I stiffen in the bushes. She doesn't want to be the Sun? What!? How does she not realize how lucky she is?

I shudder. Is Kore really the best Sun for us? Ugh. This was supposed to stop me from worrying, not make me panic even more. Plus, she seems so vulnerable and scared. It feels wrong to watch her like this. I should leave. I quickly emerge out of the bushes, with a bunch of leaves stuck in my hair.

Frowning, I leave the petite cottage, scurrying through the woods. Dust tickles my feet and I shriek, peering at my sandals. I'm standing in a pile of ash. Its gray bits rustle over my exposed toes. That's weird. I didn't see ash like this before. Or that funny-looking plant beside me. Or that tilted tree. Oh no. I must've gone the wrong way when I left Kore's cottage!

My hands tremble. This shouldn't be a big deal; I'll head forward until I reach Walend. I can do this. With a half-hearted smile, I try strolling through the woods. But between the howling wind, pointy trees, and trembling bushes, I barely resist the urge to curl up into a tiny ball.

A hissing sound erupts behind me. I bristle. What. Was. That. A shriek screeches then a long black tail whips behind a tree. Monster. That's a monster. Oh great. Sure, I've dealt with them before but the more dangerous ones come out at night. I shouldn't have stayed out this long.

I run only for a slimy substance to wrap around my ankle, dragging me backward. I scream as it spins me around. My head thuds on the ground and my vision blurs. Thousands of pointy little white teeth surround me. They belong to a snake-like monster with a long, gooey, black tail, which is wrapped around my foot, and a huge head. It shrieks, vomiting black liquid all over my head and shoulders.

"You're gross!" I yell, spitting out bits of black goo.

It doesn't like that because it hisses again, opens its mouth even wider, and pulls me closer. It's going to eat me! My heart shudders as I scramble away. It just yanks me closer. No! I

CHAPTER 3: DON'T FOLLOW GIRLS WITH BLUE HAIR INTO THE WOODS

can't die like this! I kick its tail, but my sandals slide off its slimy hide. Then its thousands of teeth swarm my face as its putrid breath smothers my cheeks. It screeches again. One tooth cuts my ear. I cover my face with my arms, trying to shield it from those wretched teeth. H-how do I get away from this!? All my kicking and squirming are doing nothing! My arms shake, only for water to splash over them. It hurdles at the monster, slamming it into a tree nearby. My eyes widen as the monster contorts and shrinks. Steam rises off its back as it screeches, slithering into a pile of goo. Woah.

"A-are you okay?" Kore approaches me. Crystal-clear water drips off her fingertips. She just saved my life! Guess I shouldn't worry after all...

"Y-yeah," I huff, scrambling to my feet.

She scowls. "Why aren't you home, villager? Walend has curfew for a reason."

My face flushes. I completely forgot about curfew. Walend's Lord rarely passes regulations. We're big on letting people be. But recently a little girl got bitten by a monster after dark, so now he decided that everyone is expected to return home extra early. "I, um, forgot. Sorry."

"Next time, don't!" Her chest heaves as she trembles. I back away from her when she points a finger at me. The stance reminds me of her grandmother, in direct contrast with the shaky girl I'd seen moments ago. "And remind all your friends too. I'm tired of having to save all of you from your own stupidity. Why can't you get it through your thick skulls that you're weak!?" Her puffy red eyes latch onto me. "Solia is dangerous and these monsters can kill you in an instant. You're not meant to be out here fighting!"

I clench my fists. Something strange rumbles in my chest

as she turns her back to me. Why is this always happening to me? Why do I have to be nothing more than a villager that everyone ignores when Kore doesn't even want to be chosen? "Well, maybe I should learn to since you don't want to be our Sun."

Kore freezes. "What did you just say?"

"I overheard you say it. I find it disgusting—" A sharp sting spreads across my cheek. I stumble backward, pressing my hand to my face. Then I meet Kore's dark, rumbling eyes. She slapped me.

"Don't you ever speak to me like that again," she growls. "You know nothing. And you are nothing. Nothing except a useless little nobody who thinks she can dare to speak to her Sun like that!"

My eyes water. Now I finally get Jorge's obsession with words. They're powerful. And they can hurt. A lot.

Chapter 4: I Stare at Glass Figurines Because I Have Nothing Better to Do

Just when I thought it couldn't get any worse, Kore walked me home. It was awkward, but she didn't want to risk another monster attack. Now we stand outside my family's shop, on a winding dirt road whose weeds prickle our thighs. Warm light leaks out of my stony house followed by bubbling laughter.

Kore furrows her brows. Cricket chirps nearly drown out her soft voice. "Did they even notice you were gone?"

I shrug. "Who knows? But thanks for walking me home."

She doesn't respond, simply glaring at me as I stumble towards my family's shop. Eventually, she stalks back to the woods without so much as a goodbye. It's probably better that way.

Inside, my mother and older brother, Homer, count coins. My two younger brothers (Gabriel and Mack) chase my furious younger sister, Nella, around the shop and into the back bedroom. Meanwhile, my two older siblings (Irene and Alec) chat with my dad, laughing with him over some obscure joke they just made.

No one bothers looking up when I enter. Sighing, I trudge over to the closet, and retrieve a broom, rolling its smooth wooden handle around my hands. I used to practice being the

THE GIRL WHO WASN'T CHOSEN

Sun with this. I haven't done that for two years now. It feels like eons ago.

I stroll over to my siblings and dad, weaving between their broad shoulders. Slowly, I sweep up shards of glass, jabbing the occasional cobweb or angry bug. Now, I'm using it to sweep up glass. Just like a nobody would. That's what Kore had called me, after all. Is that all I am? The middle child of a random glassmaker? Another little village girl whose best friend thinks she's destined to milk cows until the end of time? Who needs saving from monsters?

"I can't believe this little village girl slew the last of the dragons," Alec booms behind me. A candle flickers behind him, casting the tips of his dark brown hair in a fiery hue. "And the Skycharter didn't even choose her as our Sun!"

He points at the statue my dad wraps in a box for a customer. Sure enough a young girl reaches on her tippy toes to plunge her sword into a dragon's chest. The dragon's wings stretch out in fear, almost crashing into the delicate pine trees behind it. I've never seen that statue before, I don't even recognize her as one of our past Suns. Do they really make statues of people who aren't Suns?

"No silly, that's Thea the DragonKiller. She was our thirteenth Sun," Irene, my sixteen-year-old sister, argues, tapping him on the back. Behind her, Dad scoots to the left to avoid Nella, Gabriel, and Mack, who are chasing after each other. Once they're gone, he nervously glances from my older siblings to me.

"I know, I know, but do you know who the twelfth Sun was?" Alec asks.

"No."

Alec grins, then points at a yellow-tinted statue which

CHAPTER 4: I STARE AT GLASS FIGURINES BECAUSE I HAVE NOTHING...

collects dust on the store's highest shelf. A teen boy fixates on his image in the mirror, flexing his muscles. His boot rests on a little boy's back while a few girls blow kisses at him nearby. "Milos the Arrogant. He was so conceited because of being chosen that he focused on charming the ladies and bullying kids instead of helping Solia. Legends say the Skycharter had to return from behind the mountains to name Thea as the new Sun because she was clearly the better choice."

The Skycharter returned to choose a different Sun? No way, is that even possible? Could he do it again?

"Alright, stinkers!" Dad calls. "I think that's enough talk for tonight, we have a busy day of work tomorrow. Everybody better get to bed." My younger siblings *aww* while the older kids simply nod and say their goodnights.

As my siblings head to their bedrooms, my dad steps towards me and whacks a string of goo off my shoulder. I cough. "Must've dripped off one of the pine trees I bumped into."

Dad peers at me with dark eyes. They're the same shade as bear fur. My face flushes. Then his lips twitch into a grin. He plucks a monster tooth off my dress. "Are teeth falling off trees now, too?"

I blush. "I didn't mean to attack it, I just saw Kore and took a wrong turn and—"

"Leda." Dad grabs my shoulder, anchoring me in the chilly shop. "You need to be more careful, maybe ask an adult to walk you home at night." I open my mouth to protest, but he continues on, "I just don't want my coolest daughter to get hurt." He ruffles my hair. "If that monster had been a bandit, things could've gone much worse. People are a lot smarter than monsters."

I puff out my chest. "Jorge's handled bandits before. I could totally do it too."

He narrows his eyes. "Jorge? Oh! You mean the boy who accidentally shot a bandit in the arm and then hid in a tree for an hour until Kore dealt with them."

"He didn't tell me that…" I mumble.

"Of course he didn't. Your little boyfriend clearly wanted to impress you." He winks at me.

"Ew, gross!" I shriek, shaking my head furiously. He bursts into laughter.

"Hey, I used to lie to your mom about defeating bandits when we were little kids too." He scratches his head. "Man, they used to be bad when I was little. They kept stealing my dad's favorite pieces. Good thing we have Kore to scare them off now. But that's beside the point, Leda, can you promise me you'll be safer next time?" I peer at Dad's fluffy beard and his wide, goofy mouth that always twitches into a smile. I can't help but nod.

"Okay, I pro—"

A whimper rings out from the kitchen. My lip trembles. That sound… it sounds like someone's in serious pain. I glance at Dad, and fear flies through his eyes. Something is wrong. Seriously wrong. We both creep towards the kitchen, turning a corner. Three looming figures back my quaking family into the corner. The largest of the three, a man with wild black curls and tan skin grins madly, touching his dagger. Mom quivers. In her hand is our glittering Evin silverware. It's engraved with images of the bustling city and beautiful sun, finished off with a polished ivory handle. It's also the nicest thing we own.

The man plucks it from her fingers then laughs. "This is your nicest thing? How pathetic!" My dad freezes, as though

CHAPTER 4: I STARE AT GLASS FIGURINES BECAUSE I HAVE NOTHING...

he's seen this a million times before. They're bandits. Bandits are robbing my family. Their eyes go wild as a floorboard squeaks underneath my dad's large foot. His big belly peeks out at the end of the kitchen doorway.

"Come in, big guy!" one hollers. I shiver as my dad locks eyes with me, mouthing "Kore." I nod, my hands trembling. Kore will protect us. She'll make everything right. She has to. My dad steps into the kitchen, closing the door behind him. For once in my life, I'm grateful that someone didn't notice me.

Old habits come back as I skid into the bedroom my sisters and I share. I open my window and leap through it, only to lose my balance halfway through. With an *oof*, I fall out of the window and onto the dirty ground. I roll my eyes. Guess it's been a little too long since I last jumped out a window. My head spins before I get to my feet.

A starry night sky, dirt roads, and patches of grass surround me. To my right, are the woods separating Jorge's farm from Walend. Kore and her grandma's cottage should be inside them. With speed I didn't know I had, I rush towards the woods.

Once I reach them, I search madly for a familiar tuft of blue hair. Nothing but screeching birds, still grass, and the thick aroma of wildflowers surround me. Paper-thin leaves brush across my exposed arms as I rummage through the open woods. Where is she!? Please, don't say she's reading. Please—

"What did I tell you about being in the woods after curfew?" Kore hisses, resting under a tall, black tree. Sure enough, she holds a small book.

"Kore, bandits are at my house!" I huff.

"Bandits," she sneers, flipping through pages of her book.

"You're lying. There hasn't been an attack here in years. They never come to Walend anymore."

I grit my teeth. "They're literally at my house. So apparently they do come here!"

She rolls her eyes. "Seriously, that's your only evidence. You 'said' bandits came to your house and now I'm supposed to waste my entire night looking for these 'bandits'. "

"That's not important, we need to go before they hurt my family!"

"You—" Kore starts. A loud snap rattles behind us. It came from outside the leery woods. We both turn to our village.

"No." Cold sweat drips off my forehead. I shake my head. This can't be happening. Not here. Not now.

Peeking out at the dark woods' edges is a flicker of orange. It sends hazy plumes of gray into the sky as it skips from house to house, dancing across the streets and buildings which make up Walend. Even from here its heat dribbles over my skin and its smoky scent stings my nose. Waves of it engulf our hay roofs and beautiful wildflowers in a sea of red. It destroys them. Burns them. It's fire. Walend is on fire.

Chapter 5: Fire

This never happens. Bandits only steal. They never burn villages. Why would they when they could sell our stuff instead? Despite this, orange flames still lap around the wood's edges. I clench my fists. It doesn't matter what they normally do. They're going to destroy Walend and I can't let that happen.

"Kore!" I shout. "Let's go! Quick!"

She stands there. Frozen. Her blue strand sways in the wind.

"Hello!?" I wave a hand in front of her face. "They're burning our village. We need to go!" She continues staring blankly. "Um, this is like your moment, right? You've prepared for two years for this. It's go save the world time!"

That doesn't inspire her at all. I glance back at the village. The flames engulfing it grow by the second. I don't have time to convince her to stop acting weird! I shake her. "Come on! Stop this!"

She sags underneath me, trembling. I release my grip, stumbling backward. She's not going to do it. She's not going to save Walend. Or my family. I have to do this on my own.

In a flash, I rush towards the flames, their light expanding as I draw closer. Once there, I stop outside Walend, my chest heaving.

Everything is destroyed. Houses and shops I've known for years crumble under flames. Screams of fleeing villagers, who call out Kore's name, and the fire's mischievous cackling fill my ears. Instead of three, there are now dozens of bandits. With twisted grins, tattered clothing, and bags of loot, they slice apart houses as though they're cobwebs. They ride on black elks, knives decorating their bodies and scars covering their faces. How are there so many of them!? And where did they get so many weapons?

A bandit skids towards me, dagger in hand, as he rides on his elk. I jump out of his way. The blade still jabs my arm. I hiss, watching him ride away as my arm throbs. He barely cut through my sleeve, only leaving a tiny wound. But if I hadn't jumped out of his way…he could've killed me. I tremble. They're not here to play around. I need to find a weapon, and fast.

A bandit tethers her elk to a tree. She grins, unsheathing her claw-like blade and begins entering a house. I grab a large stone, grunting as it nearly slips out my fingers. Then, with a heave and shaking arms, I raise it above my head and hurl it at her. She dodges out of its way only to slip on the house's stone stairs and slam into them.

I wince then scramble over to the bandit. She lies unconscious on the floor, her messy brown curls sprawling across the rocky road. "Sorry, bandit lady," I murmur and retrieve her sword.

Its silver blade glints in the firelight, curling inwards like a hook. Engravings, depicting the forest engulfing Solia and the villages nestled inside it, decorate it. Awesome. I bend over again to pick up its scabbard, which I fasten to the belt in the middle of my dress. I sheathe the sword.

CHAPTER 5: FIRE

Now, with a sword to defend myself, I rush towards my family's shop. Somehow, through all the smoke of other burning houses I recognize our sign, which is now lopsided and missing a good chunk of wood. Fortunately, no smoke rises out of the shop, although it does look battered.

When I arrive, a gust of wind blows the door open, revealing a mess inside. Glass shards litter the floor, mixed with the few coins bandits forgot to steal. All of our pieces, the art Homer and Dad worked hours on, are gone. My hands curl into fists. It's infuriating, but I need to find my family. Nerves flutter through my stomach as I wade through the room, glass crunching underneath my sandals.

"Dad! Mom!" I call. For a few moments, no one responds. Then come the sobs. Faint, soft cries that seep out of the back of our shop. The kitchen. Where I'd last seen the bandits corner my family. My heart pounds as loud as an elk's footsteps and my hands shake at my sides. Vomit rises in my mouth as I notice splotches of blood on the floor.

With legs as weak as blades of grass, I follow the winding dribbles of blood. The red ooze stains my sandals' tips, causing me to slip numerous times. But somehow I reach the kitchen. Scattered pots and pans, along with thick trails of ashes, line the room. They curl in long twisted swirls, reminding me of the smoke plastering our window panes and the village's night sky.

My mom and siblings lay on the floor, forming a small barricade around something. Meanwhile the bandits who invaded my home are long gone, having left nothing but broken glass and tears in their absence. I stumble forwards, trying to figure out what they're upset about. Then I crumple to the floor, sitting beside them. Finally, I—

See something I can't ever unsee.

My dad. There's so much blood. His body doesn't move. It doesn't laugh or smile or wipe away the surge of tears running down my face. It just lays there, silent to the world it once filled with joy.

"They came in. W-we thought they were going to steal from us," Mom murmurs. "Then they took him to the kitchen and he screamed and we came back and—" She erupts into sobs, holding her husband's limp hand.

"Maybe we can save him, maybe..." I stammer.

Nella looks up at me, tears streaking her face. Even though she's little and crying to the point of exhaustion, she croaks, "He's gone."

I don't feel the scream escape my lips. It's only when Homer covers my mouth that I realize it came from me. The world blurs, and under the hazy cloud of tears I notice Homer is weeping too. I shut my eyes. I can't watch the flames dance outside our windows or see his still body on the floor. I can't think about how those bandits took him from me. How the person who once lit up any room was snuffed out. He can't really be gone. Those sick bandits can't have taken him from me. Why would they...how could they...

Shivering, a cold sweat shudders over my body as laughter abounds out my window. I look up. The bandits, they rush out of my village on their towering elks. No. My eyes blur with tears. They can't. They can't just get away with this. They can't take him away from me. I stumble to my feet. I won't let them. I'll stop them. I don't care about curfews or monsters. I don't care that Kore is who the Skycharter chose to protect us. Kore was the one who let this happen. And I'm going to

CHAPTER 5: FIRE

be the one who stops them. With clenched fists, I rush out of the house, jumping over glass shards and avoiding fallen pans. My family's sobs echo in the distance. Somehow, that makes me run even faster.

Racing through dirt roads and over burning flowers, I find the knocked-out bandit's elk. Her other friends must've abandoned her because she, along with all her stuff, still lies there. Perfect. I grab her bag and approach her elk, holding my hand out to pat the beast's soft head.

"Hey there," I murmur. "I'm going to ride you now." The elk sniffs my bag, recognizes it as her owner's, and snorts approvingly. Hoisting myself up, using a bit of her fur and the stairs nearby, I mount her.

Together, we run through the burning village. My heart aches at the sight but I continue, focusing on the bandits heading straight into the woods. A strange echoing sound rings in my ears, followed by a flash of orange and yellow. My elk rears up then bolts towards the forest.

"Wait, calm down!" I shout, clinging to her neck for dear life. I need to control her if I want to successfully follow the bandits and fight them! The elk, however, doesn't seem to care. She bolts through the forest. Ash and leaves pelt my face as we continue on. The echoing sound rings again, making my head buzz.

"No, stop!" I shout before she rears up again. This time I lose my grip and go flying off her. My head hits the ground with a thunk and my eyes flutter shut.

Chapter 6: Leafers Apparently Don't Know What Leafs Are

Ow. My head hurts. What time is it? What is going on? I open my eyes. Everything has changed. What first strikes me is the light. It's white but still chilly, dripping through pine needles and wet leaves. It must be morning, which means I was out the entire night. Squirrels dart over frosty rocks while blue jays peck at nuts. Underneath my sandals rest flattened purple flowers. I wiggle my toes in their soft petals. Then scrunch my nose as a cold dewdrop splatters onto my head. It must've leaked off one of the giant night-black trees looming overhead. They're larger than the trees near Walend, completely blocking any view of the Aurorian Mountains. That means I'm deep in the woods. Very deep.

My mouth twitches into a grin. I left Walend! A few days ago, that seemed impossible. Between Jorge not wanting to train with me and my Dad telling me to make do with what I have. Wait a minute. Dad. Tears well in my eyes and my fingers dig into the rocks beneath me. I can't think about it. I have to focus on tracking down those bandits, and putting them in prison. So that they never hurt anyone again. Which is going to be a lot harder now that I spent the whole night

CHAPTER 6: LEAFERS APPARENTLY DON'T KNOW WHAT LEAFS ARE

unconscious.

I stand up, surveying my belongings. The curved sword is latched to my belt while my dress seems to be intact. I frown. Last night I stole a bag from a bandit. It could have some sort of clue inside it. But where is it now? And where is the elk—

A nicker interrupts my thoughts.

"There you are." I grin at the elk. She reeks of sweat and grass. Probably because she's busy inspecting the plant life beneath her. Colorful wildflowers poke out near her hooves. Meanwhile, her antlers and dark gray back glisten in the sunlight. In her mouth hangs my leather bag. This shouldn't be too difficult.

I trudge towards her, sticking my hand out to pet her snout.

"Hey girl," I murmur. She kicks up, whining. "Okay. I got it, you're not a girl. You're a guy, aren't you?" He whines, bobbing his head up. I peer at his antlers' tips. They're dark black. Of course he's a male. How had I not seen that before?

"Sorry about that." I chuckle, continuing to hold my hand up. "Now, I need you to give me that bag." I point to the bag. He shoves his furry butt in my face instead. "Seriously? Give me the bag!"

The elk rears up and shoves the bag onto a large branch way above my head. Then he spins around, his beady black eyes twinkling mischievously.

"Ha. Ha. Very funny." I stalk up to the tree. Despite all my jumping, I can't reach the bag. I guess this is payback for making fun of Jorge's height.

After trying to reach the bag numerous times, I slam into the trunk. Ow. The bag resting on its branch shudders. This could work! I slam into it again. Then a third time. Finally, the bag topples down. It bursts open, spilling its content onto the grassy forest floor.

I crouch down, surveying the belongings. A flask of water, dagger, pouch, and a few glass vials lay sprawled out in the grass. I start piling the goods back into the bag, examining each of them. Unfortunately, none give me any leads on the bandits. The pouch is filled with coins and jewelry while the glass vials have ashes and—

"Gross!" I screech and drop the vial. It crashes onto a rock and shatters, splattering its red content everywhere.

Even the elk mews in disgust at the vial's content. Blood. Blood was its content. I have no idea why a bandit would keep that in her bag. Or where she even got it. My stomach churns. Actually, I don't want to know where she got that.

I sigh, trying to avoid glancing at the blood as I stuff the vial's shattered pieces in my bag. Well, that didn't help. What am I going to do now? I have no leads. And basically no idea where to go.

"Did you happen to see where the bandits went?" I ask the elk. He doesn't respond. What was I expecting? He is an elk. I plop onto a tree stump, scowling as its splintered edges poke my thighs. I need to think about this, step by step. I'm in the middle of the woods, trying to track down these bandits and defeat them. I crouch onto the ground, examining the dirt. Footprints are a no go too. Now wh—

"Lalalalala!" A high-pitched song swims through the air. What in the world? I follow the elk's gaze. A tall figure lumbers through the woods. Three-fingered hands and oddly-shaped ears wiggle at his sides. That has to be a leafer. Awesome! I've never seen one before.

Leafers are forest spirits. At least, that's what Jorge always told me. Most people don't know a lot about them because

CHAPTER 6: LEAFERS APPARENTLY DON'T KNOW WHAT LEAFS ARE

they hide in the woods separating our villages. Naturally, a lot of people invent stories about them. Some say they kidnap children while others think they hoard jewels. Nella firmly believes that they braid flowers in their hair for fun.

However, the leafer in front of me doesn't wear flowers in his hair nor does he have any jewels. The children part I can't tell by looking. But I'm guessing most child kidnappers don't sing in the middle of the woods. This leafer has feathery black hair with a couple miniature braids in it, along with peach-colored skin. He wears a sweater made of fluffy sheep wool and has two floppy ears. They twist outwards, wiggling like tiny pink worms. Plus, he would easily tower over Homer despite my oldest brother being one of the tallest people I know.

The elk stares at the leafer, and snorts approvingly. I sigh. He's right. This leafer might know where the bandits went. I just hope he's not an actual child kidnapper.

"Hello?" I call.

"AH!" he screeches, and jumps underneath a bush.

He's afraid of me? Well, I can cross "child kidnappers" off the list of rumors about leafers then. "Listen, I'm not going to hurt you, I just need to know where the bandits went. You know, the big scary people with a lot of scars."

He pops out from the bush, ears flapping up in excitement. I yelp and jump behind a tree. Previously, I'd only seen his back. Now I can see that instead of two eyes, he has one giant stitched line on his face.

"Oh no! Where'd you go, human? I saw the bandit people you were talking about and I think I can help!"

"Saw!" I squeak. "Your..."

"Don't worry about that! My eye is right here!" I peer behind the tree. He points to the necklace wrung around his neck. In the center of it is a contraption made of leather and a bronze-colored metal. A gooey glass-like surface covers the dark brown eye stuck inside it. That is weird. Really weird. "I had to take it out because I was going to the upstairs! Upstairs air makes it water too much. Um, human! Are you okay?"

"Y-yeah," I murmur. This is definitely weird, but I need to find these bandits. "Where'd they go?"

The leafer bites his cheek then blurts out, "I'll tell you where they went if you let me come with you!!"

I narrow my eyes. "Why would you want to come with me?"

From inside the contraption, his eye lights up. "Because I want to travel through Solia and meet all of you awesome humans! I've been cooped up in the tunnels for my whole life. But you humans invented all these super cool things like chairs. I love chairs! So I want to meet you and learn about your amazing ways. But I need a guide to help me find your villages and teach me all your super cool human knowledge."

"Uhh...weren't you just afraid of me two seconds ago?"

He shakes his head. "I wasn't afraid! I was just startled. I always want to look my best when meeting humans. When you approached me, I didn't have time to freshen up!"

Next to me, the elk chirps in amusement. "So you hid in a bush?" This guy is bizarre. Are all leafers like this?

"No, I freshened up in a bush." He smiles, displaying pearly white teeth. "Look! All my teeth are clean now because I rubbed them with those tiny green things on the bush!"

"You mean leaves."

"Yeah!"

"How are you a leafer and you don't know what leaves are—" I sigh. "You know what, never mind. Just tell me where the

CHAPTER 6: LEAFERS APPARENTLY DON'T KNOW WHAT LEAFS ARE

bandits went."

He crosses his arms and pouts. "Not until you let me be your travel buddy!"

"Seriously, you don't want to travel with me. I'm going to fight bandits."

"Then I'll cheer you on while you're fighting them!" He jumps up and down. "I'll be your fheerer. Fighting cheerer!"

I stare at the crazy leafer in front of me. He is my only lead on where the bandits went. But I'm probably going to regret it if I let him follow me.

"YIPEEE! HOORRRAAAYYY! LALALALALALA!!!! That's just a sample of my amazing fheering!" he boasts. I take the probably back. I am definitely going to regret letting him follow me. But I need this information.

"Okay. It's a deal."

Chapter 7: Why Won't People Take Me Seriously!?

"Lalalalala!" the leafer sings as he strolls through the forest. I have no idea why he likes singing so much. "Lalalalala!"

"Don't you think your singing will alert the bandits?" I grumble, picking leaves out of my hair.

His ears perk up. "You're right! We might scare them away!" Then he furrows his brow. "I just remembered. I don't know your name!"

"Oh, it's Leda."

"Cool, I'm Phemus!" He claps. "Now that we know each other's names, we can officially be travel buddies!"

I sigh. "So, how close are we to the bandits?"

Phemus scratches his head. I try not to stare at the long scar dotting his face. Really, it's not the scar that grosses me out but the lack of an eye. Especially since that eye is currently stuffed inside a necklace. "Ummm. I'm not sure. They were riding pretty fast on those elk things. Wait, why aren't you riding your elk? We could move a lot faster."

I glare at the elk trailing behind us. "He made it pretty clear that he doesn't like me. And it's not a good idea to try riding an animal who doesn't like you. I stole him from the bandits, and

CHAPTER 7: WHY WON'T PEOPLE TAKE ME SERIOUSLY!?

accidentally called him a girl, so I guess he has good reason not to."

"Oh no. Well, hopefully you can make it up to him and then be friends!"

"Sure," I hiss. "Are you sure they went this way?"

He frowns. "I thought so. I don't want to let my travel buddy down." He grabs the contraption encasing his brown eye. "Don't worry, travel buddy, I have an idea! I'll get you to the bandits in no time." He abruptly stops, fixating on the contraption.

What is he doing? I lean forward. Even the elk joins me. Phemus' large fingers struggle to turn a small golden knob on the contraption. It screeches and rattles as it expands like a spy glass. Bubbling grease oozes out its sides. I cough as smoke strings my nose and waters my eyes. Finally, the contraption shudders to a stop. Phemus' eye contraption now has grown twice in size.

"I can see super far with my eye-extender!" He grins and waves the eye-extender around. I duck as it whizzes over my head.

That's actually really cool. "What can you see?"

"Just a lot of leaves, right now! And some pretty birds too! Wait." With a creak, he extends the contraption again. "There's someone in the sky!"

Beside me, the elk snorts. I honestly agree with him. For once. "Phemus, people can't fly."

"Really, I see someone!" He points at the pine needles above us. "She's sitting in the sky. She looks upset, she's moving around a lot! And her body is surrounded by ropes."

I furrow my brows. "It sounds like she's in a net." I squint, cupping my hands to block out the warm sunlight. Woah. In the distance, rests a tiny net. Its pale ropes pop out against the smooth, dark pine trees.

Last I checked, bandits don't put people in nets. But they're also not supposed to burn villages, so anything could go at this point. And even if she wasn't captured by the bandits, we should still help her. It's the right thing to do.

"Well, let's rescue her."

"Yay! A human adventure with my travel buddy!" Phemus squeals. The elk whines, flattening his ears at the high-pitched sound.

"Okay," I chuckle. "Why don't you take me to her?"

He nods, scrambling into the woods. I follow him, jogging to keep up. Thick wildflowers and vines block my path, whacking my legs and arms. Finally, Phemus stops, ducking under a large bush.

"Phemus, I don't see the net—"

"Sh!" He pulls me under too, covering my mouth with a sweaty hand. The elk behind me whines. Phemus shoves his head inside the bush, covering his mouth too.

"Look!" he whispers and takes his hand off my mouth. He points to a clearing behind the bush littered with rocks and wildflowers. "Those are the scary bandits I saw before."

My eyes widen. This is my chance! In the clearing stand three bandits, all of which appear to be in their early twenties. The first is a shorter man with spiky black hair and dark brown skin. He gazes at the wildflowers, eyes glazing over. The second leans on a tree, sharpening his dagger with a sickening screech. His wild curls blow in the wind, sending shivers down my spine. I gasp. I know this man and these bandits. They were the ones who entered my house. They were the ones who— My hands clench, and shake furiously. They're

CHAPTER 7: WHY WON'T PEOPLE TAKE ME SERIOUSLY!?

who I need to fight.

Lastly, a woman with curly black hair shoved into a messy bun, and reddish-brown eyes that flicker like fire. An array of daggers line her belt, blood still staining their tips. She peers up at a net, which traps a girl my age. The girl scowls, squirming in the ropes.

"Barak," the woman addresses the shorter guy. "Cut her down."

Barak sighs and climbs up a tree nearby. He unsheathes a knife, leans forward, and cuts a rope fastening the net to the tree. The bandits laugh as the girl screeches and tumbles to the ground. All except Barak. He's too busy descending the tree.

"Alright, girlie," the second bandit sneers, spitting in her face. He grabs her bony arm and yanks her up, pinning a dagger to her neck. "You're coming with us." She glares at him. "It's nothing personal. Bone just needs a bunch of ya fast. And we need to beat everybody else by rounding up the most kids. It's pretty competitive. Every corner of Solia's crawling with us."

Bandits all throughout the country are rounding up kids? Beside me, Phemus gasps. Now I know who the real child kidnappers are. Definitely not the leafers. I grab my sword. This is my chance to defeat those disgusting bandits. Then I'll use these three to find the rest of them and stop them from hurting any more kids.

I inhale. Am I ready for this? I've never technically fought with a real sword before (Jorge never let me touch his and my family never needed one). But I've practiced techniques with a broom before. And these bandits will keep kidnapping kids and killing people unless I stop them. They'll get away with hurting my dad. I tighten my grip on my sword. There's only three of them. I can beat three bandits. I stand up.

"Stop right there, you filthy bandits!" I holler. Phemus' eye almost bulges out its contraption. Even the elk shakes his head.

"Who are you?" the second bandit grumbles as the girl writhes in his grasp.

"Leda Roubis! And I'm going to avenge my village after you burned it to the ground!"

"Seriously. You look like you're twelve. Who do you think you are, the Sun?" He laughs. I scowl. When I'm through with them, they won't be laughing.

"Mateo," the woman hisses, eyes widening as she gestures to me.

"No way, Phoebe." Mateo shakes his head. "Bone won't want her. She's not obedient enough."

Phoebe rolls her eyes, and points at the girl Mateo holds, who still struggles in his grasp. "And she is."

"More than her—"

"Enough talking!" I unsheathe my sword, causing the bandits' eyes to widen. I bet they recognize their friend's sword. Look who's scary now, Mateo! "Let's do this." I step into the clearing. The elk whines.

"Fine." Phoebe grins. "If you want to fight, we'll fight."

"But she's only—" Barak starts.

"Shut-up, Barak!" both bandits shriek, then face me. Their lips and hands curl into snarls and fists.

Phoebe unsheathes a sword identical to mine then launches. I block her. Her force alone sends ripples through my body. She's strong, how am I— She slams me into a tree. Wood scratches my back while the scent of pine needles mixed with sweat smothers me. I break the hold, ducking under her legs.

CHAPTER 7: WHY WON'T PEOPLE TAKE ME SERIOUSLY!?

Then Barak steps in. He slashes at me with a dagger. I dodge before Mateo slices my bare arm. Its cold, silver edge sinks into my skin. The slash reopens and deepens the tiny wound I'd gotten last night. I bite back my cry of pain. Their sneers and relaxed postures make it sting even more. I clench my fists. I can't give up. I can't make do again.

I launch at Phoebe. She deflects but grunts and steps backward. I slash at her legs. She skips out of its way, yawning. "Alright Mateo, let's end this." Mateo's black curls and silver dagger race towards me. I dodge. Then Phoebe knocks the sword out of my hand.

Mateo pins his dagger to my throat and backs me into the tree. Phoebe and Barak circle me, facing the same direction as him.

"Any last words?" Mateo laughs, pressing the dagger further into my neck. I feel the engravings and smudges of dirt lining its blade. I glance to my right and left. There has to be a way to escape. It can't end here. I can't really have been as useless as Kore thought I was.

"Well?" he asks. There's really no way—

With a bang, a black object thunks into Mateo's head. He crumples to the ground, eyes snapping shut. Behind him the girl he had trapped in a net grins.

"You fool!" Phoebe hisses to Barak. "You were supposed to watch the girl!"

Barak runs his fingers through his pointy hair. "You never told me that!"

"Ugh, boys," she growls. "Never mind. There's still two of us, we can easily beat you foolish children—"

"Hiyah!" Phemus charges into the clearing, a large stick in his meaty hands. "Don't mess with my travel buddy!"

"A leafer!" Barak cries as the towering Phemus lets out a battle cry. "Those things are dangerous!"

Phoebe's face pales. "Shoot. Barak, get Mateo. We're leaving!"

I latch onto Phoebe's arm. "You can't leave! I have to beat you!" She shoves me off, sending me spiraling into a tree. Why do I keep getting shoved into trees!?

"Too bad," she hisses as I lay there, my entire body sinking into the ground. The duo mount their elks, dragging Mateo with them, and ride off into the woods.

Chapter 8: I'm Dying. Who Knew?

The bandits' elks' shaggy black fur fades away as I stumble up. Sticky warm blood dribbles down my fingertips while trees sway back and forth. Next thing I know, I'm right back on my behind.

"Don't worry, travel buddy!" Phemus coos, patting my shoulder. His ears flap up and down rapidly as he drops his stick.

"Your friend's losin' too much blood," net girl says. Her thick accent makes her sound like she's hissing. She points to my bleeding arm. My ears ring and head throbs as she speaks. "That's why she's dazed."

"What do we do!?" Phemus hollers.

The girl clenches her jaw. Long snow-white blonde hair races down her shoulders. Nestled in it is a black bandana. That's weird. Why—Ow! I scream as she swiftly grabs my belt and tightens it around my arm.

"You're hurting her!" Phemus whimpers.

The girl rolls her eyes. "Rather see her die from blood loss?" Phemus frowns, his face falling. "That's what I thought."

The girl crouches down, setting a petite cauldron beside me.

She must've used it to knock out Mateo. Then she rummages through the cauldron, picking out a tiny needle and some other supplies.

"What's that!?" Phemus asks.

Instead of responding, the girl removes the belt. "Hold still." She uses a cloth to clear off the blood then slowly stitches my arm together. It hurts, but nowhere near as much as first getting that cut did. After that I can handle anything.

"Woah, you're putting her arm back together!"

"Uh huh," the girl mutters. She has large bright eyes, one of which is a forest green. The other is an icy blue. I don't think I've ever seen anyone with eyes like that. Or hair that color before. Most Solians have brown hair and brown eyes. Except for Kore. Dad says that's because of her magic. Said. He said...

"Done." She wipes off her hands on the fur cloak she wears then gets up.

"Travel buddy, you're okay!" Phemus scoops me up in a big hug.

"Ow!" I squeak. Finally, he releases me. I turn to the girl. "Thanks..."

"Val."

"Thanks, Val, for the stitches."

"Least I could do." She piles her items back into her cauldron. A rope emerges from its two sides, allowing Val to easily sling the cauldron across her shoulder. She pauses, furrowing her brows. "You ever picked up a sword before?"

"Well, no. But in my mom's stories—"

"Stories are stories," Val snaps. "There's more to winning fights than just showing up." I stare at my hands, which are caked in dirt and leather. I guess I really don't know how to

CHAPTER 8: I'M DYING. WHO KNEW?

defeat bad guys. But where do I even start? No one I know understands how to fight bandits, so it's not like I ask them for help. "Plus you don't wanna mess with those guys. You heard 'em. There's a ton of them throughout the country. Mess with one and you're messing with the whole group."

She's right. I remember them talking about bandits kidnapping kids throughout the country. And they even mentioned a guy named Bone. I wonder... "Do you think they're an organized group with an actual plan? That there's some sort of reason they're kidnapping kids and wrecking villages?"

"Don't know. Don't care." Val shrugs and turns her back on me. "I'm out. Thanks for the rescue."

"This is super cool!" Phemus squeals. He stares at the glittering golden scroll he holds. Inky black sketches of elegant birds litter its pages. Val freezes and spins around.

"That's mine!" she hisses, snatching the scroll from Phemus' hand and shoving it back into her cauldron. The girl sighs, only to jump when the elk tries gnawing on her hair. "What is that!?"

"An elk." I stumble up, scratchy wildflowers brushing against my legs. "He's a grump, so be careful." The elk mews in obvious disapproval.

She shakes her head, blonde strands flying everywhere. "That's not an elk. He's too big. And the markings on his antlers. Elks don't have those."

"Yeah, they do. If they're males."

"Female elks don't have..." She trails off, glancing at her scroll. "You know a lotta common knowledge?"

"It's called common for a reason."

"I know lots about the woods!" Phemus adds as he sits in the grass. He hops from grassy patch to patch, plucking flowers and then abandoning them.

"I thought you didn't know what leaves were," I grumble.

Phemus shrugs. "No, but I know what's underneath the forest. That's ten times more important." I squint. What is he talking about?

Val bites her cheek. "You need help? Looking for those bandits of yours?"

"A second travel buddy!" Phemus drops all his flowers. The elk snorts in disdain, narrowing his eyes at Val.

"Hold up. I'm asking her." She looks at me, her icy eyes scooping into my soul. "You need help?"

Do I? If the bandits are organized and there's more than the people who hurt my village, it would be stupid to turn down extra help. Plus, I could use someone else who isn't Phemus to make sure I don't go crazy. I shrug. "It wouldn't hurt to have help. But why do you want to help me?"

She unravels her scroll. It reeks of dust and dried ink. With a pale finger, she points to an image inside it. It's a sprawling drawing of a bird flying through the sky. Fire curls around the tips of its wings, while its head points toward the sky like a deadly arrow. Writing, which I can't read, surrounds it. I peer at the girl. She must be well educated. Like Kore.

"What is that?" I ask.

"A phoenix. I need to find it. But I don't know a lot about here." She gestures to the woods.

I frown. "I don't either, so I'm not sure that I would be the best guide."

Her eyes glaze over the scroll once again, rereading the letters on it. She shakes her head. "Not just the woods, villages too. I need someone who knows villages in and out."

Wait, why wouldn't she know about Solian villages? My

CHAPTER 8: I'M DYING. WHO KNEW?

eyes widen. Of course! "You're from Evin, aren't you?" I gasp. She's from Evin and she wants to help me. This is perfect!

"Um." Val backs away.

Phemus jumps off the grass, sending bits of dirt flying everywhere. Val continues backing away.

"You're from Evin! It makes perfect sense. Your blonde hair, light eyes, and accent. Not knowing anything about Solia. Being able to read and knowing all that medical stuff," I say. "You attend one of those prestigious schools in Evin, don't you? The ones they send special kids like Kore to." The ones Jorge applied to a year ago.

Val thunks into a tree. "Yeah." She nods. "I, um, have to find this to complete my final exam."

"Exam?" Phemus and I both ask, tilting our heads.

"It's a big test. If you complete it, you complete school," she explains.

"So, you need to find this phoenix thing but you've been trapped in that school since you were a little kid," I realize. "Now you have to travel through Solia all on your own, but because you've never left you have no idea how this place works. You don't even know what an elk is!"

Her face flushes. "Yeah."

I grab Val's shoulders and shake her. "This is awesome! My friend told me all about those schools. They teach you basically everything, sword fighting, archery, even medicine. You're exactly what I'm looking for!" Phemus giddily claps beside me. "I need someone to teach me how to fight the bandits, and I can help you find the phoenix bird, and Phemus can talk to someone from Evin. I'm sure you know how to make amazing chairs there."

"Chairs!?" Val squeaks.

53

Chapter 9: I Only Occasionally Climb Trees to Avoid People I Don't Like

Traveling through the woods is hard. Really hard. Not because there's monsters trying to attack me or because I have no idea which way to head to find the bandits. Surprisingly, no monsters have attacked us yet and as for finding the bandits...Well, if Val could speak maybe we would be able to figure out something. But currently that's looking—

"About B—" Val starts.

"I caaaannn'tttt." Phemus interrupts for the fiftieth time. Then he collapses with a huff, leaves scattering around him. Val opens her mouth, only for him to groan. I roll my eyes. At this rate we're never getting anywhere.

I sigh, pick up a twig, and poke Phemus' face. Might as well stop him from groaning. "Come on, get up."

"Nooooo..." he whimpers, putting his hands on his face. "We've been at this for hours!"

I crouch down, wildflowers tickling my nose. They smell like pine needles and roses. Awesome. "Phemus, we've only been at this for a few minutes. And if we want to find a village to rest at, I'm going to need to brainstorm with Val. See if she has any cool Evin ideas." Val coughs behind me. "So, could

CHAPTER 9: I ONLY OCCASIONALLY CLIMB TREES TO AVOID PEOPLE I...

you just be a little quieter?"

Phemus sighs, then a greasy black flap unfolds over his eye in his eye-extender. I guess that's his way of sleeping? All I know is he's quiet. Finally.

I get up, stroll to Val, and lean on a tree. Its damp wood seeps into my back. "Okay, so, what were you saying earlier?"

"Oh, I remembered somethin' they were talking about before you came. They said they're taking the kids to a cave. Apparently Bone lives there." A cave? So these bandits really are organized, they have a secret base and everything. That makes things more complicated than before.

"Wow. If they're an organized group, I'm going to need to stop all of them. But I have no idea how. In Evin, did they—" Another groan interrupts my chat with Val. This leafer!

Next to me, the elk, who's still following us for some reason, nickers at my clenched fists. Of course he's laughing at me. Then, for no reason, he approaches Phemus, leans down, and crunches on his hair.

"Waaahhh!!!" Phemus scrambles up. The elk backs away. "Okay, I'm up. Don't eat my hair, scary elk!" The elk mews, spitting in Phemus' face. "Ew!" Phemus wipes the gooey spit off his face.

"Hey, leave him alone," I tell the elk. He snorts in response, before turning around and racing off into the woods. Well, looks like he finally left.

"There he goes." I watch the elk scamper away.

Phemus frowns. "I hope I didn't offend him."

"Don't worry, he was going to leave no matter what. Especially since I knocked his owner out." Their jaws drop before I continue on, "Anyways, what I was trying to ask Val—" Phemus' stomach grumbles.

"Food..." Phemus' mouth drops open, and his bulging eye nearly pops out of its socket. "We should get food...I should get food. Food! I'm coming to get you!" He races off to the left, abandoning us in a pile of thick green leaves.

"Phemus, wait!" I shout. "We're supposed to stick together!" I sigh as the leafer's tiny floppy ears disappear into a swarm of trees.

Val shrugs. "He'll be fine."

I narrow my eyes. I hope she's right. "Alright. Well, I was going to ask you if you had any ideas about what to do with the bandits. They're clearly way more organized than I thought."

She nods, biting her lip and peering at her cauldron. Her eyes glance over her scroll, the one with pictures of birds on it. "A map. That's first priority. We'll need it to figure out where we are right now and brainstorm where their base is."

"But what about training?"

"Training? Oh. We'll use the map to find nearby villages. I'll train you there." I tilt my head. Why not train in the woods? She simply shrugs at my confused look. "Supplies." Then she pulls out her scroll and begins tracing the inky images.

We both wait for a few minutes, neither saying anything. Well, I try to start the conversation a couple of times to help brainstorm where we could find a map, but Val only gives curt responses. Eventually, I break. We need Phemus. He can warm up Val. Even if he is a bit too loud sometimes. "I'm going to find Phemus."

Val glances up from her scroll, beads of sweat forming on the edges of her forehead. "Alright," she grumbles. I race after Phemus, pine needles whipping across my bare arms. She staggers after me, hanging her head.

Sure enough, I manage to glimpse a tuft of feathery black

CHAPTER 9: I ONLY OCCASIONALLY CLIMB TREES TO AVOID PEOPLE I...

hair and familiar wiggly worm-like ears. I grab Phemus' arm. "Come on, Val and I need your help finding a ma—"

"I just saw a girl with blue hair!" he squeaks. A girl with blue hair? A familiar dainty figure flashes behind the tree's bark in front of us. No way. Not her again. I don't want to have to talk to Kore Vasil after I watched her do nothing while my village burned.

"Wha—" I cover Val's mouth before she finishes. But it's already too late. The figure shivers and Kore's voice pierces the air.

"Come out!" My fists clench. I am not waiting to talk to that girl. I grab Val's arm then pull the duo far away. Puffed breaths and the crunching of leaves grow closer. We're not going to be able to run away in time without her seeing us. Me specifically. I glance up at the trees next to us. Aha!

"Quick!" I hiss and rush up the tree.

"Why are we climbing trees?" Val grumbles. Despite her questions, Phemus and her both scramble up the tree after me, balancing on the long, daunting branches beneath us. The wet leaves dampen my legs, chilling my skin.

"Because," I whisper-shout, "we hate each other's guts. It would be very awkward if she saw me."

Phemus' jaw drops. "Why would you hate someone with blue hair, it looks—"

"Quiet, Phemus," Val whispers as Kore strolls in.

Her coal-like eyes fixate on her surroundings. "I know where you are," she declares, a large open leather book resting in her hands. My eyes widen. It's no book. It's a map... an incredible map! It glows, and images bleed off the pages, dancing through the air. The colorful pictures of tiny Solian villages and thunderous waterfalls wiggle around. I can even see people riding through the woods. They look like Phoebe and Barak. No way, I bet that thing can track anyone! Since when did Kore get access to such a nice map?

She taps on the map, directing it to the trees next to her. It slowly becomes less blurry. "Soon this map will be in focus and I will see exactly who you are, so just save me the time and come out," her voice wavers slightly. I grin. This map is perfect! Now, I have a way to find the bandits again and find Val's phoenix too. Then my gut sinks. I need to go through Kore to get it.

Kore frowns, stomping her foot. "Come on, work, map! I'll stop you stalkers in just one second!"

I bite my lip. I don't want to talk to her, but I need that map. I need to stop those bandits before they kidnap even more kids. "Follow my lead," I whisper to a still confused Val and Phemus. Then I jump off the branch and into the ground, scattering leaves and pine needles everywhere.

"You." Kore's voice sharpens. "What are you doing out here!? You should be with your family, now that your dad—"

"Don't you dare mention my dad!" I snap, eyes blurring.

She flinches then her eyes harden. "Don't mention him? Your family—" The girl stops, jaw opening as Phemus leaps out of a tree. Val follows his lead. "That's a leafer!?"

I grin, wiping my tears, and patting Phemus' back. "Yeah, he is, and he happens to be super scary." Phemus growls, though it sounds more like a puppy whimpering. Val has to cough furiously to stop herself from laughing. "So, you're going to give us your fancy map or he'll attack you!"

Kore shivers, then closes her book. "I need this map! Unlike you, I'm actually important. Solia needs me to use this to find the bandits." She straightens her back, but it looks unnatural

CHAPTER 9: I ONLY OCCASIONALLY CLIMB TREES TO AVOID PEOPLE I...

with her slightly hunched shoulders. "Now, if you'll excuse me, I have better things to do than talk with useless villagers."

"Jeez. You're rude." Val rubs her head. "Makes sense why you hate her guts," she says to me.

"Um, excuse me? Do you know who I am?" Kore shrieks, and her grip loosens on her book. Val glances at it and then at me. She's distracting Kore so she forgets about the map. Genius!

"Nope." Val shrugs, leaning on a tree. I slowly approach Kore, locking my eyes on her glistening map. It's so close!

"You fool, I'm so tired of useless people from villages nobody's ever heard of insulting me! Like you would ever understand what it's like to have any sort of important responsibility or duty." I grit my teeth. If someone actually cared enough to give me a duty, I'd be thrilled instead of complaining all the time. Especially if it was the Skycharter who gave me that duty.

Val simply rolls her eyes, waiting for Kore to finish her rant. Then she says, "I'm from Evin."

"Y-you're, what?" Kore's face pales and the book practically wiggles out her fingertips. I rush towards her and grab it. "Hey!" she screeches. Already, complex water patterns begin forming on her arms, weaving over each other like basket strands. It'd be awesome if she weren't currently trying to attack me with it.

"Phemus, run with the map!" I yell and toss the map above her. Phemus leaps up, grabs the book, and runs. Only for a loud snarl to stop him.

My entire body stiffens. Snarling wolves stalk towards us. Oh great.

Chapter 10: Glowing Wolves Attacking Me Is Not a Fun Way to Spend the Night

"They're glowing." Val's jaw drops. "Wolves don't glow."

My eyes widen. Sure enough, a blue aura hovers above the pack, seeping out of the wolves' bodies. It's an odd combination: the snake-shaped glowing blue patterns lining their sides mixed with their regular fluffy gray fur. Their bodies reek of sweat and seawater. Drool drips out of their fangs. One slimy droplet splatters onto my sandals, dampening my toes.

"Apparently they do now." I furrow my brows. There was something Jorge said about glowing wolves. Why can't I remember?

Kore steps in front of us, her head held high. "Don't worry. I'm handling this!"

"Like you handled my village?" I growl.

Her body stiffens and she looks ahead. For once her voice cracks. "Well, I'm going to handle this now." She pulls her arm up. Water drips out of her palms, pulsing up and down her arms in tiny, crystal colored streams. Then she aims her hands at the wolves. And nothing comes out. Her face reddens. She

CHAPTER 10: GLOWING WOLVES ATTACKING ME IS NOT A FUN WAY TO...

tries again. She glances at the trees behind us before running away. The wolves keep their amber eyes trained on us. Not even bothering to glance at the runaway. Seriously!

"What do we do, Leda!?" Phemus shrieks.

Something Jorge said about wolves pops into my head. "We need to back away. Slowly."

Val nods. They both mimic my movements. The wolves retreat, their blue lights bobbing across tree trunks like ocean waves. Thank goodness. Then they stretch their legs and bolt straight towards us.

"It didn't work!" Phemus cries.

"I can see that!" The wolves snarl, their hot breath plastering my ankles. "Run!"

Wind rushes past my ears and rocks crunch under my sandals. Val's blonde hair tickles my shoulder. My legs move so fast they burn.

"Separate and lose them in the woods!" Val yells.

"Good idea!" I add. "I'll take the front."

"I'm left," Val adds.

"That means right for me!" Phemus races ahead. We split, rushing into the forest. Branches slam into my arms. The rocks melt into wildflowers and cold wind stings my lungs. A wet snout touches my thigh, followed by a parade of howls. I glance back. The entire pack is following me! I groan. Why me!?

Wait a minute, I remember what Jorge told me about glowing wolves. I stop at a miniature cliff's edge and spin around. The wolves skid to a halt, watching me with smooth eyes. Behind me, a river with tumbling dark water crashes into the cliff's edges, spraying sea foam on me. I'm cornered. My fists clench.

"Come out Jorge, I know you're there!" I shout. For a moment all I hear is cricket and wolves' heavy breathing are the only sounds I hear.

Jorge ducks out from a tree. I gasp. His hair is a matted mess while he wears a brown cloak. He carries a bow, satchel, and quiver stocked with arrows. His clenched jaw, dirty cloak, and mashed-up frizzy curls look almost unrecognizable from the neat boy I know.

"Sorry about the wolves. I thought you'd remember that they glow blue after a human gives them seaflowers." Seaflowers do more than make wolves grow. Rumor is that they improve their tracking ability, giving them sharper noses and eyes. But why would they willingly listen to Jorge?

"It was kinda hard to remember that when you forced them to chase us," I grumble. "Why'd you do that? And how?"

"Why?" Jorge furrows his brows. Guess he's not going to answer my second question. "There was a leafer next to you and Kore. I had to get him away before he attacked you."

I cross my arms. "The leafer's name is Phemus. I knew him and I wasn't in any danger."

Jorge narrows his eyes, patting a wolf's head. "Sure you weren't." I open my mouth to protest but he continues, "These woods are packed with monsters. One of them was bound to attack you, which is why I used wolves to track your scent. Plus, they helped me find a cave where we can stay the night." He gestures to the eerie red sun leaking behind our arms. "Then we'll head back to Walend in the morning."

I stiffen. "I'm not going back to Walend. Not until I find the people who, who…"

Jorge's face softens as he approaches me. "Leda, I know how devastating this is. But you're not thinking straight. You

CHAPTER 10: GLOWING WOLVES ATTACKING ME IS NOT A FUN WAY TO...

have no idea the effect this is having on your family. They're terrified you're hurt, Homer sent me to find you." Of course Jorge, the only child in a family of three, would bring up family. He'll never get that my family barely even knows I exist. Homer probably just wanted to give Jorge a reason to go after me so he'd quit worrying. "And going after these bandits is dangerous. We still don't even know why they burned down Walend."

I grit my teeth. Why doesn't he get it? "It's not as simple as you think, Jorge. The Skycharter's been wrong before. And what I saw, what Kore let happen to my dad, was so wrong." My voice wavers. Then I clench my fists. "So I'm going to right the wrong. I'm going to fix this and stop those criminals."

His eyes sharpen as he moves forward again. I instinctively back up. The movement sends a few rocks tumbling into the water. "The Skycharter has to be right. Even if Kore makes mistakes. Which means Kore is destined to stop those bandits, not us. You know that, so why are you acting this way?"

"Why am I acting this way? Why are you acting this way!?" My shouts cause the wolves to wince and flatten their ears. "You never had a problem with me wanting to be a hero before. You cheered me on, taught me to use your bow. You even had your own dream of wanting to go to Evin! What happened to you?"

"I grew up," Jorge snaps, breaking our locked gaze. "I realized the same thing you need to. That we're nobodies. You weren't chosen for a reason." His voice wavers as he grits his teeth. "And I wasn't accepted into Evin's Academy for Special Children for a reason. We're not meant to do these things because it's not safe for us." He extends his hand. "Now, come on, we're leaving."

I shake my head. My frizzy braid flies back and forth. "I'm not leaving. And if you think I'm such a nobody then maybe you should forget about me and leave."

"No way. I'm not leaving you here in the woods like this." His wolves growl, approaching me. He really has changed.

My eyes water. "Fine." I glance at the river underneath the cliff. Its waves thrash back and forth, spraying water everywhere. My heart quivers. "Bye, Jorge."

"No—" I don't hear the rest of what Jorge says. I'm too busy jumping off a cliff.

Chapter 11: Floating People Are Following Me. Don't Ask.

Icy water slams into my body, pushing me deep into the river. Slimy salmon tails whip past me and the churning of water howls in my ears. It stings my eyes and legs, sinking into scars and sending rocks ramming into my toes. I kick up, only for another current to slam me into the sandy ground. Clouds of sand swirl up while seaweed and rocks jab my body. My lungs squeeze. Come on! I need to get out of here.

But that seems impossible with dark water thrashing me. At this point who knows where the surface is? A pop rings through the river followed by flashes of yellow and orange. For a moment, the dark water turns a sky blue. Ahead of me, a crumpled bird floats in the river, sinking slowly to the bottom.

"You're almost there," a voice whispers. "Just swim a little further…"

D-dad? I glance around. He's nowhere to be found. But in the clear water, I easily locate the surface. The light fades. Okay. I can do this. But what about that bird? I have to help it! I stare, just making out the reddish edges of its limp body.

"Remember, how do we swim forward?" Dad asks.

"We clear the water, like we're pushing through vines. Then

kick!" My own voice pipes. Next to me, a glowing younger girl with wild brown hair swims against the river. She looks to be seven and flickers like a candle. I was seven when Dad taught me to swim. My whole family had visited the shore near the Aurorian Mountains that day.

I follow her. Waves of water press against my arms. My lungs scream and my legs threaten to collapse.

"Keep going Leda!" Dad calls. "Always keep going!" The girl next to me huffs. My entire body aches. Maybe I should stop, and let the water collapse over me.

"Can't. Stop." Her thoughts echo through the river. "Suns. Don't. Stop."

She's right. I can't stop. I race ahead, tumbling into a warm body and ruffled feathers. Then, with strength I didn't know I had, I grab the bird and swim to the surface. Finally, I reach it, still holding the limp bird, and gasp for air. A starry night sky and brittle wind greets me. The girl disappears.

To my right rests a rocky shore decorated with trees. With the rest of my strength, I swim to it, dragging the bird with me. Then I grab onto a rock and pull myself into the forest floor. Pine needles soften my body as I drop the bird and slump to the ground. The stars twinkle above as water dribbles off my skin and onto purple wildflowers.

I turn towards the bird. It's huge, with long, curling red feathers and a twisted beak. A variety of faded oranges and reds plaster its tall body. On the tips of its feathers rest sparkly eye-like yellow rings. Their bright colors stand out like shining stars amongst the dark woods. I pat its wet chest. The soggy feathers warm under my fingertips.

"Hey," I wheeze. "Wake up." The bird twitches. I shake it again. This time its wings flap. It opens its eyes and screeches.

CHAPTER 11: FLOATING PEOPLE ARE FOLLOWING ME. DON'T ASK.

The echoing sound reminds me of ringing bells. That was the same sound from my village! The one that scared the elk I rode. Why was this bird—

I jump back when it bursts into flames. It's a phoenix! The bird Val was looking for. The fire disappears and the bird shoots upwards, now glowing orange.

I stumble to my feet. "Wait, come back!" The phoenix shrieks, disappearing into the night sky. "No!" I huff and slump onto the ground, shivering. I don't have the energy to chase after that bird right now. I'm so cold, and tired. I just want to sleep...

"If you get lost in these woods, what do you do?" my dad asks. He appears in front of me, round belly and all. The only difference is his hair looks darker and he glistens like the little girl in the river had.

"First, you need to find shelter." Eight-year-old me squints at the dark woods in front of her. "Then fire and water and..." She frowns before her eyes light up. Just like Dad, she glows. "Food! Then you need food!"

"Right, shelter is the most important. It'll get dark and cold fast." He pats her back.

"Yeah, so I need to find a cave!" she pipes.

"Exactly." He grins. "A nice, big cave."

I get up, sighing. Find a cave, Leda. Find a cave. The identical trees fly past me as I stumble through them. In front of me, bushes rustle and twigs crunch. I back up. Oh no. Fortunately, I still have my bag and sword, but I don't think I have the energy to fight a monster. My elk emerges, snorting grumpily.

I tremble. "Please, don't attack me. I can't..." The elk gestures to his back with his antlers. "Y-you want me to ride you?"

He nods. I scramble onto the elk's back and hug his neck. His fuzzy fur easily keeps me warm and he smells like roses mixed with pine needles. He charges forward through the woods. The leaves melt into blurs of green. A few splatter dewdrops on my head.

The elk finally reaches a cave, coated with thick moss and bright wildflowers. He slows down and enters it. His hooves click on the floor, echoing throughout the entire cave.

"Th-thank you," I wheeze, slumping off his back. Then I slide into the cave, still shivering. The elk chirps and sits next to me. He again gestures for me to come to him. I move towards him and lean on his black back. I fall asleep to his steady breathing.

A voice rings in my ears. "You finally listened to me." I open my eyes. Dad stands in our house, polishing one of his precious glass items. He looks exactly as he did a few days ago. Tall with twinkling brown eyes and a mouth that twitches into a smile. H-he's here…

"W-what are you cleaning?" I stutter, reaching out to touch his arm. He moves away, continuing to furiously polish the item.

"You never did care about what I did, did you?" He gazes at the statues longingly. "You spent all that time trying to be a Sun and then with Jorge at the farm. Trying to be as far away from our shop as possible. Trying to be as far away from me as possible."

"No," I whisper.

The floorboards creak underneath me as I scamper forward. The shop flickers, turning back into the way I'd seen when I last left. Coins and glass shards litter the floor while the warm

CHAPTER 11: FLOATING PEOPLE ARE FOLLOWING ME. DON'T ASK.

torchlight of my shop is replaced by cold shadows, the bright fire outside, and the smell of blood. The glass shards rattle. With a screech, they scurry towards my exposed feet.

"Dad!" I call. "Dad, please, help!"

The shop flickers again. I gasp. I'm back in the old version of it. My dad stands in front of me, narrowing his eyes. In the torchlight, they take on a golden hue.

"Help?" He laughs. "I've given you plenty of help, yet you ignore my most important advice. Just like you ignored me."

I tremble. "But D-dad, I don't think it's right. I just can't sit there and let those people get away with what they did to you. Y-you have to understand that."

He slams the statue he was polishing on a shelf. Sighing, he surveys it. "As if you care what happened to me. The only reason you're doing this is because of your useless ambition. You think, somehow, if you do this, that strange man will come back for you." He backs away from his shelves lined with dozens of statues.

"That's not true." My voice wavers. It can't be... But his grim face tells me not a word I say will change his mind. Instead, he gestures to his two shelves.

The first row holds perfectly clean statues in vibrant blues, glistening goldens, and passionate reds. They're all in various fighting positions. I recognize them: Thea, Pearce, Minta, even Damon, Solia's first Sun. At the long end of colorful statues is Kore. She's a pristine lapis blue and smiles, her sword pinned to Mateo's neck. Phoebe and Barak cower beneath her too.

On the bottom shelf is everyone I recognize. Jorge, my dad, my mom, and every single one of my siblings. At the very end is me. I'm a dinky orange, and hold a bucket.

"You aren't her. You will never be her. So quit pretending…" He grabs the statue of himself and drops it on the ground. It shatters into a million pieces. "And make do with what you have."

Chapter 12: Naming Animals Is Hard

With a gasp, I jolt awake. The elk stirs, his shaggy fur snuggling against my arms. Morning light warms my face. Birds twitter while dew drips off moss.

I sigh. Was that nightmare right? I remember the excitement I had when leaving Walend. The nervous thrill of battling bandits. Maybe it had a point. I mean, if the Skycharter came back and chose me…Is that bad to think about? My head throbs. I wish Dad was here to tell me what's right and wrong. My eyes blur. I wish he was here, period.

The elk rubs me as I sniffle. "Thanks," I chuckle. But my voice still cracks as loud as thunder. I slowly get to my feet. "Let's find Val and Phemus." Hopefully they're okay after last night. The elk seems to roll his eyes. Then he yawns, revealing a mouth full of yellow teeth. "You don't have to come if you don't want to."

He stands up anyways. I guess he's tagging along. I smile. His fluffy face is adorable. He sighs, turning his head away from me before strolling ahead. Fine then. I'll focus on the woods' other cute animals. Gray hummingbirds flutter to wildflowers, elks' hooves clank on rocks, even porcupines munch on grass. A few scamper away after I leave the cave, but most simply go about their business. Beyond the peaceful animals, sunlight bounces off wild berries, rocks, and tree trunks, lighting up the grassy area. It's actually beautiful—A screech interrupts my thoughts followed by the edges of a monster's furry green back several trees away. Never mind then.

I scoot away from the cluster of trees until the monster's furry back is out of view. I really need to find Val and Phemus soon before I become monster chow. I furrow my brows. "Okay, we'll start by retracing my steps."

The elk snorts and races away, hooves clicking across the rocky area.

"Hey, wait!" I rush up to him. His legs are twice the size of mine, so he easily strides ahead. Finally, I catch up, only for the stench of fish to waft over me. Ew. We must be near the river I fell into last night.

The elk whines. His shaggy black pelt and curling white horns glisten in the sun. "You need a name, don't you?"

He nods, giant antlers flying everywhere. I duck, narrowly avoiding being jabbed. "Alright, how about Rock?" He screeches. I cover my ears. "Okay! Not Rock, then. Jeez, you don't need to whine like that." He snorts, spitting in my face again. I narrow my eyes. "Thanks." I wipe the spit off my face. "Hmm, maybe I should call you Jerk." His eyes widen in alarm. "I'm kidding. No need to spit in my face again." Pine needles crunch underneath my sandals. I wonder…"Pine. Do you like that name?" He nickers happily.

Water droplets splatter my face. We're back at the river. In broad daylight, it's no longer black and lifeless. Instead, piercing blue water swirls back and forth. Salmon jump in and out and the scent of fish stings my nose.

CHAPTER 12: NAMING ANIMALS IS HARD

Memories of last night flood through me. Dad's advice saved my life. My gut churns. Maybe that horrible nightmare was right. Maybe I should've listened to him and stayed in Walend. But what about Kore? She let our village burn and outright said she didn't want to be the Sun! If our Sun isn't able to protect us, then who will? Who will be there to stop the bandits when they come back and burn more villages?

"L-Leda?" A voice stammers. I know that voice. Val! She teeters on the river's other side. Leaves cake her hair and shadows form pits under her eyes.

There are a few rocks in the middle of the river. I should be able to hop from across them to reach the other side. "It's me! I'm coming!"

Slowly, I jump onto the first rock, nearly slipping off its slimy surface. Then I hop from rock to rock. Murky water chills my ankles. After one final leap, I reach the other side. Pine jumps into the water, swimming across the rumbling river. Only his head and antlers poke out. Val and I chuckle at him.

After a few moments of anxious chatter, Val informs me that she spent the night in a tree to escape some monsters while I warn her about Jorge, his pack of wolves, and how I jumped off a cliff to escape him. My gut sickens as I do. I don't want to avoid Jorge like this but I need to go after these bandits. I can't be a nobody anymore and I can't make do with what I have. My eyes water. *I'm sorry Dad, but you deserve justice.*

Val nods as I distract myself by surveying the cliffs behind her. To the right rests a grassy hill littered with rocks. We should be able to climb up it and return to where Phemus, Val, and I separated. Perfect! We can retrace our steps and find Phemus and the map. Then we can find a village to rest in and Val will finally train me. I tell Val my plan as we scramble up the grassy hill, Pine racing ahead of us. As we do, my eyes widen. "Hey, Val. Last night I saw a phoenix."

Val stops in her tracks, eyes bearing into me. "You sure? They're not easy to come by."

I stare back at the raging river. "It had to have been one. It was huge and burst into flames!"

Val grins. "Guess you found one. What happened to it?"

"As soon as it woke up, it flew away."

Val studies her feet. Some strange boots cover them. Weird. They must be Evin fashion; Nella's friend visited there often and said they always wore bizarre clothing. "What'd its feathers look like?"

"Its feathers? I mean, they were orange and yellow with these big eye-like shapes on them. That's pretty much it." I shrug. She nods, takes out her scroll, and adjusts her drawing. "Don't you find those tiny markings boring?"

Val stiffens and frowns. "You can't read?"

"Nope. Most people outside of Evin can't. Defending ourselves against monsters and making sure we had food was always more important." Pine happily shrieks when we finally reach him. We both cover our ears. I groan. How often is he going to do this!?

Her eyes widen as she traces the inky words spilling across her scroll. "Never thought about that."

"Really?" Imagine not having to look after cows all day! "Evin must be so different, what's it like?"

"Oh, uh…nice." Val's face flushes as I wait for her to continue. "We mostly studied these magic rituals." Rituals? Jorge would love to know about this stuff. At least, he would've loved it. Now he's changed…"People outside of Evin aren't told about

CHAPTER 12: NAMING ANIMALS IS HARD

them. Plus they made us girls wear long fancy dresses and crowns."

We finally reach the hill's end, returning to the rocky area we lost Phemus in. I scratch my head. "Wait, how do you run around in a stuffy dress?"

"You don't." Val clenches her jaw. "Anyways, let's find Phemus." Her tone lets me know she doesn't want to say any more. I wish she would say more, her life sounds awesome! Except for the stuffy dresses.

Val and I shout Phemus' name. Even Pine joins in by shrieking. Unfortunately, the leafer doesn't respond to our calls. I seriously hope he's okay. We keep calling until our throats are sore before deciding to travel further into the woods. Pine follows us closely behind. I glance at Val. While we're together I might as well ask something I've been wondering. Even if she doesn't usually talk a lot, maybe she'll be willing to share some of her special Evin knowledge. "Hey, Val?"

"Yeah?"

"Why do you think those bandits are rounding up kids?" Maybe if I understand them better, I can figure out how to defeat them. Outsmart the bad guys at their own game. "I mean, stealing makes sense. Burning villages, sure, if you're trying to create chaos while you steal. But kidnapping kids and taking them to a mysterious cave so a guy named Bone can see them? It doesn't add up."

She snorts at my rambling and continues searching the ground for Phemus' footprints. "Who cares? Let's just get in and out. You defeat the bandits. I find the phoenix. Phemus gets whatever chair thing he wants. It's simple. Don't make it take longer than it needs to."

I groan. "The bandits are the ones making it complicated. They're too confusing."

She pats my back. "Try working with magical rituals."

"Well, do you have any ideas Miss I Study Magical Rituals!?"

She rolls her eyes. "Seriousl—" She stares ahead, freezing. I follow her gaze, frowning as I make out the figures in front of me. I gasp.

Phemus lies unconscious on a long wooden cart. A woman, who's surrounded by multiple larger men with swords, pushes the cart forward. The group marches ahead until they disappear out of sight.

"Oh great," I mutter.

Chapter 13: Crale. Grrrrrr…

Phemus has been kidnapped. Wonderful. Just wonderful. It's not like I didn't already have enough to worry about with those bandits running around kidnapping children and my best friend hunting me down with glowing wolves. Now, I've got to free him from a bunch of random kidnappers if I want to get that map to find the bandits. And help this leafer. Come on Phemus, why did you have to get caught?

Val pokes me, whispering, "Where are they goin'?" Her eyes fixate on the map Phemus clutches, which gets further and further away with each step the people take.

"Umm…" I squint at the figures, and gasp. "Crale!"

"What?" She scampers ahead, following the kidnappers from a safe distance. I join her. Pine even bends his head, ducking in between trees. If I've learned anything over the past few days it's that I can't just charge in and fight people. Val and I need to find a different way to rescue Phemus and get his map. But first, we can't lose this group in the woods.

"The clothing they're wearing. See, how long and dark it is?" Val nods. All of them wear long black leather cloaks which lack a hood or sleeves. "Only people from Crale wear those coats. Of course they kidnapped Phemus! All the people in that village are jerks," I whisper-shout. Then cross my arms. Ahead of us, one man tugs at Phemus' ear, causing the rest of the group to erupt into laughter. "See, jerks!"

Val narrows her eyes. "Jeez, relax."

"Relax? How can I relax when I have to face the most annoying village ever? They think that since they have a big wall and those stupid fancy coats they're so much better than Walend. Well, the Sun was born in our village and we have lots of cows. And leather. We never needed their stupid Crale leather—"

"Okay. I get it," Val grumbles.

I sigh. "Whatever. It's hard to explain to someone who grew up in Evin. You guys are basically like your own country."

Val's face flushes. "Guess we are."

The kidnappers stop at a large wall. Its thick, dark wooden spikes remind me that we've reached my least favorite village. Flanking the wall is an arched wooden door decorated with silver. Silver, huh? Who even cares about silver? Kore has exotic frogs in her house!

A kidnapper claps. For a few seconds, silence follows. Then the door swings open and the group scrambles inside, dragging Phemus into Crale. I gulp. What are we going to do!? There's no way we can sneak past that huge wall.

I turn to Val. "You're from Evin. Do you have any ideas on how to get inside? Or past that?" I gesture to the giant wall.

"Right, um…" Val glances at the wall's top.

A few guards are there, but most look to be sleeping. Crale has about the same population as Walend but produces a lot more. Unfortunately. That means most people are overworked and tired. Yet another reason why Walend is better.

CHAPTER 13: CRALE. GRRRRRRR...

Val scrambles to the backside of the village's wall. "You up for climbing a wall?" She pats the wooden structure. Multiple ropes link it together, each row a person's length apart.

"No. I am not going to climb those ropes."

Val shoots me a coy smile. "Alright." She jumps up, grabs onto some ropes, and hauls herself up.

"No. Absolutely not." I shake my head furiously.

"Guess I'm saving Phemus by myself," Val calls from above, her blonde hair whipping around in the wind. "Better hope I can do it even though I've never been here before."

I grumble. She's not going to know how to navigate Crale, is she? Fine. I turn towards Pine. "You can't climb this so you're going to have to wait here, sorry." He snorts, rolls his eyes, and disappears into the woods. Hopefully, he'll come back again.

I sigh. Slowly, I approach the thick rope, and heave myself up. The wood and rope scratch against my palms as I ascend higher and higher. My body quickly tires, but I ignore my arms' aching and continue on, doing a victory dance in my head each time I pass another row of ropes. And then another, and another.

Blue jays zip around me and dozens of pine tree tips lay beneath me. I'm so high! I can't think about that. I'm doing this to find that map, save my country, and put those jerk bandits in jail. Plus, if the Skycharter comes b—Wait, I made it!

After one final pull I'm on top of Crale's wall, in a small path that is smothered with dust. Wooden spikes line my vision along with bushy treetops. The wind howls, rustling my long braid and chilling my spine.

I pump a fist in the air. "I made it!"

"Took you long enough," Val snickers as she leans on a spike, checking her nails.

"Hey!" I yelp.

She chuckles, only to clear her throat. "Let's focus on finding Phemus."

"Yeah, you're right." I point to a trapdoor stuck in the middle of the pathway. "We can use that to get off this stupid wall before a guard finds us." Fortunately, the nearest one is sleeping. Val nods.

I lean down and pull on the trapdoor. It flaps open, revealing a small room packed with dozens of shelves. Glittering clocks, thick shields, and maps are stuffed on nearly every row. Looks like no one's inside. I jump down. The shields pinned to the walls rattle. Val follows me, closing the trapdoor on her way. Except she falls on her back by accident.

I burst into laughter as she lays on the ground, groaning. Then I offer her my hand. "Payback is sweet." She rolls her eyes, takes it, and gets up.

We survey the room. Torches' glow illuminates it while intricate maps of Solia cover its walls. A string of red flags with lions on them drape across the ceiling. Ew. Crale flags. A boy looks up from polishing a sword and glares at me.

His hair is slick and black like ink and his skin is the same shade as mine, tan. He wears the typical Crale cloak, dark pants, black sandals, and a scowl. My fists clench.

"Belen," I growl.

"Leda," he hisses.

"Oh great." Val facepalms.

Belen crosses his arms. "I knew it! You Walend kids always wanted our beautiful Crale leather." He pats his leather coat. "So now you're sneaking into our village to steal it."

CHAPTER 13: CRALE. GRRRRRRR...

I scoff. "Your leather. Why would I ever want your flimsy leather? Walend's leather is ten times stronger!"

"Please." Belen shakes his head. "I've seen Jorge's little farm and his weak cows."

My fists clench. "How dare you insult my best friend's cows!" Only I get to do that! "Especially when I've seen the cows at your family's farm. They're so small I can fit them in my hands."

"Those are my mom's cows!" He shouts and points his sword at me. "You stupid thief, I'll fight you myself to protect my city!"

"I'm not a thief!" I roar. Belen starts charging anyways.

I unsheathe my sword in defense. Oh great. I just got myself into another sword fight, didn't I? Despite having not practiced at all. Why do I do this to myself!? I grab a shield. Belen swings at me. His sword clanks against the shield.

"Val!" I yelp. "How do I win a sword fight?" If only she had a sword too and could help me fight!

"You don't know how to sword fight?" Belen laughs from behind my shield. "Oh, how could I forget? All of the villagers in Walend are helpless since they rely on Kore for everything!"

"Argh!" I growl and break our hold, tossing the shield to my side. I may hardly know how to fight but I'll prove him wrong! I start to launch at Belen.

"Stay calm!" Val shouts.

She's right. Plus, she's probably been in way more fights than me. I hold back from launching at Belen. He jabs at me. I block his bow, inhaling. *Keep cool, Leda.* I watch his twitching wrists and mimic his movements, countering them. At first, his blade nearly slashes me. But with each blow, my blocks get better and better. Belen's face reddens and he growls, pushing harder. I'm actually holding my own against him! But I can't just hold my own against Belen. I need to beat him. I look towards Val.

She shrugs. "Umm...use your environment?"

Okay. I can do that. Next to me is a wooden shelf of weapons. I duck behind it. Instead of hitting me, Belen's sword rams into the wooden shelf, sinking inside the wood. Yes!

"Come on!" He hisses as he tries pulling it out. It stays wedged inside.

I leave the safety of the shelf and launch at Belen. He grabs a shield in the process. Swordless, he reaches for a rock resting on the shelf to his right.

"Don't let him get a weapon!" Val shouts.

I kick his knee. He grunts, dropping his shield and slipping onto the floor. I pin my curled sword to his neck.

"Who's the bad sword fighter now!" I grin.

He groans and gestures to Val. "You had help. What do you want, thief?"

"I'm not a thief. Your people kidnapped a leafer I know. Where is he?"

On the ground Belen narrows his black eyes. "You want to help a leafer?"

I frown, keeping my sword pinned to his throat. "Just tell me where he is." Val joins me in glaring at the boy.

He scowls, then points to the left. "There's a map over there of Crale. Can you at least let me show you where the leafer is on it?"

I nod, sheathe my sword, and help him up.

"Thanks," he mutters, rubbing the back of his head. He walks over to the giant Solian map then opens up a smaller map resting on the desk underneath. A chair is snuggled

CHAPTER 13: CRALE. GRRRRRR...

underneath the table. I wonder if Phemus has seen it. He'd be thrilled.

Belen clears his throat and points to a gray square on the map. "Okay. All our enemies are kept in here."

"Why is a random leafer your enemy?" I grumble.

"Because he's a leafer. You never know how they'll act," Belen snaps. When Val shoots him a look, he continues, "Kore isn't able to single-handedly defend our entire village here, so we actually have to be competent."

"We have it rough too," I hiss. "She wasn't able to defend our village either."

Belen frowns. His face softens. "Wait, what happened?"

My eyes water before I grit my teeth. Now isn't the time to cry or think about…think about what happened. I need to find Phemus. "Just. Be careful. There's some bandits rampaging through villages."

He nods solemnly. "Thanks for the heads up." Then he hands me the map, his face returning to its normal scowl. "Take this. Find your leafer friend and get out of my village."

Chapter 14: I Love Cauldrons Almost as Much as Phemus Loves Chairs

"Can you see anything?" The torch I hold barely lights the narrow hallway we stroll through.

"Nope!" Val pipes, waving her torch around. I think I found a match to Phemus' love for chairs.

Damp wood presses against my arms and rims my vision. Two sky-high wooden walls flank our sides. I squint at Belen's map, trying to determine the prison's location. The door to the prison should be inside Crale's giant wall. But I have no idea how we're going to find it if we can't see anything.

"I bet Belen purposely gave us bad torches," I mutter.

"Is there such a thing as a bad torch?" Val hungrily watches the flame in front of her.

"Yes." I glare at my torch. "Ours." My torch whittles down, leaving me in the dark. I groan then sigh. "Guess I shouldn't have complained."

"Hey, look at this," Val calls.

She holds her torch up to a large map of Solia. Sprawling drawings of dense villages, towering mountains, thick woods, and glistening rivers cake its surface. I frown. The map only reminds me of one thing. Solia is huge. There's no way I'm finding the bandits without Kore's map.

CHAPTER 14: I LOVE CAULDRONS ALMOST AS MUCH AS PHEMUS LOVES...

"That's a lotta villages," Val murmurs.

"Doesn't look like more than the usual thirteen." Wait a minute. "They forgot to include Walend! Ugh, I hate when they do that. There were thirteen explorers and thirteen villages. Why is that so hard to remember?"

She shrugs. "I've only seen one—two now. The rest all blur together when you rarely hear their names."

I scowl. "Then I'm going to make sure you never forget Walend."

"Leda, I don't c—" Val starts.

"Number one. We have the best spices in our food because we memorize all these different properties about the plants that grow near our village and then use them in our food. Number two." Val sighs, glaring at me through slitted eyes. "We wear super cool fingerless leather gloves because they protect our palms but still let us grab onto rocks when we climb the cliffs near our village. Number three—Ow!" I pick up my foot and whimper while Val fixates on the object which whacked my foot. Guess that ends my trying to make somebody actually remember my village's name.

"It's a trapdoor," she murmurs, kneeling down. Her torch-light glimmers across the trapdoor's silver surface. She fixates on a padlock resting on it, which must've been what my foot banged into.

I peer down at my map. "That trapdoor must lead to the prison." It makes perfect sense based on this map! "But how do we find that padlock's key?"

Val furrows her brows. She takes her cauldron off her shoulder and removes her scroll. A bunch of colorful vials rest inside the cauldron. She retrieves two vials: a glowing green tube and a sparkling yellow one. Then she opens both with a pop. She mixes them together in her cauldron, which now glows.

"Woah…" I lean in to peer at the cauldron.

She pushes me back. "Don't do that."

"Sorry," I whisper. Why? I don't know, it just felt like a whisper moment.

With a hiss, the cauldron steams and shoots out a golden liquid that smells like vanilla. Val catches a few droplets in an empty vial with a grin. She pours the liquid onto the trapdoor's padlock. Her hands are surprisingly steady as she ensures the liquid only touches the padlock. Finally, she backs up and watches the padlock melt into a black puddle.

"How, what?" I stammer, staring at the puddle. Val scoops the rest of the liquid in her cauldron into another vial and puts all her materials back.

She snickers as I gawk. Then she opens the trapdoor, revealing a long stone staircase.

"You coming?" she asks before scrambling down the stairs.

"Evin is awesome," I finally mutter before following her inside and closing the trapdoor behind her.

The stone steps are slimy, covered in thick moss and annoying weeds while the hallway narrows even more. Val's torch is our sole light source, tinting the whole area with orange. We quickly reach a long prison. Similar to the steps, it is narrow, dim, and stuffed with overgrown moss. A single Crale flag droops from the ceiling while cells line both sides of the room. Only one, frankly exhausted guard, watches the prisoners.

"Don't fight him," Val hisses.

We both stand behind at the staircase's edges, peering into the room. I roll my eyes. "I won't. I'm not a child that needs

CHAPTER 14: I LOVE CAULDRONS ALMOST AS MUCH AS PHEMUS LOVES...

basic instructions." Sword fighting advice is helpful, but this is just annoying!

She narrows her eyes. "You're twelve, right?" I nod. "Then you're a child."

"You're the same age as me!" I whisper-shout.

"I'm thirteen." She grins. "That makes me a teenager."

"You—" A yawn interrupts my whisper. The guard dozes off. I smile. "Yes!"

"Keep your voice down." Val points at the guard. "He could wake up."

I cross my arms as we enter the room. "I knew that."

She snorts. "Uh huh."

I glower at her before we search the cells for Phemus. Unfortunately, the cells I pass by are all littered with criminals. Some of them beg for me to free them while others are too busy sleeping. I shiver at one guy. His muscles basically fill up the entire cage while scars drench his arms. Even asleep, he looks like a monster. Honestly, it makes me grateful that we didn't have to deal with this in Walend. At least, before—before everything happened.

I grit my teeth. Now is not the time to think about that stuff. I need to find Phemus. A whimper from the cell next to me interrupts my worrying. A familiar whimper. I race over to the cell.

"Phemus!"

The leafer huddles in the back of the cell. His contraption lays sprawled on the stone floor, split into various pieces, while his eye is now back in its socket. It's rimmed with red and he keeps itching it. His limp ears perk up when he sees me.

"Leda!" he shouts and races to the bars, pressing his face on them. "I knew you would come back! The other humans said you wouldn't b-because humans don't care about leafers and I got really worried for a bit. B-but now you're here! Hooray!"

"Quiet!" Val hisses only for the guard to rouse. Oh no.

"Hey!" he yells, waving at us. "Get away from the prisoners, kids!"

"See, even he thinks you're a kid, Val!" I shout.

Her eyes narrow and her accent somehow increases. "I'm a teen. Thirteen makes you a teen."

The guard's face scrunches up. "Please, you're a kid." He points at the now glowering Val. "But that's beside the point. Get out of here, it's not safe for kids to be near prisoners."

"But Phemus didn't do anything wrong," I explain, pointing at his cell. "He was kidnapped and jailed just for being a leafer."

The guard sighs. "I know it's hard for a child like you to understand, but leafers are dangerous. They eat people."

"No we don't!" Phemus protests. "Why are you saying such mean things about us?"

"Be quiet, leafer!" The guard snaps, causing Phemus' ears to droop. Okay. That's it. I officially don't like this guy. I unsheathe my sword. I still haven't trained like Val recommended but I have her right here to give advice, so I should be alright.

"Just leave us alone!" I shout.

The guard shakes his head. "Listen, I'm not fighting a kid."

I clench my fists around the hilt of my sword. "Too bad."

He groans. "Fine. If I defeat you, will you leave? And go back to doing whatever kids do these days?"

"Deal."

The guard unsheathes his sword and approaches me. I look towards Val but she just shrugs, leaning on a cell door. "You're

CHAPTER 14: I LOVE CAULDRONS ALMOST AS MUCH AS PHEMUS LOVES...

not a child, right? You don't need basic instructions."

"Val!" I growl and dodge one of the man's blows. "I will kill you when this is over!"

The guard and I spar for a few minutes, but just one of his blows tells me he's way stronger than me. If we keep going, I'll easily lose. I glance at the moss growing on the wall next to me. Then at the flag hanging from the ceiling and the table to my left. Val did recommend using your environment...

I dodge another blow and rip moss off the wall. Then chuck it at the guard's face.

"What the!?" he shouts and starts furiously wiping the moss off his face. While he's busy I jump up and grab the flag of Crale. "Stop that!" he hollers, having successfully cleared off the moss. He scrambles towards me.

I duck and crawl underneath the table, still carrying my flag. Once I reach the other side, I rush up and whack his head from across the table with the flag's pole. With a thunk, he crumples to the ground.

"Sorry," I huff to the guard, before dropping the flag.

Val's eyes widen as she leans on the wall, moss hovering around her hair. "Not bad." I glare at her as I sheathe my sword.

"Not bad? That was super awesome!" Phemus shouts. My face flushes.

"Thanks, Phemus." I turn away from Val. She sighs then waltzes up to Phemus' cell. With a click she unlocks it, using a key she must've found on the wall.

Phemus scampers out of the cell and scoops Val into a hug, picking her up off the ground. "Thanks Val! I'm so happy you came back!!"

"Um. You're welcome," she squeaks. Her face turns pink as

she struggles in his grip. Once the leafer finally releases her he turns to me, basically crushing my bones as he wraps me in a giant hug.

"Leda, I've been holding onto this just for you!" With a swooping motion he grabs Kore's map and hands it to me. "Now we can beat those super scary bandits!"

"You want to defeat the bandits?" A deep, wheezing voice growls behind me. Phemus' ears jolt up as I spin around to face the man. He's tall with curly black hair stretching to his shoulders and an eye patch covering practically half his face. Not exactly the nicest-looking guy.

"Y-yeah. Why do you care?" I grit my teeth. Only for him to burst into laughter.

"Good luck, we've already raided three coastal villages. Kidnapped loads of kids." Three more villages? At this rate they'll kidnap every kid in Solia! "Not a single one of them defeated us and you, a tiny little girl, think you can beat us? You're a nobody, you're better off going back to your mommy."

"Well I have a secret weapon." I try not to let my voice waver as I open the book containing Kore's map. He's going to regret calling me a nobody after he sees this awesome map! My jaw drops.

"What's wrong, Leda?" Val asks

"It's... empty."

Chapter 15: Why Do People Kiss?

Why? I stare at the blank pages of the book, warm torchlight dancing across them. Even though we're back in Crale's walls, the jailed bandit's laughter still echoes in my ears. It makes me want to visit one of Phemus' underground tunnels and never come back.

"I told ya, it's enchanted. No amount of staring's gonna make the map appear." Val sighs, stroking her scroll. She wasn't too happy about the map not working either. She'd planned on using it to find the phoenix, but now we're both back to square one.

"Phemus," I say to the leafer strolling next to me. He cradles the remaining parts of his eye-extender. "Could you ask Val to actually help by using one of her potions?" I didn't forget about how little help she gave me when fighting that guard!

"Seriously," Val grumbles.

"Val, could you help—" Phemus starts, still staring at his broken contraption.

"I heard her say it."

Phemus' ears droop. "Oh, right, sorry." He sighs. He's been acting upset since we first rescued him. Hopefully leaving the jail will lighten his mood.

Val glares me down, her torch's orange glow tinting her face.

"I'm not usin' my potions cause they might ruin the map—" She stops, her eyes widening.

What is she—? Oh... In front of us stands Belen and another girl. Belen holds a torch and is a head taller than the girl, who has bronze skin, and frizzy hair stuffed in a big bun. He leans in and kisses her. Ew! Val's face flushes while I immediately cover Phemus' eye.

"What's going on?" Phemus asks. The couple break off, turning beet red.

Belen growls, "Leda, you were supposed to leave Crale!"

"We were going to leave after finding Phemus," I stammer, drop my hand from Phemus' face, and try to pat his shoulder instead. I'm too short to reach so I settle for tapping his back instead. "But our map doesn't work anymore, so we're just kinda wandering around trying to figure out how to fix it," I nervously laugh, fiddling with the edges of my dress.

Belen rolls his eyes so much I worry they're going to go back into his head. "Are you kidding me, how can you be dumb enough to break a map?"

"We didn't break it. It's enchanted and none of us know how to open it."

"Maybe Kore can help. She's in our village," the girl Belen kissed murmurs. Her voice is soft and high like a baby animal. Her eyes stay trained on the ground. "My dad said the scouts helped her in this morning." Kore's coming? We're definitely not asking her for help, but maybe we could spy on her and figure out how to unenchant the map. Plus, Val did say she wanted to train me in a village. Crale might be our best option. Unfortunately.

"I don't know about that, Penelope..." Belen chuckles softly. "Leda's, uh, leafer friend here will get attacked." I don't think

CHAPTER 15: WHY DO PEOPLE KISS?

I've ever seen Belen act this nice. Ever.

"Your mom does have a pretty big barn. We could sneak him in there with one of my dad's old hats." Penelope glances at him shyly, batting her eyes. "It'd be really sweet of you to help out your friends and let them stay there."

Belen's face flushes. "I, um, I—"

Penelope touches his arm. "I mean, ever since you and Evan stopped being friends you've just been moping in your mom's barn for days." Belen's face turns cherry red as I snicker. "It would be nice to see you happy again."

"Happy? With them?" Belen squeaks so high it makes him sound like a chipmunk.

Penelope, however, pays him no mind. Her eyes flicker to Phemus' contraption, which lays disheveled in his arms. "What's wrong with your contraption?"

"Oh." Phemus sighs. "The, um, guards that took me to the cell didn't like me. So, they weren't very nice to my stuff... And now my eye hurts because of the upstairs air. Tunnel air isn't like this air at all." His ears droop as he trembles.

"Penelope," Belen murmurs. "What does this have to do—"

"I might be able to fix it." Her soft voice cuts through his nervous one. "My family are blacksmiths," she explains. "The contraption isn't too complex so I can probably put it back together in my family's shop. I'll just need your parts."

"Really?" Phemus jumps up then hands her his eye-extender. She nearly buckles from the parts' weights. "Thank you so much!"

"Wait, you can't just offer to—" Belen starts.

"This is so kind of you to help your friends and this leafer you don't even know." Penelope smiles. Belen's cheeks flush. I grin. He already knows he's lost. Looks like we're going to be staying in Crale for a while. Sorry Pine.

Chapter 16: Kore. Just. Kore.

I pull the hat over Phemus' head for the millionth time. "Keep it on! Otherwise you'll blow our cover."

"Sorry!" The hat's thick cloth muffles Phemus' voice.

We enter Crale's center, finally leaving the chilly walls. Cobblestone replaces the dirt pathways and red-rimmed buildings pop up on our sides. Crale flags with proud lions flap outside nearly every building. I almost vomit. For once I miss Walend's pretty purple flags with blue seaflowers on them.

The villagers around us glance at Phemus' large hat. They slump in and out of shops, while dark circles swarm underneath their eyes. Wow. I never realized how tired people in Crale really were. Probably because I only see them when they come to Walend to trade goods.

Val reaches up to poke the large red hat covering Phemus' entire head. "Sure this'll disguise him enough?"

Belen stiffens while Penelope shoots Phemus a warning look. Too bad he can't see it underneath the wool hat. "Of course it will disguise him. This hat idea is genius, no one will ever—"

"Mom!" A little kid tugs on the edges of his mom's cloak, sandals skipping on the polished stone beneath him. "That person has one eye."

Belen grabs Phemus' hand and pulls him into an alleyway, just before the kid's mom glances at the leafer's partially-exposed eye. We quickly follow him. A few stained-glass windows and sturdy red buildings surround us. To our right is a stone staircase, leading into someone's basement.

"You three wait here," Belen grumbles. "We're going to find a less busy pathway to my barn." Then he takes Penelope's hand and the two disappear into the crowd. I sigh, opening the book while Phemus slumps to the ground. Val has to shove his hat back to stop him from looking at the bustling people outside the alleyway.

It's still blank. Infuriatingly blank. I try shaking it. Once. Twice. Even three times. It doesn't work. I can't believe we put in all that work to get this map and we still have to spy on Kore to make it work. But at least I'll have time to actually train with Val. Her advice already helped me a lot. I grin. Yeah, once I finally see those bandits, I'll be able to kick their butts once and for all.

"Guys." Phemus' eye widens as he stares at me and Val. His voice turns quiet as he trembles. We both lean in. "I just figured something out. Belen kissed Penelope, didn't he?"

Val snickers and blurts out, "Yup," before I can stop her.

I press my hands to my ears, trying to block out a bunch of Crale kids' annoying clapping. I always hated the clapping games they played with us when coming over to trade. But they were the closest village to us and we needed the minerals and lumber so we always put up with it. "Ugh. Don't remind me about all that gross stuff."

"You've never had a crush?" Val narrows her eyes, leaning back on the alleyway. A bright red flag flutters just past her

CHAPTER 16: KORE. JUST. KORE.

shoulder. The lion on it scowls at me.

"Um." I fiddle with a strand of hair. "I don't think so. The guys in my village are all weirdos." Phemus gasps in horror.

Val raises an eyebrow. "You're talkin' to me now?"

I shrug. "I can't hold grudges forever."

Finally, Phemus, who looked like was going to explode while we talked, bursts out, "How can you turn your back on love? It's the most amazing feeling ever!"

"Well, most of the guys in my village don't even know my name."

Phemus' jaw drops. "But you're super memorable." My face reddens. H-he really thinks that? "You saved me and Val, how could anyone forget someone like that?" I smile, my chest warming. He's right, I did save them, and if I save more people… Then maybe I can have even more friends. Maybe people will smile when they see me and remember my name and call me interesting. Does that mean Dad is—was—wrong?

Phemus' head tilts, reminding me to give him an explanation. "I'm the middle child of seven kids. There were always so many of us that everybody only remembered the interesting ones."

"Who cares what everyone remembers?" Val says, picking at her nails.

"Easy to say when you go to a fancy Evin school. I'm sure no one's ever forgotten your name." Val doesn't respond, simply staring at the floor.

Phemus glances between us, clears his throat, and then chirps, "Val, you have to have like-liked someone, right?"

Val's eyes glaze over. For a moment, I'm worried she's not going to respond again since she just keeps staring at the cobblestone. "Once."

"Really? What was he like?"

Val clenches her jaw. In a tone as sharp as a dagger she says, "Selfless."

Phemus backs away from the rigid girl. Okay, we definitely hit a nerve. And I don't want to upset the person who's going to train me later. Even if she is oddly closed off about things. I clear my throat. "Have you ever been in love, Phemus?

He puts his hands on his face, one eye watering. Then he sighs dramatically. "Back when I was young and foolish, I like-liked this girl."

Young and foolish? "How old were you?" I sigh.

"Ten."

"How old are ya now?" Val chimes in, voice softening. Good, looks like she's feeling better.

"Eleven." He clears his throat. "Anyways, she was super nice. She baked the best fresh stones I've ever tasted! And we always used to hold hands in the red tunnels underneath the oogly flowers. Then she found out about my love for humans and she made fun of me!" He sniffles. "After that we never spoke again."

I pat Phemus' back. "That sucks."

"I guess, we were never meant to be." He wipes a tear away, slumping back in the barn. "I just wanted to meet humans and their amazing chairs…"

"Everybody knows chairs are stupid," Belen grumbles, poking out from the edge of the alleyway. "Now, come on, we found a different way through Crale."

Penelope beams next to him. Everyone perks up. "We're going to the basement."

* * *

CHAPTER 16: KORE. JUST. KORE.

Apparently, Crale has a basement. Basically, Crale is built on a series of jagged cliffs. Underneath said cliffs are a cave system which a few busy Crale civilians rush through. According to Belen, they're so cold, damp, and generally unpleasant that only people in a real hurry actually go through them.

Goo drips off a slimy vine above us and splatters onto my face. It reeks of rats and cockroaches. Yeah, I see where Belen's coming from. For once. Penelope, however, doesn't seem to mind the goo, misty curved cliffs, or hissing bugs. She skips over puddles and gawks at the houses lined above us.

"Back before Belen and I first started dating I used to use these tunnels to visit his house everyday." She smiles, nudging his arm. "Don't you remember, Belbel?" Belbel? I snicker, only for Belen to shoot me a death glare.

Suddenly, a thundering wave of clapping rushes over us. Unlike before, they're loud and pound across the stony walls nearby. They form elaborate patterns as the Crale villagers above us crowd together.

"What is that?" I gawk.

"We only clap like that when someone important is visiting," Belen says. The applause echoes in my ears. I wonder what it would feel like for people to clap like that for me.

"But we should be able to hear who's talking underneath the village in case you're curious about what's going on. The voices always echo across the rocks here," Penelope adds.

Phemus squints at the houses perched above the rocky terrain, pulling his hat up slightly. Although we're technically in a cave system below the city, there are a few openings in the ceiling which allow us to see above. "If you squint really hard you can even see them too!"

Val tugs at his arm. "Who cares? We've gotta go."

I follow Phemus' gaze to a person standing above the crowd. They ride an elk. Its white fur glistens like fresh snow, sparkling in the sea of black leather coats. Its rider is the opposite, short with tan skin, freckles, and—

A streak of blue hair.

My fists clench. Kore. The girl riding the elk is Kore. The girl with a stupid grin smearing her face as she moves through the crowd is Kore. The girl who the villagers rejoice upon seeing is Kore. The same Kore who watched my village burn to the ground. Who abandoned us when wolves attacked us. Who called me useless.

I freeze. Phemus, Belen, and even Penelope do the same. Val sighs, her hand dropping from Phemus' arm as she too watches the crowd with wary eyes.

A man emerges at the crowd's front. He wears a long Crale coat, which is red instead of black, and a funny hat with a green feather.

"K-Kore…" He bows. "Our beautiful Sun, as the Lord of Crale I am humbled to welcome you to our village. If there is anything we can do for you…"

Kore's eyes never leave the sky throughout this whole ordeal. Once he finishes, a faint smile dots her lips. "I am pleased to be here. But I am not here for favors, but to warn the good people of this village. Dangerous bandits have burned my home, Walend. I do not know their intentions, only that they pose a threat unlike anything we've ever seen in Solia."

Of course she pretends to care now. I roll my eyes.

"Through my research, I discovered that the bandits not only destroyed Walend, but ransacked three other villages along the eastern coast. Oddly enough, kidnapping kids has been their main objective, despite them only burning and

CHAPTER 16: KORE. JUST. KORE.

murdering in Walend," Kore rambles on. So Walend's the exception. Why? "As such, I have made it my mission to eradicate these bandits and rescue the children they have stolen. Unfortunately, a thief has stolen the map I plan on using to locate these revolting bandits' base, which is why I have visited the noble village of Crale to see if anyone here has seen her."

The villagers nod solemnly as my guts sinks. Val shoots me a look. Looks like we're gonna have to fix this map and train soon. Otherwise, the village might turn us into Kore.

"What does she look like, our dear Sun?" Crale's Lord coos.

Even from here, I can see Kore's expression shift. Her icy black eyes harden. "She's my age, but tall with tan skin and an athletic build. She typically has a long braid of shaggy brown hair and matching brown eyes. The type of person you'd forget about in a second." My fists clench. I'm tired of this. Of being the type of person people forget about. I want to be a hero. Someone everyone cheers for. Someone everyone remembers. Someone who would've saved my dad!

"However, the map she's carrying is enchanted." She pulls out a glistening object woven together by twigs and laced with morning dewdrops. "Meaning only the person who wields my translator will be able to turn it into a map." That's it! I grin. All I need to do is steal that translator from Kore and I'll know exactly where the bandits are taking these kids! "Otherwise, it will simply look like a large leather-bound book."

Belen groans, staring at the large book I'm carrying. "What did you do this time?"

The villagers, however, begin screeching above us as Kore sighs dramatically.

"I'll find her for you, Kore!" a man shouts.

"No, I will!" shrieks a woman.

"Of course you found a way to get the entire village after you." Belen ruffles his thick black hair. "This is going to be a lot harder than I thought." I probably shouldn't tell him about Jorge chasing after me with glowing wolves either then…

But wolves, angry villagers, and a stiff Kore can't bother me right now. Because I'm going to prove her and everybody else wrong. I'm going to be a hero. But first I need that translator.

Chapter 17: Apparently, Magic Is More Complicated Than It Looks

I do have to admit, Phemus kinda has a point about these giant hats. Or maybe I'm just irritable because my entire body is sore. Val made me train all day inside Belen's barn. And she did not go easy on me. She made me teach every move to myself, which took twice as long and was twice as hard.

I fidget with my orange hat, barely avoiding slamming into a house. The fact that they're made of dark wood (Crale actually cuts down pine trees, unlike Walend) and it's pitch black doesn't help.

"Are you sure about this, Leda?" Phemus frets. "It's just Belen didn't want us leaving his barn. At all."

"Phemus," I grumble, glancing at the houses underneath the rim of my hat. I just need to find the most glamorous house here. Kore's pretty easy to find. She doesn't blend into the background, unlike me… I clench my fists. That's going to change. "We need this map to find the bandit's base. Otherwise, we'll just be wandering around the woods for hours."

Our sandals click along the cobblestones. The windows are all dark so far. At least there are hardly any people around.

"Do we have to defeat these bandits? They seem super scary!"

I stiffen. "You don't have to do anything. But those bandits wrecked my village. I'm going to make them pay, no matter what." A sliver of silver catches my eye. Sure enough, a gorgeous three-story house lined with silver and carved wooden statues rests in the distance. I grin. Perfect.

Phemus looks to Val. She shrugs. "This map'll help me see where the phoenix went. That's all I need." I make a sharp turn into an aisle of houses. Then prance towards Kore's. Next thing I know, we're outside and in front of the towering black house. "This is the place Kore's staying at, see!" I point to an open window. Crale's Lord snores inside the bedroom. "She's the Sun so she'd have to sleep at the most respected person in Crale's house."

"You're so observant!"

"Thank you, Phemus." I grin, placing my hand on the door's silver-rimmed knob. Man, Crale's Lord must really love silver.

Val rolls her eyes. "The door is gonna be lock—"

The door creaks open as I smile. The one thing Walend and Crale share in common (besides their leather production) is unlocked doors. Walend considers everyone family and Crale is too cocky about their wall to think they need to lock their doors.

"Wh—"

"Shh!" I shush Phemus before he can say anything. We definitely can't let Kore know we're here. Here consists of a long wooden table (that's embroidered in silver too, of course), several monster heads, and a lot of Crale flags. Ew.

I gesture for the others to start searching. Phemus immediately begins rummaging through everything. Val follows his

CHAPTER 17: APPARENTLY, MAGIC IS MORE COMPLICATED THAN IT...

lead, ducking into another hallway. Now, where would Kore store a map translator?

Probably in her room, which means I need to find a staircase. Our Lord has a two-story house too, and all the bedrooms are on the second floor. I duck into one hallway. No staircases at the end. But Phemus is there, noisily rummaging through chests.

"Phemus—"

"Um, I've been meaning to ask you something, Leda. Why did those guards hate me?"

My eyes widen. "What?"

Phemus' head hangs low. "Back in the forest I was scared and alone but I saw some humans. So I waved at them, only for them to yell and attack me! They banged my head into a tree and then I woke up the next morning being dragged down to this dark scary box. The whole time they were laughing and poking me and calling me mean names and when I told them to stop they broke my eye-extender." He sniffles. "But I love humans and I know they're all amazing, so why were those people mean to me?"

I bite my cheek. "Not everyone is nice. There are lots of bad people out there."

"W-What?" he stammers.

The floorboards creak above us. Is someone up? "Listen, Phemus, we need to do this quickly, maybe we can talk about this later?"

He nods and whimpers "Okay" as I duck into another hallway. This one contains a pretty bored-looking Val. She's searching under a painting of two men arguing on top of a cliff. A Walend cliff. Ha, I knew Crale could never forget my village!

"See!" I whisper to Val. "That's another reason why my village is better."

"What?" Val hisses between rummaging through the Lord of Crale's sweaty leather coats. She winces at the stench. And Crale has the nerve to say we smell.

"Crale is totally jealous of us because a long time ago our founders fought over this strip of land and we won."

"Don't care," Val grumbles, rummaging through more clothing.

"And now we have it, which means we get to watch pretty ocean sunsets every night. Not that I did, because my house wasn't close to the cliff. But my friend visited it a few times. Oh! And these pretty glowing flowers called seaflowers grow out of it."

"Still don't care." Val examines a tiny shoe in front of her. She's never seen Crale shoes, has she?

"And its grass is great for cows, so we'll never have to rely on their stupid Crale leather. We're the only village in the country that doesn't have to!" I pat her head. "See? Isn't Walend super cool?"

Val narrows her eyes. "No. Getting this translator so I can find my phoenix is cool."

"Jeez, that's what I've been trying to do. You didn't happen to see a hallway with a staircase, did you?" She points to a third hallway whose entrance is only a few feet from this one. "Thanks!" I duck into the other hallway. One day I'll get that girl to start caring about things other than finding that phoenix.

Finally, I arrive in a hallway whose wooden planks are coated in red paint. At the end of the hallway is a steep stone staircase. Yes! I rush through the hallway, passing paintings of

CHAPTER 17: APPARENTLY, MAGIC IS MORE COMPLICATED THAN IT...

old Crale lords. All of them share the same hooked nose and choppy black hair. Makes sense since they're all descended from Crale. I wonder what it must've been like to be one of those thirteen original explorers. To go from living in the old Solia, the real Solia, with beautiful hills and never-ending food to being trapped here. To meet Evin, the explorer so intelligent, strong, and kind that the city she founded became our capital. To live in a time with no Suns. A time before the first Skycharter crossed the mountains to save us all.

I shake my head, then scramble up to the wooden stairs. Who would want that? There'd be no one to save you when the monsters came. It'd be so easy to lose someone to bandits. My chest squeezes. No. I'm not thinking about that. I can't think about that or I'll freak out. And I can't freak out while those bandits are still out there. While other people's dads are in danger.

Kore's room is pretty easy to find. Silver lines the ceiling, forming tiny little stars that glint in the moonlight from Kore's open window. Finely carved furniture and a wool blanket encase her in her bed. Sure enough, she lies fast asleep, a book draped over her chest. She looks so…peaceful, snuggled with a book in her lap. Her face is smoothed out. Her hair is scattered everywhere on her pillows and her arms loosely grip her book. Even her normally defiant bright strand of blue hair is somehow duller.

I frown, glancing at the translator she's shoved on top of her book. She won't mind if I take this, right? It's not like she even wants to be the Sun anyways. Ugh. Why am I even thinking like this? She let my village burn down and did nothing!

With that thought, I grab the translator, only for a cold clammy hand to seize mine. Kore's eyes pop open. "I knew you would come here, thief!" She outstretches her arm, ready to aim a bolt of water at me.

Without thinking, I slam her book into her shoulder. She grunts and lets go of my hand. A jet of water buzzes by my ear, barely missing my head. Then I grab the translator and rush out of her room.

Kore's right on my heels. Shoot! I unsheathe my sword and her eyes widen.

"You wouldn't, that's not a fair fight," she growls.

"You can shoot water out of your hands! Plus, you could call the Lord of Crale any moment."

She scoffs, rubbing her wet hands. "I don't need to call the Lord, I can defeat you on my own."

"Like you defeated those wolves?"

"I—" she starts, only for Phemus to slam his body onto her. She groans underneath him, completely unable to move.

"I got her!" Phemus rolls off the stunned girl. Then he grabs her shirt and hoists her into the air. "What should I do with her?"

I furrow my brows as Kore continues groaning. "I have an idea."

* * *

Val can't stop snickering as she watches Kore struggle on the hook we put the edge of her dress on. I giggle in between holding my sword to her neck so she doesn't use her powers on us.

Finally, she stops giggling. "You sure we should do this in here?" Val shakily holds the translator since she's the one who knows how to wield magic.

CHAPTER 17: APPARENTLY, MAGIC IS MORE COMPLICATED THAN IT...

"Just in case Kore was lying and there's something else we need. We'll quickly try it."

She nods, furrowing her brows as she fixates on the woven mess of twigs. She shakes it, once, twice. Then starts frowning.

"What's wrong, Val?" Phemus murmurs.

"It won't." She fiddles with the translator again. Its dark branches squeak under her grip. They're the opposite of her fumbling pale fingers. "Work." All our eyes turn to Kore, who sighs.

"It's a moonstar." We all tilt our heads. She rolls her eyes, blowing at her faded blue strip of hair. "They're the second type of magic. I have the first type, it's much rarer. It only occurs when a person naturally produces magic in their blood in such high quantities that they can cast spells through vessels."

"Vessels?" My head spins.

"Tiny holes in a person's arms which allow magic to shoot out. Mine allow me to produce water. But that's beside the point." Kore shakes her head, shivering in her hook. "Moonstars are items with certain chemicals in them that can react with a person who possesses even a small amount of magic in their blood to cast spells."

"So none of us except you can use this, can we?" I scowl. Curse our magicless blood!

Kore squints at the blade in front of her. "I mean, not technically," she blurts out. Then her face reddens. "Wait, I didn't mean—!" She gulps as I press the blade closer to her neck. She tries to kick my blade away. I dodge her blow but she does manage to make my satchel fall, spilling its contents onto the floor. Val's eyes narrow at the vial of ash but I keep my blade on Kore.

"Which one?"

"The leafer," she squeaks. "He can't cast magic but forest spirits technically have enough that they could..."

"Hooray, I can help!" He smiles in between his whispers. Then he grabs the translator and fiddles with its center. With a click, the translator rises up above the map, spraying out a hazy silver glow as it flies over the map.

"Awesome," I whisper.

The map lights up below it. Solia, its buildings and glorious woods, rise out of the map, flickering like candlelight. A tiny phoenix zips right past me, while a group of petite bandits rests under the tree it's perched on. I can even see Walend, freshly charred, with its familiar gray beaches and bustling wildflowers. My mom's outside of our house, sobbing, Homer grabbing her shoulders. My fist clenches. I'll make this better, I'll avenge him.

I turn my gaze to the rest of the bandits. This is perfect! I can see where all of them are and that they're all heading in the same direction. Towards a jagged cave system. So that's their base.

"Humans are so cool!" Phemus squeaks as I grin.

"This is perfect. Now we know exactly where the bandits are and where your phoenix is, Val!"

Val, however, is frowning, her whole body trembling. "Why'd you have a vial of ash in your bag, Leda?"

"No idea. I stole it from the bandits." Phemus gasps dramatically. "You should've seen the other stuff in it. There was a vial of blood. It was gross."

"Blood!?" Val's eyes widen. Her face looks older without the fluffy coat to balance out her sharp jawline. "Leda, what'd the

CHAPTER 17: APPARENTLY, MAGIC IS MORE COMPLICATED THAN IT...

bandits do to your village?"

"I already told you." I tilt my head. The silver sheen of the map flickers across our faces. "They burned it."

"Are you okay, Val? You're acting very intense!" Phemus worries.

"This is important," she growls. "Leda, did they kill anyone?"

"Th-they—"

A growl hisses out the front door, which we left slightly open. It belongs to a bristling gray wolf.

Chapter 18: Angry Wolves Are Following Me Again

A gray wolf approaches us, snarling. It has long, shaggy fur and black markings all over its body. It snarls, waltzing through the house.

"Why do evil wolves keep attacking us!?" Phemus grabs his hat's tip and lurches it upwards to stare at the gray figure.

"Why's a wolf in the middle of Crale?" Kore hisses, still struggling on her hook. Val traces her cauldron. Whatever she was trying to say earlier is going to have to wait.

"Jorge." My mouth goes dry. I don't know how he figured out how to convince the wolves to sneak into Crale.

"Who's Jorge!?" Phemus squeaks as the wolf snaps at him. Shoot. We're going to wake up Crale's Lord with all this commotion. "Please be nice, puppy!"

Val rolls her eyes. "Bow boy. The guy you jumped off a cliff to escape, right?"

"You jumped off a cliff!?" Phemus whisper-shouts. Kore rolls her eyes as if she'd already expected it from me. "I knew humans were awesome!"

"Yeah, that's him. And he may or may not be trying to bring me back to Walend, where it's safe." My face flushes. "He's kind of a goody-two-shoes."

CHAPTER 18: ANGRY WOLVES ARE FOLLOWING ME AGAIN

"A goody-two-shoes shoes who sics wolves on people—" Val mutters, only for the wolf to leap onto her.

She screams. I unsheathe my sword and slice at its side. It screeches when my blade sinks into its fur and slams into a bookshelf. Above us, figures rustle. Kore's calls for help and Crale's Lord's shouts intermingle.

"Val! Are you okay!?" Phemus pulls her up. She nods.

"Guys, we need to get out of here, they're up!" I rush over to the book. In a quick swoop, I pluck it off the table. The wolf slowly gets up, still staggering from the blood loss. Then he scrambles towards me. Fortunately, the bloody wolf is too wounded to reach me in time. I'm already rushing out the door after Phemus and Val. The wolves follow us, so we don't have to worry about helping Kore.

A scream echoes in the air as we scramble out of the Lord's house.

"Woooolf!!!" the Lord screeches. Then he shrieks a second time when he sees Kore stuck on a hook. Immediately, lights pop up in every window. Villagers creak open their windows and doors. A shaggy, bloody wolf bounds out of the house and straight towards us. Of course, he's somehow okay. There's gotta be a way to escape this, right?

"The basement!" I huff. There was a door we used to get down there. If we close that door in the wolf's face, it shouldn't be able to get through. Even if it did, we'd be long gone after going down that steep staircase. "We can head in there to escape!" The others nod.

We turn a corner, ramming open the door, and rushing onto the staircase which Val scrambles down through. I unsheathe my sword as the wolf approaches us again, growling angrily. But between my nerves and trying to hold the map, the sword ends up slipping out of my hands and clattering all the way down the stairs.

Double great. Phemus nods grimly. "Don't worry, I got this Leda!" But instead of fighting the wolf or closing the door, the leafer yanks me backward, and I go sliding down the stone staircase. "Catch her, Val!"

A shocked Val rests at the staircase's end. I slide down. I never noticed this before, but she's tiny and scrawny and much, much shorter than me. I barrel down the staircase, crashing into Val. Fortunately for me, but unfortunately for her, her small body breaks my fall.

"Ow…" she grumbles as we both get up.

"I'm comiiinnnnggg!!!" Phemus calls and scrambles down the stairs.

Behind him, the wolf barks. It cautiously extends its paw onto a stair.

"Phemus, close the door!" I yell. "The wolf's right behind you!"

"Aaaaahhhh!!!" Phemus screams as the wolf almost snatches his hat. In a fit of pure panic, he grabs the doorknob and slams the door in the wolf's face, whacking its poor paw in the process. Fortunately, Phemus reaches the end of the stairs completely unharmed. The wolf's barking fades away.

"Thank goodness!" I laugh. The others join me. We all slink between the cave walls. A few lazy green bugs buzz by us. For once I'm happy to see them and sit in goo. Meanwhile, a wolf's howl continues pounding through the air as villagers scramble around trying to stop him.

Eventually, it dies down, but Val's worrying glances haven't. Before that wolf had attacked us, she'd asked me… she'd asked me if—

CHAPTER 18: ANGRY WOLVES ARE FOLLOWING ME AGAIN

"Leda." Val gets up and starts pacing in the empty cave system. "Did they kill someone?"

I gulp. My eyes blur and my entire body shakes. I'm not supposed to think about this. I'm supposed to stay strong, but for some reason, I blurt out, "My Dad. They, he…" Phemus pulls me into a hug. Val's eyes soften, only for her to begin pacing even more. I sniffle, breaking Phemus' warm hold. "I'm fine." I rub my eyes. "Sorry, I don't usually get like that."

Both of them shoot me concerned glances. But if either has a problem, they don't say anything. Val, however, looks like she's going to vomit.

"What's going on, Val?" I ask.

Val shakes her head. "This is not good."

"Val." I grab her shoulders, stopping her pacing. "Tell us what's wrong."

She pulls out her scroll and points to its small letters. "Ash from a new flame and blood of a freshly-killed soul. That's how you summon a phoenix."

Chapter 19: Phoenixes Are Way Scarier Than I Thought

Phoenix. My mind races back to the bird I rescued in that icy river, with its long feathers, firey glow, and sharp beak. But why would bandits want that bird of all things?

"Hold up." Phemus frowns as we rush through the cave system. We can't risk those villagers or Jorge's wolves finding us. "None of what you just said made any sense! But maybe that's because I can hardly hear in this stupid hat..." He scratches at the floppy object.

"The vials." Val reaches into my bag and pulls one containing ash out. She pours the black flakes out, rolling them in her fingers. "Ash of a new flame. The ash's gotta be from something that's recently burned. Like your village. Then the blood needs to come from a freshly killed soul. That's why they killed..." Val avoids my gaze.

That's why they...my eyes water. "W-why would the bandits want a phoenix?"

Phemus crosses his arms. "Don't the bandits like stealing? That's what I heard the guards say!" I nod. "Couldn't they sell the phoenix for lots of money?"

I shake my head. "I literally just found out phoenixes existed

CHAPTER 19: PHOENIXES ARE WAY SCARIER THAN I THOUGHT

a few days ago. And my best friend is a farmer, he has a book detailing every monster out there that Solians know about. Plus, I've never heard anyone talk about them before. There are a lot of animals like that. Entirely new species that exist in the woods but no one knows or cares about because there's no demand for them. Most Solian traders wouldn't be willing to buy, much less spend thousands of mintas or damians on a bird they know wouldn't sell for much."

Val paces back and forth through the street while muttering under her breath, "Not good. Not good."

"Could you stop and explain to us what's going on?"

Val finally exhales and says, "There's a reason I need a phoenix for my exam. They're powerful. And do lots of damage."

Phemus shivers. "What kind of damage!?"

"If you think your village burning was bad…imagine the whole country burning." Phemus and I both tremble. "That's what phoenixes can do."

I remember the clump of matted feathers underneath my fingers followed by the bird bursting into flames. "The phoenix must've gotten away, because I found it in the river after they burned my village."

"You saw a phoenix! That's so cool!" Phemus cheers as he tries touching one of the jade-colored bugs flying next to us. The bug squeaks and flies away from him, ramming itself into a wall.

"What's stopping them from burning another village? There's a reason regular people aren't supposed to know about phoenixes." Val grits her teeth as my gut churns. Right. Regular people like me aren't supposed to know anything. Val begins twirling a strand of her long blonde hair. "There's no way to stop them from gettin' the phoenix."

"Unless we take out Bone. Together." They both stare at me. Defeating the bandits was supposed to be my goal. My way of being a hero. Of saving all the other people they want to kill. Of giving justice to my dad. But these bandits are way more organized and dangerous than I thought. I'm going to need their help if I want to defeat Bone.

Val nods. "Deal. Can't have those bandits stealin' my phoenix." We both turn to Phemus, whose ears have flattened as we continue strolling towards Belen's barn.

"If they're bad humans like you say, Leda," Phemus whimpers looking at me. "Th-then maybe I could help."

"Awesome." I tap my map. "Now that I know where their base is, the plan is simple. We sneak into the base, and defeat Bone. Since he's their leader, we can force him to order the rest of the bandits to turn themselves into the Evin Guard." Aka the best guards and jail system in our whole country. They're tasked with protecting Solia's head governors, the Lords and Ladies of Evin, for a reason.

Val nods as we stop at the ladder to Belen's barn. A rather annoyed Belen is right next to it. "We'll leave tomorrow. First thing."

Belen scowls at us. Then glances up at the trapdoor we'd previously entered through to sneak into his barn. His hair is unkempt and he's dressed in gray pajamas. "The whole village is awake! Why do you keep causing problems?" I don't meet his eyes as I climb up the ladder. "Hey, answer me!" Val and Phemus follow my lead, both exhausted from the night. We all three have one goal in our minds at this point: go to sleep after a crazy past couple days. Hopefully, this time I'll actually get a good night's sleep instead of another nightmare.

CHAPTER 19: PHOENIXES ARE WAY SCARIER THAN I THOUGHT

"Guys, I said answer me!"

* * *

I'm back in the river. Dull blue water illuminated by a fiery bright light engulfs me. Instead of whipping past me, the pink salmon stay frozen in the river. I try touching one. But my hand won't move. All my body can do is shiver and try not to gurgle river water down.

My head throbs as a piercing screech echoes everywhere. Muffled and distorted by the river water, it sounds eerier than anything I've ever heard before. Like a mix between a child screaming and an old dog wheezing. It comes from a giant ball of flames in front of me. In the center of that ball rests the phoenix. I'd recognize those long, curling feathers anywhere.

It shrieks and swims backward. Until a long pale hand grabs onto its chicken-like legs. My eyes widen. At least, I think they do. I can't move anything so maybe nothing is happening at all. Either way, the person tugs on the phoenix, dragging it up towards the surface. I'm struck by her stringy black hair and sharp reddish eyes. Phoebe. Phoebe is taking the phoenix! I have to stop her.

Finally, my legs and arms tingle again. Yes! It's go time. I kick as fast as I can after the bandit only for someone to tug on my sandal. I look down and nearly scream. It's Jorge. Except it isn't him. Instead of his usual alert black eyes, his are a milky white with no pupils. There's no person behind that endless white.

I turn back towards Phoebe, trying to loosen Jorge's grip on me. But she's too fast for me and Jorge's grip is too strong. The woman escapes into the surface, and both the phoenix and her disappear into the glittering sun. Cheers shriek above us. They're just as loud as the ones Crale gave to Kore. What is going on up there? Did someone defeat her? Are they cheering for her? Is anyone going to come back for me?

Another person tugs on my sandal. My entire body shivers when I glance at him. Dad. Lifeless, soulless, Dad. How he was when I saw him back then. My heart hammers. I can't look at him. I can't see him like this again. I just want to be up there, away from this scary river with these lifeless people. I want to be with the cheering crowds and laughter.

Dad's meaty hand sinks into my ankle and my body turns motionless again. All I can do is watch as he drags me down. And hope that someone above hasn't forgotten about me. But as the light grows dimmer, I realize no one's coming to rescue us. Instead, I hear the cheers grow more muffled and muffled. Until they're gone.

Chapter 20: Belen Can Actually Be Nice?

I gasp, slamming into a stall door. The hard wood thunks against my head. Ow. What a great way to wake up. Itchy hay scratches at my legs and cows moo, reminding me I'm back in Belen's barn.

"Are you okay, Leda?" Phemus' head pops up from the stall next to me. His black hair is a scrambled mess. Whether it's from sleeping in a barn or still left over from the hat he wore yesterday, I have no idea.

"Yeah." I pat the stall door. "I won't let this stupid door keep me down."

"Oh! I meant, upset. You seemed really sad while you were sleeping."

I rub my eyes, shivering. I remember the silence. Floating in that cold river. And my dad. His eyes. He was so limp and he looked like how I saw him before. I gulp. *Don't think about it, Leda. Don't think about how you saw him, his laughter and smiles gone forever. If you do, you'll go crazy.*

"L-leda—" Phemus starts. An elk in the stall behind him shoves her head in his face. He scrambles away. "Don't spit in my face!"

I laugh. At least Phemus can distract me from those awful

thoughts.

"All right." Belen enters the stable. He carries a tray of steaming food while Penelope trails behind him. "Time to finally leave my barn!"

Phemus and I both exit the stalls we were standing in. With a jolt, Val startles awake and leaves hers too. Belen sets the tray down, which contains three bowls of soup. Phemus, Val, and I all down them. Turns out being hunted by wolves makes you very hungry.

Penelope giggles, and a large contraption rattles in her hands. "You ate that fast!" Her voice is as quiet as ever.

Belen touches Penelope's shoulder, causing Phemus' eye to nearly bulge out of its socket. "Penelope finally finished fixing your, uh, machine-thing, and I'm guessing you already solved your map problem, which means it's time for you to leave Crale. Finally." Penelope narrows her eyes at Belen, who stiffens.

"For once we're on the same page." I glare at him. Time to defeat Bone.

"My eye-extender!" Phemus screeches, scrambling to the girl. She hands him a glistening eye-extender which he swirls around. With a squelch, Phemus opens the eye-extender and reaches towards his eye.

"Phemus!" Val and I both shout.

"Oh, sorry." Phemus waltzes to the back of the room and turns around. Once complete, he faces us again. Belen's jaw drops. Phemus' eye has returned to its rightful place inside the tiny contraption. Already, the pops of pink normally surrounding its edges fade away. "Hooray! My eye was starting to get all itchy because of the upstairs air. It was really annoying."

CHAPTER 20: BELEN CAN ACTUALLY BE NICE?

"H-how..." Belen stammers. I lean on the stall wall, then grab my bag. I hoist it over my shoulders and walk past him.

"You'll get used to it," I snicker and leave the barn.

Val, Phemus, and Penelope tag behind. Belen stumbles onto the empty dirt path, still carrying his tray. To our right rests Belen's family home, a small red house, while behind us stands Crale's looming wall.

Penelope glances at the wall. "Are you sure you'll be able to leave Crale safely by yourselves?"

I touch my scabbard. "We should be okay. Thanks, both of you."

Belen's face flushes. A breeze ruffles his feathery black hair. "You're thanking me!?"

"You both helped us a lot, giving us a place to stay, food, fixing Phemus' eye-extender. If there's anything I can ever do to repay you, let me know."

Penelope smiles. "It was no problem." She elbows Belen.

"Um, you're welcome, Leda." Belen stares at his feet. I smile. Turns out he can be nice, with some encouragement.

"Byeeee!!!" Phemus yells as we leave.

Penelope and Belen both wave goodbye. Penelope beams and even Belen cracks a smile. Finally, we reach Crale's wall. Val somehow figures out which loose board lets us inside it. Then Phemus and I clamber in. Val follows us, closing the wall's new hole behind her.

We're immediately coated in darkness, sharp rocks jutting out underneath our feet. Cold air mixed with the stench of sweat engulfs us.

"Anyone remember to bring a torch?" Val grumbles. Nobody responds for a few seconds.

"No..." I realize. "Phemus?"

"Oh! I just shook my head, but I guess you can't see that." Phemus chuckles.

I poke Phemus' sagging arm. "Wait, can you see right now?"

"Yup! This is exactly like the tunnels!"

"You have night vision? That's awesome." Is Val nodding in agreement? Instead of rolling her eyes? No, the darkness must be tricking my eyes.

"Thanks, Leda!"

A flickering orange-red illuminates the room. It seeps out of the creaks in the stone walls next to us, flickering across our faces like fire. Following it is the thunderous roar of screams. Children's screams. No. Not again. It can't be—

"Hey kids!" a voice calls. I spin around and am met with Mateo waving his hands around. "If ya know what's good for you, you'll freeze." He unsheathes his sword.

Barak, Mateo, and Phoebe's eyes widen when they recognize us. Barak trembles, gripping his torch while Mateo traces his sword's hilt. Both of them scowl while the tips of Phoebe's mouth curl into a grin.

"It's you, what's your name, Leda?" She snickers. "It's so forgettable, I have a tough time remembering." Okay, that's it! How dare they insult my name?

"Ugh..." Mateo grumbles. "Why do we always run into her or that stupid boy who sics his wolves on us instead of a kid Bone could actually use!?" Jorge is attacking the bandits with his wolves? Really? Phoebe swats Mateo. "Ow!"

"Neither of you have any brains," she grumbles, unsheathing her sword.

Barak mimics her. "W-what should we do, Phoebe?"

Phoebe leans down, grabs a rock, and hurls it at Val. The girl immediately slumps unconscious.

CHAPTER 20: BELEN CAN ACTUALLY BE NICE?

"Val!" Phemus and I shout.

"Kidnap the kids," Phoebe orders. "The others are already kidnapping the rest of those Crale brats. We want to show them up, don't we?" The flicker of firelight oozes in between the wooden rods once again. Even more screams screech through the air.

My heart squeezes. They're doing it again. Burning everything to ashes, hurting people. But now Penelope, Belen, even Kore, they're all at risk. If the bandits aren't lying, then any of them could be kidnapped, never to be seen again. My fists clench around my sword's hilt.

"This ends now," I grunt.

Mateo giddily grins. What is with this guy and liking to fight me!? He launches while Barak charges towards Phemus. Phoebe simply leans on the wall, smirking. I deflect Mateo's blow. He follows up with an even stronger one, which I barely dodge. With a thud, it slashes against the wooden wall. I attempt slashing at his legs, but he dodges.

Oh great. He's clearly a much better fighter than me. How am I going to win— He slashes right next to me. As I dodge, I trip over a rock and tumble to the ground. With a grunt, I spit dirt out of my mouth, quickly rolling onto my back. As I do, Mateo pins his sword to my throat. My eyes widen and blur with tears. I couldn't win against Mateo even after Val's training. How am I supposed to beat Bone too?

To my left, Barak jabs his torch at Phemus, backing the leafer into the wall. Mateo grins. "Gotcha." He whacks the hilt of his sword into my head and my vision goes black.

Chapter 21: Ugh...

The rattling of wheels and clicking of hooves wake me up. That and the fact that Phemus' entire body slams into me.

"Phemus," I grumble.

"Sorry!" He rolls off me, waving his arms in the air. They're bound by thick rope. "I couldn't use my arms to balance when this cart ran over a rock."

I peer down at my bound hands. My bag, map, and Val's cauldron are long gone, but Phemus still has his eye-extender. All three of us rest in a cart with long metal bars locking us inside. Behind them rests the Solian woods, with its tall dark trees, fresh morning sunlight, and blue wildflowers. Val sits at the cart's end, her head burrowed in her knees. Moving the cart forward is an elk with shaggy black fur. He's almost identical to Pine except he's entirely black while Pine has a white underbelly.

"Those Crale guards were so easy to defeat. Good thing too, because now we get to use their prisoner carts. Crale's obsession with trapping people in jail came in handy for once," Mateo blabbers. He, Phoebe, and Barak sit on a wooden ledge attached to the cart's front. Next to them is a cloth bag, which likely has our stuff inside.

CHAPTER 21: UGH...

"They all seemed pretty tired. I think they're overworked." Barak scratches his hair, which sticks up like a tree.

"Really?" Phoebe grumbles. "I hadn't noticed."

Mateo snickers while Barak's face flushes. He stares at the grass the cart flattens. "S-sorry, Phoebe."

The cart rumbles over another rock. I slam into the bars of the cell, using my legs to orient myself. Fortunately, I don't topple over like Phemus did. The movement jolts Val out of her knees. Her eyes are glossy, only for them to sharpen as she focuses on me. Phemus tries getting up, but the movement sends him tumbling to the floor.

The bandits could be taking us to their base, which would be a good thing. However, there's no guarantee they're taking us there at all or that we'll be able to escape without our weapons. That settles it. "We need to find a way out of here. There's no way we can defeat Bone if we're stuck as his prisoners. So let's all search the cage for clues. And try to do it quickly." The sooner we stop these bandits, the less they can do with that phoenix and the poor kids they kidnapped. But am I really a match for Bone? I couldn't even defeat Mateo. I shake my head. Now's not the time to think like that. Now's the time to escape.

All three of us fixate on the cage. Phemus' ears flick up and down while Val stares at the bars with her icy eyes. I rub my hands together, itchy rope scratching against my wrists. Firstly, we need to escape these. I wiggle my wrists, but it doesn't do much. Okay then. Let's try another strategy. I bring the rope to my mouth and gnaw on its pieces, continuing to wiggle my hands. Eventually the rope loosens and I drag my wrists out. Yes!

"H—" I cover Phemus' mouth before he cheers, pointing to

the bandits sitting a few feet away.

Val follows my lead, freeing her hands. Then we help Phemus escape his ropes.

"Alright. One step down," I whisper. "Now we need to get out of this cage. Any ideas?"

Phemus gestures to the cage's back. "That door has a fancy thing on its side. The humans used that to trap me in the cell." He shivers. I pat his shoulder. Crale people can be jerks. Even if Penelope and Belen were surprisingly nice. I hope they're okay.

I squint at the door's thick black lock. "It's called a lock. It keeps the door from opening." My gut tightens. That lock looks very complicated, with its numerous parts and tall height. This is going to be difficult.

Inside its circular contraption, Phemus' eye widens. "How do we break it?"

"We need to pick it." I scratch my head. "But it looks complicated. And I'm terrible at picking locks."

"I can pick it," Val murmurs. "But we need my cauldron first. There's a lotta valuable stuff in there."

"Okay." I peer at the cloth bag Mateo forages through. "That's going to be—"

A howl interrupts me, followed by the whoosh of an arrow. Jorge! It thumps into the ledge the trio of bandits sit on, barely missing Barak's leg. He yelps. So the bandits weren't lying about him attacking them. Jorge. Nervous, cautious Jorge is actually willing to attack bandits for me. My chest warms.

"The freak's back." Mateo reaches over and yanks the arrow out of the ledge. A few gray wolves dart out of the trees. They scamper in front of the cart, stopping the elk in its tracks. "You got lucky last time! But we'll get you..." Mateo continues

CHAPTER 21: UGH...

hollering at the trees. There's no response.

I snort as we watch a grown man yell at trees for three minutes straight. Phemus' ears flatten from the sound. Val bursts out laughing. Finally, Mateo stops and someone whistles from behind the trees. He hurls Jorge's arrow at the trees, only for it to thunk into a branch, its tawny color blending with the smooth wood. The whistling continues.

"Why you little—!" Mateo jumps off the ledge, unsheathing his sword. Immediately, he slashes his way through the wolves, becoming a blur of black hair.

Meanwhile, a stream of arrows flies towards the ledge, forcing Phoebe and Barak off. Now, on the ground they too have to fight the pack of wolves. Perfect!

"Val, pick the lock!" She nods and I scamper towards the cage's front. "Phemus, help me!"

We both extend our arms through the bars and open the bag resting on the ledge. Together we grab Val's cauldron and pull it inside the cage. Yes! We do the same for the map and the translator. I reach further into the bag. Now all that's left is my sword.

The elk shrieks after a wolf bites its leg instead of a bandit's. It bucks up then charges. The wolves and bandits scamper out of its way. The movement sends us tumbling onto the floor as trees whip by us. A wolf chases after the cart, howling.

I grab onto the bars to orient myself, only for the elk to come loose. The cart trips over a rock and topples over. We all scream as we go crashing down and the cell door bursts open. Oh, so now it opens! My eyes slam shut as I curl into a ball, covering my head with scratched-up arms. I screech when metal bars ram into them.

Then everything goes silent.

A stream of cold water tickles my cheek. My eyes flutter open. The cage lays on its right side, resting in a small river. The stream is nowhere near the depth of the one I almost drowned in, meaning its cold water only reaches just past the right side's dark bars. It sloshes against my sandals as I get up, careful not to bang my head on the cage's left side.

Phemus pumps a fist in the air. "We're alive!"

Val groans, rubbing her eyes. The edges of her stringy hair drip with water. She grabs her cauldron, puts all her materials back, then slings it over her shoulder, sighing.

"Yeah, and we fixed the door problem." I point at the once locked door, which now swings back and forth.

"Yes!" Phemus cheers as we exit the cage. I spread my arms out. We're finally free, at last! And to think I was actually worried we—

The bushes rustle as a wolf jumps out of them. He growls at us, exposing a ray of sharp white teeth. Not again. I touch my belt. Except my sword's gone. Stupid bandits!

Val fixates on her cauldron, retrieving a bottle of some sort of gas. "Hold your breath. This'll last five seconds."

She opens the bottle and a cloud of dark green gas swarms my vision. The wolf yelps as he staggers back and forth. Finally, he howls before collapsing. The gas fades away.

"That is awesome! Is the wolfie okay?" Phemus pats its furry head.

"It only knocked him out. He'll be fine. Just outta our hair." She bends down, tracing his black markings. The same ones which glow blue when he eats seaflowers. I grin. So she is interested in some stuff besides her exam and saving that phoenix. Val's face flushes when she catches my glance and she stumbles upwards, rubbing her hand on her leather pants.

CHAPTER 21: UGH...

I squint at the girl. "Wait, how do your potions work? Are they moonstars?" No, they can't be. Val didn't have magic in her blood since she couldn't use Kore's translator. Val bites her lip as she stuffs her vial back into her cauldron.

"Nah. It's a special type. Only taught in Evin." She glares straight ahead, avoiding my gaze. That's all I'm going to get out of her, isn't it?

"A special type of magic! I thought only the Sun had special magic!" Phemus' one eye widens. "Wait a minute, Val, are you the Sun!?" He immediately bows, flattening at least a dozen wildflowers. I facepalm.

"Uh, no?" Val squeaks.

"Phemus. Kore is our new Sun." My gut churns. I used to hate calling her that. But am I any better? I did nothing while the bandits hurt Crale. I couldn't even escape the cage without Jorge's help! "You literally just saw her in Crale. Did you not hear Crale's Lord announce that she was the Sun?"

"The girl I tackled..." Phemus' eye widens as he ignores my question. I swear, that leafer has selective hearing. "You mean I accidentally tackled the Sun?" We both laugh but beads of sweat already form on Phemus' forehead. "B-but she didn't even look fighty. How was I supposed to know!?" Phemus stammers, stumbling to his feet, dusting off his pants. "Suns are supposed to save people, right? Defeat all those bad guys..." Phemus stops to punch an invisible enemy. "But she looked too frowny. Now Val looks fighty. She has the fight eyes!" Right, Val's the one who has fight eyes. I lower my head.

"Good to know." Val chuckles as she squeezes water out of her hair.

"Plus Leda just said you have special magic. I thought only the Sun had special magic!" And she has magic too.

"Lots of people have magic like Kore," I say. This time my voice doesn't crack. Thank goodness. "Except they're all supposed to be sent to Evin as babies and trained at a school there."

"Really? Did Kore go to that school too?"

I shrug. "I don't think so. It's weird though, she was ten when she was chosen, so she should've spent at least the first ten years of her life there." How bizarre. Well, I guess Kore has had a pretty bizarre life. Lucky her.

"Leda!" Phemus yells. I jump, only for an arrow to wham through my dress, pinning me to a tree trunk. Shoot. It's Jorge. Of course, he's still after me. But I can't face him right now. Not when the bandits are planning to capture a phoenix. And not when his doubts may have been right.

I yank the arrow out of the trunk. "It's my friend. He's after me again." I narrow my eyes. I was always the faster runner of the two of us. My eyes fixate on a large tree within walking distance. "Meet me back at that big tree. I'll distract him and get him off my trail."

"But—!" Phemus protests.

"Don't worry about me. I've got this." I hope. I race into the woods before any of them have a chance to protest.

Chapter 22: Patient Jorges Are My Enemies.

I rush through the forest, thick grass flying under my worn sandals. Jorge races after me, struggling against the greenery which latches onto his cloak. I have a head start, but he's quickly catching up. My hands tighten around the arrow. Its light feathers tickle my fingertips. I need to lose him. I glance up. A tree with branches too high for a normal person to reach stands in front of me. That's it!

I jam the arrow into the tree's trunk, ensuring it's above my head. Then I grab onto the arrow, pulling myself upwards. It cracks, almost snapping in half. Quick! By extending my leg up, I grasp onto a branch seconds before the arrow breaks. With a grunt and trembling arms, I pull myself onto the branch, tossing the map and translator up before me. The branch scratches against my knees. Sweat and blood stings my mouth.

Jorge finally catches up, stops at the tree's base, and glances up at the broken arrow. He folds his arms. "Did you seriously use my own arrow against me?"

"Did you seriously send a pack of deadly wolves after me? On numerous occasions!" I yell, almost falling off the branch.

"They weren't going to attack you." I scowl. He scratches his head. "Just make sure you didn't jump off a cliff. Again."

I shiver, rattling the branch. "Trust me, I'm never doing that again. I almost drowned. And then I started seeing glowing people. It was weird."

"Really? What happened—" Jorge shakes his head, curls flying about. "Gah! Stop distracting me. Get down here, we have to go before those bandits come back. Did you see what they did to Crale?"

I lower my eyes. How could I forget? "I was there, Jorge." I clench my fists. "But I have to stop them. They're not just kidnapping kids. They're burning villages to capture a phoenix." If I let them burn down Solia like they burned down Walend and Crale, I'd never forgive myself. Even if I'm not as good a fighter as I thought. Even if I might be as bad as Kore.

Jorge leans on the tree trunk. "And how is that our business?"

"It's our business because that phoenix could burn down Solia!"

"That's Kore's job, not ours." He furrows his brows. "I told you about this at the cliff."

"You told me I needed to grow up. And that I'm nobody," I murmur, eyes watering. Jorge bristles. "I didn't forget." Now more than ever, Jorge and what my dad said keep haunting me. Those nightmares and my own doubts prove that. I fiddle with a leaf. If only my dad was here to explain what he meant and help me through this and hug me and call me his coolest daughter— I can't think about that. Not now.

"I'm sorry." Jorge sighs, bringing me back to reality. "I shouldn't have snapped at you like that."

I hug my knees, the branch's wood scratching against my bottom. His apology is nice but for some reason his words still tug at me. I don't know why, since before I lost to Mateo, I'd had no problem drowning them out. Well, at least during

CHAPTER 22: PATIENT JORGES ARE MY ENEMIES.

the day. "It's okay."

"Thanks. Now get down from there!"

"Nope." My braid swings off my shoulder and brushes against his nose. He bats it, sighing.

"Fine then, I'll just wait here. You'll get tired of sitting up there eventually."

"Ha! You'll get tired of standing first!"

He slumps onto the ground, leaning onto against the tree trunk, then peers up at me, a stupid grin on his face. "Oh, really?"

My chest tightens. If there's one thing I know about Jorge, it's that he can be patient. Very patient. After all, he sat through the entire Skycharter ceremony just for me when he was ten. Back when he barely even knew me. I need to escape this branch or I'll be stuck here forever, doubting myself even more.

A tiny black head pops out of the bushes beneath me. Pine! He glares at Jorge then stares at me. He snorts, and turns around, gesturing with his antlers to his exposed back. Woah. This is awesome! I leap off the branch and onto the elk's back. He kicks up before charging into the woods. I turn around. "Byeeee Jorge!" I wave.

"That is not fair!"

I laugh, hugging Pine's shaggy black fur. "Thanks Pine, sorry for staying so long in Crale. We kinda got sidetracked." He sighs, shaking his antlers in disbelief. "I said sorry!"

Pine stops abruptly, kicking at a rock underneath his hoofs. What? Why would he— Phoebe, Mateo, and Barak surround us. Their clothes, littered with tufts of gray fur, are ragged and torn. A clump of Mateo's hair is missing, while Barak sports a scratch on his cheek. Even Phoebe's hair is undone, spilling over her shoulder in scruffy black waves.

"Thanks, Oscar." Barak pets Pine's head, offering him some berries.

"Oscar!?" I screech.

"You seriously stole one of our elks and expected him not to answer to us in the end." Phoebe laughs. She joins Barak in petting Pine. Oscar? Maybe I should call him traitor.

"You really are stupid!" Mateo approaches Pine's side. Before I can fight, he grabs my braid and yanks me off the elk. I screech, trying to writhe out of his grasp. He pins a dagger to my throat. My eyes water. He captured me so quickly.

"Maybe she felt a connection with him," Barak continues, stroking the elk.

"Shut up Barak," both bandits hiss. He flinches, gazing at the ground.

Mateo's eyes widen, as he continues pressing the cool metal against my throat. He laughs. The crazy sound sends shivers down my spine. "Come out, freak! I know you're there!" He tightens his grip on the dagger. "Come out or I'll slit her throat." And now he's using me as a hostage! What kind of hero am I? If the Skycharter came back, he'd never pick me at this point.

I whimper, only for the bush to rustle and Jorge to scramble out, holding his hands in the air.

"Drop the bow and quiver," Phoebe sneers. Mateo grins.

Jorge scowls, dropping it along with his quiver onto the grass.

"Maybe he should take off his cloak too," Barak suggests as he grabs a rope and throws it around Pine's (the traitor!) neck.

Phoebe nods. Jorge bristles but his eyes flicker to me. He does what they say. Underneath his cloak are his normal

CHAPTER 22: PATIENT JORGES ARE MY ENEMIES.

clothes and a bulging satchel. Phoebe raises an eyebrow then gestures for him to take off his satchel. He does and she opens it, retrieving a heavy leather book.

"What is this?" She flips through the pages.

"Who cares? We've finally got that stupid freak. He's been getting under my skin for too long." Mateo shoves me to the ground. Phoebe unsheathes her sword and pins it to my back. Then Mateo cracks his knuckles and approaches Jorge. He spits in his face. "No more wolves for you, huh?" Jorge shakes as the bandit turns back to me. "Pity we couldn't catch the blonde too. Three kids would've made all this hassle worth it."

Phoebe grins, looking between both of us. "Oh, this will be more than enough."

Chapter 23: Rivers Continue to Nearly Freeze Me to Death

And I thought the cage was bad. Apparently, the bandits couldn't salvage its broken remains. Instead, they decided to tie us up like we're elks. No worse than elks. At least Pine, the annoying traitor, doesn't have his arms bound to his sides. Well, he's an elk, so he doesn't have arms. But he still has more freedom than Jorge and I do. We're both essentially on a leash, with our arms tied to our torsos by thick ropes that the bandits use to force us forwards.

"I'm sorry," I mouth to Jorge as Mateo drags him along. He grits his teeth and shakes his head, glaring at the bandits. I sigh. At least he doesn't hate me. And he understands my hatred of the bandits for once.

Meanwhile, Phoebe studies Jorge's leather book. She flips through the numerous pages, which contain various drawings of animals. "This is very detailed but I can't..." She turns towards Jorge, causing me to stumble forward since she holds my rope. "Can you read this?" She narrows her eyes at him. He clenches his jaw. "Huh, never would've guessed you could read. You don't look like you're from Evin."

"We're here!" Barak claps, pointing at a rushing waterfall. It topples over a stony cliff in blue waves. Water sprays my face

CHAPTER 23: RIVERS CONTINUE TO NEARLY FREEZE ME TO DEATH

until all I can taste is fish pee and cold droplets. A few dark rocks jut out of its bottom. It forms a pathway that leads to a sliver of stone behind the waterfall. Slimy moss and white-tinted wildflowers grow out of a few wet rocks.

"Thanks for bringing us here, Barak." Phoebe smiles.

Barak blushes, kicking at some rocks underneath him. "N-no problem."

"Come on, let's go!" Mateo shouts, shoving the two apart. He jumps from rock to rock, dragging Jorge with him. The boy barely manages to follow him without being submerged in water.

Phoebe follows his lead, but moves slower, giving me time to hop from rock to rock. Even then, I have difficulty balancing on their slippery backs with my arms tied together. By the time Mateo reaches his third rock, Jorge tumbles into the sparkling river.

"Jorge!" I shout, rushing to the edge of my rock. He can't swim! I struggle against my binds, peering at the dark water. If I dive inside I'll be of no use since I can't use my arms to grab him. I turn to the bandits. Why aren't they doing anything!?

"He can't swim, y—"

Phoebe pushes me into the water. Its icy grasp numbs my entire body as I kick around, only for my feet to fall on solid ground. I stand up, my head bursting out of the water. It's shallow. Of course, the bandits wouldn't go to all that trouble to kidnap kids just to kill them. Next to me stands Jorge, whose normally puffy curls stick to his face in matted tiny black swirls. We both glare at the bandits, who snicker on their rocks.

"That's payback for attacking me with those wolves, freak," Mateo sneers. Jorge continues glaring at Mateo, only to break eye contact, his face turning red. "That's what I thought. You're weak."

Jorge turns away from the bandit and wades through the water, shoulders hunched over. I move to join him, only for the rope to tug me back underwater. I manage to regain my balance and stand up again. Phoebe chuckles atop her rock.

"Don't think I don't have a score to settle with you, too. How's avenging your village going?"

My fists clench. "When I escape I'll take all of you down. Even Bone." I have to believe that. I have to. Every hero fails sometimes, right?

Phoebe rolls her eyes and jumps to another rock ahead of me, not bothering to look back. "Sure, little girl." None of the other bandits pay me any mind. I scowl, trying not to whimper.

A jet of salty water splashes into my face. A playful snort follows it. Pine nudges me as he races around in the water. He's awfully familiar with this place. Not that I care. I'm still mad at that traitor! I turn away from him and say, "Hmpf!" then speed ahead. He shrieks in the background but I pay him no attention.

After an eternity we finally reach the waterfall. Phoebe drags me out of the river and onto a rocky platform. Mateo does the same for Jorge, but much rougher, while Barak helps Pine out of the water.

Phoebe turns to me. Against the foaming white waterfall's roar, I barely hear her words. "I don't want to hear a word from you after we enter these caves, understand? No yelling, no threatening. Nothing! And if I do..." She unsheathes her sword, pinning it to my throat. "You know what'll happen." I gulp, trembling at the cold blade. She grins. "Glad you

CHAPTER 23: RIVERS CONTINUE TO NEARLY FREEZE ME TO DEATH

understand." Then we enter the caves.

Behind the foaming waterfall is an elaborate cave system. A cave system I recognize. The bandits' base! Kore's map really is accurate. The water casts a blue hue on the black rocks and dampens the floor. The walls reek of fish and moss hangs in its dark corners. Parts of the cave's walls are hollowed out into holes and have prison bars flanking their front. Inside them are children, some look to be as young as five while others as old as sixteen. Grime covers their faces while their clammy hands grip the cell's bars. They quiver. I can't meet their sullen eyes.

I shiver. This is where they keep the children they kidnapped. This is what they're going to do to us. I glance at Jorge, whose face is now bone-pale. That's saying something because of his olive complexion. But being fearful isn't an option. We're here at Bone's base. Sure, the way I got here wasn't ideal. And I haven't been as good at defeating bandits as I hoped to be. But now's the time to escape, defeat Bone, and free those poor kids. My gut churns. Am I really ready for this?

"Where have ya been?" one of the bandits, a woman with short spiky brown hair, asks. Tiny pink scars dot her cheeks, while she wears a thick belt containing numerous daggers and keys.

"Alessia!" Phoebe hugs her. "Good to see you again. We need some cells for these kids."

A few bandits swarm the group. Barak and Mateo start talking to them and eventually walk off, leaving Jorge, Pine, and me with Alessia and Phoebe.

"Well, lucky for you we just hollowed out some new ones in the back. I'll take you to them."

"Great." Phoebe tosses Jorge's rope to Alessia, who scowls at its damp surface.

"Ew. It's wet. What happened?" She tugs on Jorge as she and Phoebe stroll through the cave systems. Water drips from the ceiling while slimy moss squelches under my feet. Pine follows closely behind. Why? I have no idea.

"They had a little fun in the river," Phoebe snickers.

"Seriously? They had to be pretty bad to warrant that." Her eyes flicker about as she plays with a tuft of her hair. "What'd they do?"

"Long story short, they distracted us a lot. The duo kept rescuing other kids." Alessia turns a corner. We head up a rocky staircase carved into the cave. Pine has some difficulty following along but he manages to shove his way through the narrow passage. "Mateo's real mad at him. He wanted to kidnap five of them like Adrian did, but between burning Crale and dealing with these kids, we barely managed to get two. Now Bone's plans are almost complete and we'll have hardly helped at all." Almost complete? I've got to act soon. Even if I'm not ready. But how?

Alessia chews the inside of her cheek as we enter the top of the cave. A gaping hole rests to our left, spraying the gray cave with sunlight. Vultures sit at its edges, pecking at dead animals. To the right stands an empty cell. "But if they fought well... it might not matter that you only got two. Quality's better than quantity." Quality?

Phoebe nods, cutting off my ropes. Her shiny sword and sharp eyes let me know that there's no running away. She does the same for Jorge. "That's what I thought. But you know how Mateo is."

Alessia plucks a key off her chain. It is long, crooked, and

CHAPTER 23: RIVERS CONTINUE TO NEARLY FREEZE ME TO DEATH

gray, matching the cave's walls. She opens the cell door. Then Phoebe shoves us both inside and Alessia locks the door. I tremble. How are we going to escape this?

"There we go. All locked up," Alessia declares, leaning on the bars. "Say, is Barak still obsessed with you?"

Phoebe rolls her eyes. "Yeah. It's annoying."

I turn away from the duo, sitting on the cold stone floor. I'm not going to sit here and listen to bandits rant about their lives. Jorge glances at me and we both frown, trying not to tremble in fear at our circumstances. My eyes flicker back and for just a second they meet Pine's.

He shrieks. A loud, wailing shriek.

Phoebe scrambles over to the elk. "Shut up, Oscar!" He continues shrieking. She grabs a bit of his fur and pulls him down the stairs.

"Quick!" Alessia calls, glancing at the open hole in the cave displaying the dark green Solian woods. "Get him downstairs before he lets the whole country know we're here!"

Chapter 24: Is It Bad to Change My Mind? About a Lot...

Our legs are flying. Well, that's what I'm telling myself so that I don't panic about how high up we are. Not only is our cell surprisingly large (because the bandits have yet to put other kids in here) and bright but it also has bars on both its right and left sides. And, as it turns out, our cell is above the rest of the cave system so we're able to peer down at everyone else. But the wailing kids and angry bandits aren't a pretty sight.

The gaps between the bars are so large that Jorge and I can both shove our legs through them. Which is what I'm doing right now as we peer down at the bandits scurrying beneath us.

"Guess we're not getting out that way." I shrug, pressing my face to the cell's cold bars. "It's too far down." I sigh and stop swinging my legs, getting to my feet. I dust off my hands. We'll have to find another way out.

I race off to the other side, fiddling for the fifth time with the padlock. Unfortunately, my sandal's laces aren't any good at picking it. That, or I'm just a bad lock picker. Probably the latter.

I rattle the bars, scaring a few vultures. Maybe I could use

CHAPTER 24: IS IT BAD TO CHANGE MY MIND? ABOUT A LOT...

one of the bones of the animals they were eating to pick the lock. "Hey! Vultures! C'mere!" With a squawk they all fly away in a flurry of black feathers.

"Jorge," I grumble to the boy who still sits at the back of the cell, legs dangling over the surface. "Can you control vultures too?"

"It doesn't work like that."

I cross my arms, kicking a rock into the wall. "Well, it should." I sigh. "Do you have any ideas on how to escape here?"

He doesn't respond.

"Fine." I pick up the rock I was kicking. "Maybe this'll work." Then I wham it into the clunky padlock. It rattles, shaking like an angry black cat, but doesn't burst. I try again. And again. And again.

"Leda. Stop," Jorge growls. "It's not going to work. We're stuck." He slumps over.

I slump over next to him. "Stuck." I shake his shoulders. The cave's stony floor scratches at my legs. "We can't be stuck. There has to be a way out." I can't fail again. Not when so many lives are at stake. So many other kids' dads. "Were you stuck when you tamed an entire wolf pack? Were you stuck when you rescued me from bandits?"

Jorge sighs. "I guess not."

I grin. For once he's listening! "Jorge, you're awesome! I mean, do you think Kore could do the things you do?"

"No," he murmurs. "But that's only because—" I cover his mouth with my grimy hand.

"No buts. She couldn't. So why sit around and wait for her to rescue us? We can get out of here on our own. But I'm only going to be able to do it if you help me." I lock eyes with him before flicking his forehead. "I need your brains on my side." I need all the help I can get to defeat Bone after making all these mistakes.

He sighs, leaning over. "I-I don't know…"

"Hey, Leda. I leave you in here for one second and you've already damaged our new padlock?" a voice asks. Next to me, Jorge stiffens. I spin around.

Phoebe stands at the edge of our cell, the battered padlock in her hand. She scowls and taps her foot before gesturing to me. "You. Come with me."

"No way." I stand my ground. I need to stay with Jorge so we can figure a way out of here. I'm not leaving him. Not again. Not when I'm so close to getting him on my side and fighting Bone with him.

"Oh really," she sneers, her red-tinted eyes glinting like fire. "What did I say about talking in here?" With a click she opens the cell, grabbing me.

"Get off me!" I yell, struggling in her grasp. Jorge gets to his feet, fist curled as his eyes dart about the room.

Phoebe pins a dagger to my throat. "Cut it out." With that she forces me out of the cell, leaving Jorge locked inside. He races to the other side, pressing his face to the bar to glimpse me as Phoebe drags me down the staircase.

"It'll be okay!" he calls as Phoebe pushes me down the stairs after binding my hands with rope. I scoff. How can he say that!? Oh right, I forgot, he's not the one being dragged down a staircase so narrow he can feel the slimy moss on its walls tickling his skin.

The staircase goes on for an eternity. When we finally do reach ground level Phoebe turns and forces me even further into the ground. I shiver. What does she want from me?

CHAPTER 24: IS IT BAD TO CHANGE MY MIND? ABOUT A LOT...

"We're here," she murmurs, pushing me forward. I stumble into a strange room, and am immediately greeted by the roar of a waterfall.

To my left, the end of the waterfall rushes down in place of a cave wall. The outside sunlight slamming through its waves lights the room. But unlike torchlight, this light is blue. It paints our faces and the remaining cave walls, which are covered in drawings.

They portray images of Solia, the Solia before we were trapped in these woods by the Aurorian Mountains. Our farms are filled with thousands of cows and juicy grapevines while the sea is a beautiful clear blue instead of the dark, cold rivers we have now. Instead of woods with monsters, we have strong villages made of stone and wood, all tightly packed together. Most importantly, the sun rests above it, casting its strong rays on the backs of hard-working citizens, protecting them from the monsters who would soon devour their country.

Phoebe traces the images, shaking her head. "We were once beautiful, weren't we?" Her fingers leave the stone, rubble rubbing off on them. "We had everything. There was no famine or monsters or darkness. Our villages weren't divided by these despicable woods, ruled by Lords instead of a King. We were united. All protected by our beautiful sun." She traces the image of the beaming sun casting its rays onto Solia.

I narrow my eyes. Why is she telling me all of this? I already know all the old stories. I was obsessed with them when I was little. She tugs me along, exposing me to another picture.

It's of the same kingdom and people, but this time swarms of enemies round them up, dragging them away from their beloved kingdom and sun. Phoebe's eyes sharpen. "Then they took us away. Those selfish outsiders. They dragged us away from our beloved sun and kingdom." Her fingers trace the image as she follows it to its sequel. Mountains swarm the Solian people. "Then they trapped us behind these horrific mountains. Because of their jealousy, they let the rest of us rot in here like animals. Yet we still trust them."

"W-what are you talking about?" I ask. Water sprays my back.

She leads me to another image. This one is of the Skycharter faithfully trudging through the mountains, his robe fluttering in the wind behind him. She follows the images of him painted onto the cave's walls as he reaches the other side of the mountain, our side. All the way until the image shows him conducting a ceremony and painting the picture of the sun onto a boy's face. Damian. Solia's first hero. The Skycharter called him our Sun since he would protect us just like our old sun did.

Phoebe bends down to retrieve a rock burrowed in the sand beneath us. Then she uses it to mark a white x over his body. "The Skycharter," she growls. "He's one of them. One of the outsiders who first trapped us in this wretched place."

"No he isn't." I shake my head. "Even if the first Skycharter was. There's a new one every fifty years. The Skycharter who chose Kore wasn't one of the original foreigners who trapped us here." Why is Phoebe so fixated on the original outsiders? They trapped us here before the thirteen explorers founded our villages. Before our first Sun. That was so long ago that we've forgotten why they put us here.

Phoebe chuckles. "It doesn't matter. You've seen the way he acts. Like he's better than us. The outsiders say they have superior knowledge to us. That they're smarter and stronger.

CHAPTER 24: IS IT BAD TO CHANGE MY MIND? ABOUT A LOT...

But not one of the Suns they've chosen has destroyed the Aurorian Mountains. Not a single one." She scowls at the rock in her hand. "If they're so smart then why haven't they helped us? Why haven't they chosen a Sun actually capable of destroying the mountains? Or used their 'superior' knowledge in some other way to save us?"

I peer down at the sand, a shiver spilling across my spine. What she's saying actually makes sense. A lot of sense.

Phoebe throws her rock into the waterfall. "They don't want to help us. They're jealous and afraid, just like they've always been. And if they have it their way, they'll keep us trapped in these mountains, under their palms, begging for them to choose our Sun for the rest of eternity."

Bile rises in my mouth, but Phoebe tugs me closer to the cave's wall anyways. "Why do you care about this anyways? You're bandits, all you want is money."

Phoebe grins, tracing the wall. "It's a nice cover, isn't it? Bandits." She chuckles, shaking her head. "We're not bandits, we're rebels. But Bone said it would be safer that way, we'd be seen as less of a threat to the Lords and Ladies of Evin. Our glorious governors who have the nerve to ally themselves with and actually trust an outsider."

Phoebe bends down, digging in the sand until she retrieves a yellow crystal shard. She holds the crystal to the cave's wall. With a hiss, the cave rattles, then a small rock whizzes out of the wall. I jump out of its way as it steams up in the sand, releasing a cloud of gray smoke.

"Kore and those stuck-ups in Evin aren't the only ones who can use magic." She smiles holding the crystal in her shaking hand. My eyes widen. That must be a moonstar like Kore talked about.

"So, you have magic in your blood?"

Phoebe narrows her eyes. "What are you talking about? Bone taught us how to use these, nobody had a problem using them, and none of us have magic."

D-did Kore lie? Or is Phoebe lying? I grit my teeth. All of this is so confusing! "W-well, Kore's magic is still way stronger than your crystals will ever be. You're nothing to be afraid of."

Phoebe laughs. "You're right, Kore's magic is stronger. But soon our magic will be far stronger than hers."

Phoebe reaches into the hole exposed by the cream-colored rock. She grabs a glass box with a beautiful feather inside. The feather glistens, golden sparks caking its edges. It smells like burning wood and a hole resembling a flaming eye rests in its center.

"A phoenix feather," I inhale.

"If you know what bird this belongs to then I assume you know why we burned your village, don't you?" I nod, my forehead throbbing. Why would they want a phoenix feather of all things? "Of course. I should've known you would've figured it out." Phoebe grins at me. Wait, why is she grinning like that? "After we burned Walend, Bone was supposed to return here to summon the phoenix using the ashes and blood we collected. He did, but the bird managed to get away. Fortunately, he was able to grab this feather." She traces the box. "A phoenix's feather always points towards the bird. We can use this to track it down."

"Can't you use the ashes and blood you collected?" I narrow my eyes, tilting my head.

"Not exactly. It needs to be fresh. After a few days the items "expire" and won't summon the phoenix. We don't want to cause more of a scene or hurt any more Solians than

CHAPTER 24: IS IT BAD TO CHANGE MY MIND? ABOUT A LOT...

needed so we figured this would be better than murdering more civilians." Rebels? Actually wanting to not hurt Solians? Is what Phoebe saying true? I shake my head. "You look confused."

I squint at the tall bandit next to me. Or rebel? "But why do you want a phoenix if you don't want to hurt Solia?"

"Well, that goes back to our first point." She taps on the box. The sharp click of her nails sends shivers down my spine. "The Skycharter made the wrong choice. That's why Bone intends to make the right one."

"W-what!?" My hands shake, rope scratching against my wrists. There's no way...

"He's going to choose a new Sun, a real Sun. Someone who cares about our country. Someone capable of actually destroying the mountains." Phoebe grins, her eyes glinting like lava. "Bone's already collected countless children to choose from. But you're right. The person we choose needs to have magic as strong as Kore's. And the only way to do that is to infuse them with a phoenix's magic. Magic powerful enough to burn the entirety of Solia."

Phoebe continues carrying the box, waltzing to another image embedded on the cave's walls. I gasp. A child stands there while a swirling phoenix flies above him. His chest is exposed and the phoenix's fire swarms into it. "Once we find the phoenix, Bone is going to throw a glorious choosing ceremony. Just like the Skycharter had to pick our new Sun. Except in this one, after choosing our Sun we will weaken the phoenix then infuse its magic into the body of our Sun. That Sun will essentially have the same magical abilities as Kore. They'll be on par with her and since Bone intends to choose someone actually competent, they should have a much better chance at rescuing Solia from the grasp of these mountains."

The roar of the waterfall, along with Phoebe's words, disorients me. Bone's going to host another choosing ceremony, pick a better Sun, and give them Kore's powers? Why…why does that sound exactly like what I've always wanted? "Why are you telling me this?"

"Because out of all of the other kids, I think you have the best chance of being chosen." Phoebe nonchalantly places the glass box with the phoenix feather back in the wall. Then she uses her crystal and the previous rock to smooth together the wall, locking the glass box inside.

"Um…w-what??" My face flushes.

Phoebe snickers and points to me. "You. You have the best shot of being chosen."

"R-really? Me? Everyone tells me I'm ordinary and forgets my name and ignores me…" I trail off, sweat dampening my face.

She tilts her head. "You know I was teasing when I said I forgot your name, right? I mean, you were the only kid I tried to kidnap who challenged me, who wanted to not only save yourself but take down Bone as well. It's like…" Her eyes sharpen. "Like you're the one who likes it. Who wants it. It comes naturally to you. Being our Sun is like breathing to you." She really thinks that? Even after I've made all those mistakes?

She takes my arm and waltzes me away from the cave wall. Then guides me to the waterfall. We both watch it spray drops of water on our faces. She gestures to the cave wall behind her. "I know you hate us because of what we did to your village. Which is why I wanted to bring you here to explain what we're doing. To show you that we're not bad people. I want you

CHAPTER 24: IS IT BAD TO CHANGE MY MIND? ABOUT A LOT...

to see that if you join us instead of fighting, we can do great things. To make you understand that you could be our Sun." She exhales, smiling at me. "So what do you say? Will you stop this hatred and fighting and join us?"

Stop fighting? If I do, I could have a chance at being the Sun. At being what and who I've always wanted to be. If I got that power from the phoenix, I could finally be on Kore's level. I could finally free Solia.

For some reason, my dad's voice pops into my head. *Make do with what you have.* And then his body. His poor broken body. These people murdered him. And my dad? He was so kind to me. He teased me about Jorge and laughed at my bad jokes and cheered me up when I was sad. He would never hurt a soul. He would never lie to me. And he's been right so far. I have made mistakes. I wasn't the perfect hero I thought I could be. I don't even know if I'm any better than Kore.

So, maybe I should try listening to him. Just this once.

I spit in her face. "I will never join you."

Chapter 25: I'm Giving Love Advice to a Bandit. What Is My Life.

"You did this to yourself," Phoebe growls as I glare at her. My fists clench around the cell bars. Their cold surface chills my palms.

"He has nothing to do with this," I snap. Jorge stiffens in her grip, keeping his eyes locked on me.

"It's going to be okay," he murmurs.

"Listen to your friend," Phoebe sneers. "You need some time to think about everything."

"No, I don't!" I shout, only for her to drag him down the staircase, far away from my cell. I slam into the cell wall, crumpling onto the floor. It was so close. Everything I worked for, everything I wanted was right there. It had to be the right choice to give it up. Right?

My eyes drift to the empty cell. And now I'm alone in a cave packed with bandits, all of which are as good at fighting as Mateo. According to Phoebe, they can use magic too. My head spins. Should I listen to my dad's advice again? Should I give up and wait here for someone to save me? No, I can't, not when so many people are in danger. But I also can't do this alone anymore. I'm not as competent a fighter as I thought I'd be.

CHAPTER 25: I'M GIVING LOVE ADVICE TO A BANDIT. WHAT IS MY...

I furrow my brows. That settles it. I need to find Val, Phemus, and Jorge again before I try to take down this ceremony. If we work together and have a plan, we might be able to do this. But Phoebe said that Bone is going to finish his plans soon. I have to do something to delay this ceremony and buy time. That's it! I'll destroy the phoenix feather, then they won't be able to track the phoenix.

I get to my feet. *Okay, Leda. Get out of this cell. Find Jorge. And destroy the feather.* Should be simple. I hope.

* * *

It. Was. Not. Simple. I slam another stone into the cell's bars. It screeches and rattles but still, nothing happens. I groan, scratching my head. How am I supposed to get out of here?

A figure scampers up the staircase. I squint. It's Barak, holding a flower. What is he doing here? He sniffs the pink flower, eyes watering. Then he watches a few hawks fly around the sky from the hole in the cave. He eventually sighs, plucking at the petals. It's then I notice a silver key on his belt. Aha! That's my way out!

"Um, what are you doing here?" I ask.

"Gah!" Barak jolts up, almost scrambling out of the room.

"Wait, don't go!" I yell, racing over to the bars. *Come on Leda, think of something to get him to stay here.* "I, um, like your flower?"

He stops and twirls the flower in his hand. "Yeah, it is pretty. It'd never look at someone like me..."

"Well, flowers don't have eyes, so it can't look at you." I lean closer to the bars, reaching my hand out as he continues not facing me. If I can just lean a little further...

"It's a metaphor," he grumbles, then turns around, sighing. I quickly retract my hand, letting out a nervous laugh. He clenches his teeth, sunlight illuminating his thick hair. "Hey, you're a girl. D-do you know what girls like?"

"Uh…" Oh great. I don't have time to listen to lovey-dove stuff.

He scrambles up to the bars. "Or maybe, do you know why they ignore you? Even when you do everything to help them? When you agree with them and always do what they ask even if you don't… If the things they do you're not so sure will help other people like they say it will," he stammers then laughs. "I don't know. That was stupid. I should get going."

"No!" I reach my hand through the bars and grab his arm. Quick, think of some good advice, Leda! Uhh. "You should… maybe…umm…stick to your own ideals. You shouldn't have to change who you are for someone else, you know?"

"But what if you really like her?" Barak scratches his head.

"I don't know." I shrug."I'm just saying it'd be sad to spend your whole life pining after someone else, always trying to fit who they want you to be instead of being someone you want to be." Barak's eyes widen. Then he hunches over, confused.

"I never thought of that before." The keys jangle on his belt as he stares off in thought. I pluck them off him. Yes! I hide it behind my back and smile. "Maybe I'll give it a try. Thanks for the advice."

"No problem!" The bandit stalks out, leaving me alone in the cell. My fingers grasp around the silver key which I then use to escape that awful cell. Grinning, I pump a fist in the air. Finally, I'm free!

Okay. Now I need to find Jorge. I race down the staircase. The moss still rustles my arms. Ew. Anyways, I continue until

CHAPTER 25: I'M GIVING LOVE ADVICE TO A BANDIT. WHAT IS MY...

I reach the main entrance, where dozens of bandits reside. Or rebels, as Phoebe would call them. Some stand in front of cells, poking and laughing at the scared children inside them. Others polish weapons or compare stolen jewels. I grit my teeth. There are too many of them. I glance to my left, which contains a narrow hallway lit by torchlight. Guess I'll go that way instead. Why does everything have to be so narrow in caves!?

I rush through the hallway, tracing its damp sides. If it's anything like the cave Phoebe showed me, then there might be items stored in these walls. I wish I could use magic like her to figure out their secrets.

"Hey, kid! What are you doing out!?" Alessia snaps in the hallway. Oh great. She unsheathes her dagger. Double great. Out of sheer panic, I stomp on her foot. She drops her dagger, which I grab and pin to her throat. Yes! "Seriously!?" she fumes.

"Can you use magic?" I demand.

"W-why would you ask that?" Alessia laughs, glancing at her pocket.

"Open your pocket!" She does what I say and a few yellow crystals clatter to the floor. "I knew it! Can you use those crystals to open some holes in these walls?"

"How do you know that?" she murmurs as I release her, still pointing the dagger in her direction. She picks up the shard and holds it to the wall. Gray mist swarms through the cave, and sure enough dozens of rocks pop off it, exposing cells filled with swords and items. Awesome!

Alessia scowls as I race over to the wall and grab a familiar bag and sword. I shove the dagger into my old bag, sling it over my shoulders, and put the torch on the wall. Then I grab some rope and tie Alessia's hands to a hook on the wall.

She scoffs. "You know, you won't get very far. You're just an ordinary kid. Phoebe will beat you in a sword fight in two seconds flat!"

An ordinary kid. She's right. But if I stayed here, maybe I wouldn't have to be that. I shake my head. I already made my decision and I need to rescue Jorge. I'll just try to avoid fighting Phoebe. I ignore the bandit and rush through the hallway, only to exit the cave, and find myself in the presence of another roaring waterfall.

Dark, lush vegetation flocks the area I've entered while the smooth waterfall spills into a cool, black lake. Rocky walls surround the area but instead of a ceiling like a cave would have, there's nothing but a blue sky stuffed with hawks.

"C'mon, the rest of the caves are this way!" a voice shouts. I know that voice. Phoebe! I fight my way through the thick plants. Vines scratch my legs and leaves whack my arms, but I continue on. Finally, I reach a clearing filled with thick grass and wildflowers.

Phoebe yanks on Jorge's arm, tugging him towards another tunnel leading to yet another cave. He stiffens, then tries to writhe out of her grasp. I grab a rock nearby. Maybe I can knock Phoebe out with it.

"Seriously," Phoebe grumbles. "I've already had one of you give me an attitude. I'm done—" I launch the rock at her. She easily dodges it. Uh oh. She locks eyes with me in the bushes. Then unsheathes her sword, shoving Jorge to the ground. "Come out Leda."

With a hammering heart, I unsheathe my sword too. Time to win a sword fight against a bandit.

Chapter 26: Water Hurts

I launch first, trying to throw her off guard. Instead, Phoebe matches my blow. With a clank, our swords rush into each other. They're both crooked, causing them to get hooked on each other's edges. Both of us yelp when they get caught together, only to pull the swords apart. That causes us each to slam into the ground. Phoebe immediately gets up and swings at me. I roll to my side. Grass, dirt, and flower petals get stuffed in my mouth. I spit them out then get up.

I race into a bush, using its thick leaves to hide from her blow. Her blade whizzes through the leaves, shredding them apart.

"Come back here, Leda!" Phoebe yells. She tears through the bush. I get up and slash at her shoulder. She grunts, barely blocking my blow. "I know you care about our country. And your village. So, why can't you understand?" She jabs at me. I block her blow, heart hammering. She's so good! How am I going to beat her? "Why can't you see the good we're trying to do?"

My blade clings against a cave wall as I slash my sword at her. "Burning villages. Kidnapping kids is not good."

Phoebe delivers another blow. This one knocks the sword out of my hands. I trip over a rock and slam into the ground as she pins her sword to my throat. "How many more people will die from Kore's incompetence?" I bristle at her words. She makes a good point. Was I wrong? "We're doing the country a f—" A sharp whistle interrupts Phoebe's monologue. She turns to Jorge who stands there, whistling. "What are you doing, boy?"

For a moment, nothing happens and Jorge whistles again. Phoebe rolls her eyes and taps her foot, crushing a yellow wildflower underneath it.

"Stop that whistling," she hisses. "It's annoying."

Jorge does it again. A hawk flying above caws and dives straight towards Phoebe's hair. Her eyes widen and she shrieks. She drops her sword and runs away, screeching.

"You can control hawks!" I grin. This is awesome!

"It worked!" He smiles as I grab my sword. He then grabs Phoebe's and takes my hand. We race through the clearing and re-enter the tunnel I came from. Alessia still remains tied up on the floor.

Once we're far away from Phoebe, I finally ask, "How did you do that? And control wolves in the first place?"

Jorge huffs, catching his breath. "My book. I...It's hard to explain, but I figured out how to do it from there. I need to find it."

I smile, gesturing to the wall. "Well, you're in luck." Almost immediately, I spot Jorge's cloak, bow, arrows, book, and satchel in one of the cave's holes. My map and translator are in a nearby hole.

"Woah. It's like a storage compartment system." He traces the edges of the cave wall before grabbing his stuff and putting it on. I grab mine too. "Okay, let's get out of here."

"Wait. We need to do something first," I murmur, bending

CHAPTER 26: WATER HURTS

down to pick up some of Alessia's yellow crystals she had scattered over the floor. It shouldn't be too hard to figure out how to use them. "Follow me. It's something Phoebe showed me." I race off in the direction of the phoenix feather.

"Wait, Leda!" Jorge calls, but I've already turned the corner and find myself descending down the deep, dark staircase. Soon, I arrive at the cave's basement. The familiar spray of water, roar of a waterfall, dusty sand, and intricate wall paintings greet me.

I twirl the crystal around my fingers. Yellow dust leaks off it, sticking to my fingertips.

"Can you not run off like that!?" Jorge grumbles as he enters the room. "Wow. This place is beautiful."

I nod. Beautiful, but it hides a deadly secret. I hold the glinting crystal to the cave wall, willing it to hiss and pop like it did when Phoebe made the same movement. Nothing happens. Oh great.

"Umm. Jorge. I know we don't really have time for you to explain exactly how you control animals, but can you use your magic to open this wall thing and—"

"Me controlling animals has nothing to do with magic. Also, it's not controlling, it's more like asking," he explains.

Why does magic have to be so complicated!? My hands clench around the crystal. Fine, I'll go and get Alessia, then. Making her do this is going to be a chore since this phoenix feather is important to the bandits.

"Wait here—" I start to tell Jorge only for a jet of water to hit my face. It soaks my entire braid and fills my mouth with foul-tasting water. I spit the water out, glaring at the waterfall. What in the world?

"Stay back, fiends!" Another jet of water rushes towards us.

This time it hits Jorge, soaking his thick curls.

"These just got back to normal," he growls, grumbling as he picks up a strand of wet hair. I shudder. Whoever did that should know better than to mess with Jorge's hair.

The waterfall parts to the side and a figure enters the cave, floating on a stream of peaceful blue water. Kore daintily lands on the cave's sandy shore. Her thin hair casts a stringy halo around her face. Although her blue strand has faded even more than before. Weird, it's almost like it's disappearing. Water drips out of her palms. It's clear and thin, unlike the waterfall

Jorge drops his arrow, which he was planning to load into his bow. Like I said. No one messes with Jorge's hair. "Kore," he murmurs. "You're here..."

"You!" She points at me. Her eyes are wild and desperate, darting around the cave system. "You keep getting in my way! You keep trying to do my job," Kore's voice cracks. "I'm supposed to do this. I'm supposed to be the Sun. Stop it! Stop trying to be me!"

My fists clench. "Stop trying to be you? I'm not trying to be anything like you. I'm not trying to be the girl who froze when my village burned. The girl who ran away when wolves chased me. The girl who lost a fight to the most peaceful leafer I know. The girl who doesn't want to be the Su—"

"Shut up!" Kore screeches. A ball of water crashes into me, flinging me backwards. I slam into the cave wall and my vision rattles for a moment. I groan, suddenly finding myself lying on the floor. My entire body shakes in the sand. Everything, my muscles, arms, legs. It all hurts like nothing has ever hurt before.

"Leda!" Jorge yells, drawing his bow. He aims the arrow at

CHAPTER 26: WATER HURTS

Kore's face, hands trembling. "What is wrong with you?"

Kore quivers as her face pales. "I didn't mean to... I-I swear. I can't control it." She backs away from us, the waterfall almost engulfing her. My vision continues blurring while my eyelids turn heavy. If it weren't for the fear of what's going to happen coursing through me, I'd drift to asleep from exhaustion.

"I don't care what you meant." Jorge keeps his bow trained on Kore. He grits his teeth. "Get away from us." His eyes flicker to the staircase. Kore glances that way in response. "Now."

Kore shivers, her body still shaking as she races through the stand and up the staircase. I watch her white dress disappear against the gray stone and reach out my hand, only to groan from pain.

"She can't..." I try to talk, try to point to the cave wall or the shattered fragments of yellow crystal now burrowed in the sand. But my own body rebels against me. "Leave. Magic... She has magic..." She needs to open the wall and destroy the feather! I don't care who does it. Someone needs to or the bandits will create a pawn more powerful than her!

"Leda." Jorge appears in front of me. He must've run over here when Kore left. I was too focused on her. He cradles my body then his eyes sharpen. "We need to get out of here."

"No..." I whisper, but my voice is so faint even I can't hear it.

He slings my arm over his shoulder then tries picking me up. Only to grunt as he nearly drops me. He shakes his head. "You're taller than me. I can't pick you up. You're going to have to walk, okay?"

I whimper as I try standing. Even then I have to heavily lean on him. How am I going to do this? Overhead, bandits shout while water drips from the ceiling. I grit my teeth. It doesn't matter how. I have to do this.

I bite back a scream as I start hobbling forward. Jorge does most of the work by pushing me ahead. He laughs. "There you go. We're here. We did it! We're at the staircase." He glances up. I follow his gaze. Above us is a winding stone staircase with shaggy moss and shadowy halls. "Oh great…"

I clench my fists. *Keep going, Leda. Always keep going.* I stumble forward, nudging Jorge.

"Okay." He inhales. "You're right. Let's go."

I don't know how we do it. But we make it to the top. It takes an eternity and we nearly slip fifty times along the way but we make it. By the end, Jorge is sweating and his face is red from nearly dragging me up the staircase. We both lean on the wall, huffing.

In front of us, Kore fights the bandits. If you can call it that. Clear water flies everywhere at odd angles, slamming into the occasional bandit's face along with spraying the kidnapped kids with water. I meet eyes with Kore for a second. She looks away like she's the one afraid of me. Even though she blasted me with water.

"Alright. Enough resting." Jorge gets off the wall and drags me through a tunnel. "I saw another exit in the clearing Phoebe took me to. All we've got to do is get there."

Orange torchlight flickers against our faces. Alessia is still tied up and yells at me as we limp through the narrow hallway.

"Hey! What's going on out there? What happened to you! Let me out of this!" she screams. It's nearly drowned out by the shrieks of bandits and splashes of water throughout the cave. Everything's so chaotic that no bandits bothered to help her.

CHAPTER 26: WATER HURTS

Jorge continues dragging me away from all of it until we finally reach the clearing. It's still. Curls of Phoebe's hair lay on the ground, while hawks caw above us. Other than that, not a soul is in the area. Phoebe must've left to go fight Kore.

Jorge lays me on the fuzzy grass. "Okay, I can't remember the exact place I saw the exit. I'm going to go find it. You wait here." He pats my shoulder, his brows furrowing. "It'll be okay. She'll be okay," he mutters to himself and scurries off.

Once he leaves, I'm left to do nothing but peer up at the clear sky. Sunlight warms my face while puffy clouds float around in its sea of light blue. Why is the sky always clear and beautiful when everything is going wrong?

A familiar snort sounds next to me. With a groan, I turn my head. Pine stands to my right. What does he want? His black eyes water.

"Don't..." I huff. "Don't tell the bandits..." My eyes nearly flutter shut. He whimpers, nudging me with his furry black snout.

"Woah," Jorge says. I try to cock my head backward to see him, but I can't move it. "Leave her be." The rustling of grass tells me that he's slowly approaching Pine. Pine gestures to his back then at me, whimpering again.

"Do you want to help us?" Pine snorts then gestures again. He actually wants to help me. But the bandits are his owners. Why?

Jorge, however, doesn't question it. "Great. Thanks, bud." He pats Pine's back, who spits on his face in return. Jorge wipes away the goo, scowling. "Seriously." Pine snorts playfully. "Whatever." He hoists me onto the back of the elk then hops in front of me to give directions.

Pine snickers and rushes off, somehow already knowing

where to go. He carries us out of the cave system and into the bright sunlight.

Chapter 27: Jorge Spends His Free Time Talking to Birds

Crale's on fire. And I'm in the middle of it. Screams echo around me as the once proud red buildings topple onto stragglers. Bandits rush on furry black elks. They tug giant prison carts packed with crying children. My heart lurches as I rush towards them, unsheathing my sword and slashing at elk legs.

A bandit atop one laughs. I look up. Mateo. "You can't even beat me, worthless brat," he jeers. "Who'd ever want you to rescue them?" Then he kicks off and his elk races through the sky, carrying the prison cart behind it. The rest of the elks follow suit, forming a sea of thick black fur and glinting cages in the sky.

Crale civilians gawk at the scene, scurrying out of their houses and wiping the tears off their faces. Then they turn to me, thousands of black and brown eyes latching onto me. An elderly woman starts laughing wildly. Vultures circle over her head while her stringy black hair flies around her face. "You got them to go away, Leda! You're our new Sun!"

"Hooray!"

"Glory to the Sun!" Their echoing cheers, hollow laughter, and endless clapping just chill my spine. No, this isn't right. I back away from their sweaty bodies. "Leda, Leda, Leda!" They kept chanting my name, strolling closer and closer. Then they grab at bits of my hair, ripping my dress and scratching my skin.

"Dad!" I scream as they keep whacking me. All I can see is skin and smell is sweat. "Dad, help!"

Everything freezes. The people, the fire, even the elks in the sky. A round figure emerges from the tips of a frozen fire, and floats through the crowd. His eyes are empty and his steps make no sound. Even weirder is the fact that he walks through countless people until he finally reaches me. I peer up at him and reach out to hug him.

"Th-thank you for coming." I smile. He dodges my embrace, eyes still empty. "D-dad?"

"You like it." He gestures to the crowd. I shake my head. He's wrong. He has to be. Right? "You wanted this, didn't you? You cared more about this than you ever did about me."

Tears spill down my cheeks. "You're wrong D-dad… I do care about you. I love you. I miss you…"

He snorts. "Did I not tell you to make do with what you have? You should know better than to love somebody that doesn't exist." He disappears and the crowd comes closer.

* * *

I jolt awake. Thick fur scratches at my arms while a starry night sky twinkles above me. A fire whisks at the rims of my vision, pressing heat onto my face, while a wolf snarls nearby. Its big black eyes peer into my soul. I screech. Why am I next to a campfire and why is a wolf facing me!? What's going on—

"Nightmares, huh?" The wolf scampers to the voice behind

CHAPTER 27: JORGE SPENDS HIS FREE TIME TALKING TO BIRDS

me. I spin around. Jorge sits in front of me, leaning over his book. I must've fallen asleep when riding on Pine. Jorge closes his book and shoves it into his satchel. A pack of wolves surround him while hawks perch in the air. Even a few mice scurry at his feet. My eyes widen. His relaxed posture, the animals surrounding him, the book in his lap. He's like a completely different Jorge.

I grit my teeth, remembering Jorge's question. The nightmares still won't go away. This time that crowd was terrifying. It was the first time I'd ever been scared of people. And my dad, he told me he didn't exist. But that's not true. It can't be true! "Yeah," my voice cracks. My fingers twirl around a blade of grass.

"Did they start happening after..." His face flushes.

"Yeah." I pluck the blade off the ground. I don't have time for this. I can't think like this. I get up, only to grunt and nearly fall down again. Jorge quickly catches me.

"Woah! You can't do that. Kore really roughed you up. You need time to heal."

"Kore," I croak, leaning on Jorge and a nearby tree trunk. "Did she...defeat the bandits?"

"I don't know. When I left, I didn't see anything on my way out." He shakes his head then hoists my arm over his shoulder. "Come on. Now that you're awake, you can ride that elk. You were so restless in your sleep that we couldn't keep you up on his back. Seriously, you kicked me like five times."

I snicker. "Even in my sleep I'm a better fighter than you."

Jorge whistles and Pine scampers away from a few other elks. He snorts and rolls his eyes upon seeing me. But his eyes let me know he's happy I'm okay.

"Uh huh. My bow beats your dorky sword any day."

I tap my sword's hilt, which rests on my belt. "What are you calling dorky! This could slice you in half in two seconds flat." He clicks his tongue. Ha! He always does that when he can't think of a response. A few wolves tussle behind him. "So, are the wolves following the both of us now that I'm finally with you again?"

"Oh." Jorge's eyes widen, as if he just noticed that basically the entire wildlife population of Solia is following him around. "No, I was just talking to them for a bit."

"You can talk to animals!?"

"That's not important." Jorge wipes his dirty palms on his pants. He gets up off the log he rested on, circling the campfire. The flames bend and fold like the wings of a bird, casting orange light over his face. "We need to discuss getting back to Walend without those bandits catching us again." He whistles. A hawk nods and flies into the sky. "That hawk should help look after us when we leave on your elk tomorrow morning, but—"

"Hold up!" I try getting up, only for my entire body to ache. Kore really did a number on me. I grunt. Trembling, I continue standing, towering over Jorge. "I am not leaving tomorrow morning. In fact, I'm not leaving at all."

"Are you kidding me, Leda!?" Jorge's voice thunders with a deep tone he's never had before. Every single animal turns their heads towards me, staring at me with their beady black eyes. Seriously? Can't they give us some privacy? This is just rude. "You're still talking like this after everything? I mean, look at you, you can barely stand up!"

"This isn't about me. It's about saving Solia." I steady myself on Pine's sweaty back. "These bandits aren't just rampaging villages and kidnapping kids for no reason. They

CHAPTER 27: JORGE SPENDS HIS FREE TIME TALKING TO BIRDS

have a purpose, a ceremony they're planning for. If I let them complete it, they'll be more powerful than Kore, free to wreak havoc over everything!"

Jorge's eyes widen in horror. Even the wolves beside him scamper backward, whimpering. The hawks squeak nervously on their branches. "I-it's still not our job. We're supposed to stay in Walend, where it's safe."

"Not our job?" I sigh. "Listen, Jorge, I get it. I'm far from the ideal hero, but Kore isn't going to save us. And people are in danger. Someone has to step up."

Jorge stiffens, then sighs. He grabs his book and tosses it to a hawk. The hawk flies onto me, talons sinking into my shoulder. Then it drops the book into my hands. I frown at the soggy book.

"I can't read. And what does this have to do with anything?"

"You'll see. Now, open it. I drew pictures in the margins."

I sigh. Of course he did. Then I crack open the novel, and am immediately greeted by a short man. He almost perfectly resembles Jorge with his square jaw and alert black eyes.

"That's my ancestor," Jorge murmurs. "My family dates back hundreds of years."

"Before the Sun existed?"

"Yeah, turn the page." I flip through the pages, settling on a page with a young boy. He whistles. A hawk then flies towards an Ocean Eater on the verge of biting his leg. "Every village has a different way of protecting themselves from monsters. Crale has its giant wall. Evin is filled to the brim with magicians. And my family figured out how to communicate with animals to protect Walend."

"And you do this by whistling to them? Or...is it magic?"

"Neither." Jorge shrugs. "And both." I turn the page again. It shows a pack of wolves hunting together, hawks scouting the terrain, and even the phoenix at the top of the woods. "We call it the order. We don't know where it comes from, maybe it's magic, maybe it's just plain nature. Either way, it's the idea that everything in this forest, in Solia, is linked. Every animal, every person, every monster. And that there's a purpose for each and every one of them."

He whistles again. Hawks circle above us, scouting out the area and warning us with screeches. "Hawks are lookouts. Wolves are hunters. My family protects Walend. Yours creates beautiful glass." Beautiful glass. That's all? "In order to work with these animals, we have to understand their nature and work with them, not against them. We have to make do with what we're given."

My gut sickens. That phrasing…He didn't know. He couldn't have. My eyes water and I rub them. Shoot. I can't think like that right now!

Jorge's face softens. "Listen, Leda, I get it. I r-really do. But we have to have faith in Kore."

I cross my arms, sighing. Jorge may think all this order stuff is an excuse for us to not stop these bandits. But I don't care. I'm not giving up. Not when so many people could get hurt. However, for once, I realize I'm surrounded. I know Jorge. And I know there's a reason he kept all these animals around. He knows I might run away, so he purposefully surrounded me with them. Wolves and hawks I have no hope of outrunning. So, I need to be smart. I need to go with what he's saying for now and figure out how to escape him some other way. "Okay. I get it."

"Really?" I half-heartedly nod. My best friend beams. "Well, now that I'm thinking about it, it might be better for you to

CHAPTER 27: JORGE SPENDS HIS FREE TIME TALKING TO BIRDS

get some rest. You got really hurt yesterday." He yawns. "And I'm a bit tired, too." In a few moments he's already asleep, his hood pulled over his head. I, however, am left staring at the fire, unable to fall asleep. The animals still stay nearby. If I leave they'll wake up Jorge. I'll have to find a way to escape tomorrow when I'm well-rested.

I keep staring at the fire. Its flames are mesmerizing. My eyes water from its ashes. Wings stretch out of its edges. A caw pierces the air. The kind that chills my spine and rings around my head like a bell. My eyes widen. No way.

The phoenix. I don't know how it got in there. But I knew those flames looked too sharp to be regular flames and not wings. Its chimes tickle my spine while its smooth black eyes stare deep into my soul. It emerges from the fire, locking eyes with me. Then it launches on its hind legs and flies into the air. Bits of fire curl around its wings as it screeches.

One by one, Jorge's animals bow to the phoenix. Even I feel myself lowering my head in front of the flaming bird. It glitters like a fiery jewel in the night sky. I gawk. It's beautiful. I can't let this ceremony turn it into a weapon for the bandits. The phoenix races into the sky and I try not to think about the fact that one of its feathers is in their hands.

Chapter 28: Pine's New Name Hurts My Soul

With a grunt, I hoist myself onto Pine's back. Jorge joins me, furrowing his brows as he whistles to the hawk on his shoulder. Eventually, he lets the hawk fly ahead. "This hawk should show us where Walend is. But why'd Oscar help us, anyway?"

"Oscar! His name is Pine," I grumble. Snowflakes flurry above us, pelting my face like tiny icy daggers.

Jorge pats his back and the elk sets off into the woods. Long trees whisk by us. "Um, I'm pretty sure it's Oscar. That's what the bandits said."

"No, it's Pine." I rub my fingers through his shaggy mane. "Which one do you like better, Pine or Oscar?" He doesn't respond, keeping his eyes trained ahead and panting.

"Guess we'll never know." Jorge shrugs. I groan. Why does this elk never listen to me!? "Anyways, do you know why he came back to help us?"

"Honestly, he confuses me. I knocked out his owner then he hated me then he found me a cave and basically saved my life and then he betrayed me for bandits. And now he's helping me again…it's complicated."

"Good to know you have a complicated relationship with

CHAPTER 28: PINE'S NEW NAME HURTS MY SOUL

an elk," Jorge says.

"Well, at least I don't talk to wolves. And a hawk." I scratch my head. Talking to Jorge is nice but that's not what I'm trying to fix right now. I need to escape from Jorge and his many, many wolves. Otherwise, I have no chance of stopping that ceremony.

A few wolves behind us jump up, licking at the snowflakes. I grin. Perfect! If they're distracted, that means all I need to do is get Jorge off Pine.

I survey the boy in front of me. Jorge has always been shorter than me but he's also leaner. He's not as used to riding Pine, barely holding onto tufts of his fur. It wouldn't be too hard to…I sink my hands into Jorge's cloak and push him off Pine.

"Hey!" he yells.

"I'm sorry, Jorge! Run!" Pine tears off and we rush off into the woods. Yes, he finally listened to me for once! "I love you, Pine!" I screech as the elk snorts in approval.

Wolves bark at our sides, and Jorge scrambles after them. Snowflakes wet my lashes, blurring my vision. Pine's furry chest heaves underneath me. Thick green leaves flap across my bare arms. Suddenly, Pine screeches and topples over. I crash into the ground. Wet mud and snow splatter across my dress.

"Pine!" I call, stumbling to my feet. A chill sweeps across my entire body. The taste of mud in my mouth makes me want to vomit.

He whines, stutters to his legs, and gestures with his muzzle as if he's telling me to go on without him.

"Thank you," I murmur to him. Then I take off. My heart pounds and heat rushes to my face. My sandals squeak in the mud, splattering over my legs. I leap over a log. Then a long white object I've never seen before and don't have time to care about.

I find myself in a large clearing. Littered with giant…animal bones. Flowers sprout out of them while snowflakes flurry towards them. Woah. I stop for a minute, only for the barking of wolves to send shivers through my spine. I rush forward.

Suddenly, two figures dart in front of me, standing at the edge of the clearing. One of them has golden hair and the other is huge. No way. "Val! Phemus! It's meeeeeeee!" I screech.

"Leeddaaaa!!" Phemus charges into the clearing. His eye extender is all wound up, expanding far beyond his body. He pauses to catch his breath, clearly having run a great deal. Slightly behind him is Val. She also stops running and rummages through her cauldron. "We've come to rescue you!"

"What—"

Behind me, the wolves stop while Jorge gasps. I spin around as he loads his bow.

"Jorge, no!" I shout. The boy doesn't hear me since he loads his bow and aims it at Phemus anyways. The leafer's ears flop downwards as he whimpers. Behind him, Val races into the clearing, a vial of sizzling goo in her hand. She pushes me out of the way. Then she clenches her jaw and her icy eyes narrow in on Jorge's loaded bow. Her eyes flicker to me.

"Get away from her, wolf boy," she hisses.

Jorge's fists curl around the bow. Icy air blows across his face. He scowls and keeps his bow pointed on the duo. "No way."

Phemus continues whimpering as Jorge keeps his bow trained on him. Not only are his floppy ears lowered, but he shivers as well. Does Jorge's bow really scare him that

CHAPTER 28: PINE'S NEW NAME HURTS MY SOUL

much? His ripped sleeve flutters across his body. He looks roughed up. A lot. I turn to Val. Her blonde hair is scattered about and scraps of mud paint her face. Even her leather pants are torn. What happened to them?

"Fine." Val twists the cork off her bottle, throwing it into the snow. A stream of yellow smoke, followed by rising foam, hisses out of the top of it. Jorge keeps his hands trained on the bow, scowling.

I have to stop them. But Jorge is trying to take me back to Walend, and if Val wins then maybe he'll leave me alone. If anyone can take down an entire pack of wolves, it's the girl from Evin. My gut shudders as I take a step back towards Phemus. *I have to do this. I'm sorry, Jorge.*

"Let her go with me and I won't shoot. We can all leave this unharmed. I don't want to hurt anyone."

Val scoffs. "Let her go? I'm not holdin' her back from anything, she's with me for a reason. And I wouldn't worry about you hurtin' me."

Jorge's eyes flicker to me and I nod. They widen. For once they look hurt. My gut churns and I look away. "Listen, your friend here looks like an adorable puppy and you're a girl, I don't want to—"

"Imma girl?" Val's eyes widen as she shakes with fury. "What's me being a girl got anything to do with this?" Oh no...Jorge, not this...

"I don't fight girls. Not unless I absolutely have to. It's against my family's principles and I've already broken it too many times." I shove my face into my hands from embarrassment.

"Oh, yeah? You think you have to go easy on me for being a girl, huh?" Jorge looks away. Val shakes, tilting her blue vial to add droplets to the yellow one.

Phemus' eye widens within its eye extender. "Val! No! That'll hurt the human a lot!"

"Some humans deserve to be hurt." Val's eyes sharpen as she adds the droplet to the potion. Wait, what is she doing!?

"Val, please don't hurt him—"

The potion hisses and Val thrusts the top part, which was exposed to the blue droplet, at Jorge. In a flash, the liquid bursts into blue flames that rupture in the air. The flames stretch out and touch Jorge's extended arrow, immediately burning the arrow's tip. Jorge releases the arrow, trying to keep the rest of the bow from burning. The burning arrow lands in the snow, the flames so hot that they melt part of the snow before fizzling out. Wow. I didn't know flames could be that powerful. I didn't know Val was that powerful.

"Who are you?" Jorge's eyes latch onto Val, studying the bony girl. I sigh. Thank goodness. They're both okay. That wasn't nearly as bad as I thought—Jorge lets out a loud whistle. A familiar one that mimics the call of a hawk. Seriously?

Sure enough, a hawk dives through the sky, heading right for Val's head. The girl stares ahead, likely searching for wolves.

"Val! Look up!" Phemus calls, keeping his eye-extender trained on the sky.

"Phemus, what—" Val gasps as the hawk's claws slash at her. They're both going to seriously hurt each other. I need to stop this! She puts her leather-covered arms in front of her face but it does little to protect her from the hawk's bright yellow talons.

"Guys stop this, you're going to hurt each other!" I yell.

They ignore me.

Val snatches another vial from her cauldron. Phemus tries

CHAPTER 28: PINE'S NEW NAME HURTS MY SOUL

to yank the hawk off her, but the bird's wings flap rapidly in his face, scaring the leafer off. Val cracks the vial against the beak of the bird, dripping orange goo all over its brown feathers. With a crack, the orange goo hardens around the hawk's wings. He squawks and tumbles into the snow, thrashing as the goo continues hardening around him, trapping him on the ground.

Jorge's fists clench and he whistles again, the sound mimicking a roaring howl. Val dives through her cauldron, looking for more potions.

"That's it, I'm going in," I growl. But Phemus grabs my arm before I can. "What are you doing!?"

Meanwhile, Val retrieves a lean purple potion. She twists the cork of the bottle off as I struggle in Phemus' grip. "Last chance, wolf boy. Leave us alone."

Jorge snorts before whistling again. Great. And I thought he wasn't a hothead...

"Phemus, let me go. Someone is going to get hurt!"

"But Val isn't a bad person," he murmurs. "A-and she told me we had to do this."

Is he actually worried about this now of all times!? "P—"

Val grins, letting a droplet of potion fall to the ground. The purple juice reacts with the snow, forming a silver bolt. It's like a jagged scar and shoots through the snow with the energy of a hurricane. I gasp. I've never seen something like that before. It reminds me of the lightning bolt which struck Nella's best friend Lyssa's house back in Walend.

The bolt slams into Jorge, sizzling through his body. He yells as it thrashes him back and forth before he crumples into the snow.

"Jorge!" I scream. Phemus whimpers, letting go of my arm.

The boy grunts, trembling on the ground. He slowly gets

to his feet. Thank goodness he's okay. Behind him a wolf leaps out, baring its teeth at Val. Jorge whistles again while Val retrieves another potion. I need to stop them, fast.

I race across the bone-filled terrain, finally reaching them and jumping right in the middle of their battle.

"Stop!" I yell, holding my hands out. Both kids instinctively freeze. Even the wolf and hawk (who's still struggling in the snow, poor guy) stop at the sudden sound. Finally, they're listening to me! "Guys, there is no point in fighting each other when the bandits at any minute could destroy our country! We need to focus on the priority here."

"Whatcha talkin' about?"

"I'm talking about the ceremony they're holding to choose a new Sun. The one where they're going to kill the phoenix and infuse its magic into their Sun to make them more powerful than anyone in Solia."

Both Jorge and Val's faces pale. "They're choosing a new Sun," they both murmur, then shoot a worried look at each other.

"That's bad," Val says.

"Really bad," Jorge realizes, dropping his bow.

Chapter 29: Dragon Ribs Are Easy for Short People to Sit On

Jorge and Val still hate each other. At least, I think that's why they're sitting an entire rib cage apart.

"What did these bone thingies belong to?" Phemus wonders, knocking on the large bones. We both sit on the same rib cage in between the two. Snow coats the edges of it, still dancing in front of our faces.

"Dragons. They went extinct after Thea, the thirteenth Sun, killed the last one-off." I used to love hearing the stories about her. It's so weird to think that she wasn't originally chosen as the Sun. "They were really bad in her time, plus DragonKilling used to be a huge tradition here. You'd get a lotta money and fame for killing one." Val tilts her head, inspiration sparking behind her eyes before she goes back to fixating on her nails.

"Ohhh yeeeaaahhhh. All the leafers are super mad about it. We have a dragon memorial day and everything."

"That's interesting, Phemus." I nod, trying to smile. Val and Jorge don't say a word. Great, this is going to be awkward. "So, I had us all sit down and take a breather because I think this whole fight was a big misunderstanding, right?"

Both of them avoid my gaze, continuing to glare at each other. I groan. "Well?"

"I shouldn't have fought her but I don't regret trying to protect you," Jorge says.

"I don't regret fightin' him." Val shrugs.

Phemus' wiggly ears flap down. "Val!"

The girl wipes a smudge of dirt off her cheek. Then she jumps off the rib she was resting on and locks eyes with Phemus. "We went after ya, Leda. All the way to the bandits' base. You're right. Those people are crazy. They kidnapped Penelope." Jorge's eyes widen. He must've traded with Penelope before. We both traded with Belen together, but his family always had extra goods to sell. "And Kore ain't gonna do anything. We got there when she was trying to stop them. Her powers were outta control! She nearly killed us with them and barely escaped gettin' kidnapped by those bandits."

Jorge tilts his head. The wolves curled around his lap him flatten their ears. He turns towards Phemus. "Is this true?"

"Yeah, it was really scary!" He jumps off the ribs. Then he karate chops the air. "She was spraying water everywhere. It even hit my arm." He jolts his arm up, revealing a long, nasty bruise. I grit my teeth. Just when I thought Kore couldn't make me any madder. "I'm not sure that she's a very good Sun…"

Jorge stares at the ground. Snowflakes settle on the hood of his cloak. "I know she isn't a good Sun." Yes, people are finally on my side! Now all I've got to do is convince them to help me stop this ceremony. Then everyone in Solia will see who's the better hero. Jorge's voice cracks and for once he leans towards me. "You s-said they want to choose a new Sun. Why?" Woah. This is the first time he's actually cared about what the bandits' plan is.

CHAPTER 29: DRAGON RIBS ARE EASY FOR SHORT PEOPLE TO SIT ON

I climb up the dragon ribs. Their bones are slippery and wet with snow under my hands. But I don't care. I can think clearer when on top of them. I stroke the bone's ivory surface, telling everything—and I mean everything—the bandits told me. Then I add a bit of my own insight on how with a kid more powerful than the Sun in their hands, the bandits could do anything they wanted and wreak havoc on even more cities. The trio's faces all pale as they tremble. Finally, I ask, "Do you really think we should just stand by and let them do this?"

Jorge sighs. "Well, do you even have a plan or the skills to fight off an entire organized group of bandits?" The wolves at his feet look up at me with big black eyes. I won't let their little beady black eyes judge me.

Clearing my throat, I exhale. This is my chance. This is what I've been preparing for. "I know in the past I've been impulsive, but this time I want to defeat the bandits with a real plan. According to Val, they have a technique for summoning the phoenix, which means no matter how many times we save the phoenix from them they'll just resummon it. That means our best bet on stopping them is to wreck the actual ceremony instead."

An image of those poor kids pops into my head, reminding me of what I'd been mulling over as soon as I left on Pine with Jorge. "I think the best way to do that is through the kids. If we can loosen their bindings right before the ceremony, then during the ceremony they'll cause complete chaos. In the midst of everything, Val, Phemus, and I'll all work together to defeat Bone and any other major bandits. With their leaders gone and their ceremony in complete chaos, the bandits will be forced to surrender."

I clear my throat as Jorge narrows his eyes at me. "Phoebe

said they're holding the ceremony in one week. That means we'll have one week to train and rescue the kidnapped kids. Plus, Val is from Evin and has incredible fighting skills, so she'll be able to train us." Val's face flushes.

"And how do you plan on doing that without a layout of their base?" Jorge taps his foot.

I open my map book. Phemus leans up and touches the translator. The book glows, once again displaying the vivid map of Solia with moving animals and everything. Jorge gasps. "This is an enchanted map of Solia, it shows every living creature in the country. We'll know exactly where the bandits are heading on the day of the ceremony and the layout of their base. So…" All three of us turn to him with wary, but hopeful eyes. "What do you think, Jorge?"

For a while, he doesn't say anything. His hawks dart from dragon rib to rib. Then he shifts slightly and says, "If the bandits are really trying to do everything you say they're planning. And Kore is as bad as everyone says she is. And no one else is stepping up. And your friend here is from Evin. And you actually follow the plan you've made. Then I wouldn't oppose waiting to go home for a little longer."

I leap off the top of the dragon's rib. Then I rush over to Jorge and smash him with a giant hug. Phemus has definitely given me some expert friend-crushing skills. "I knew you'd come through! This is awesome, it'll be just like when we were kids. Defeating bad guys left and right!"

Val sighs behind me, tapping her foot. "We've gotta get going. We only have one week to plan this attack."

I release Jorge, who glares at the girl. "You're right, Val." I crack my knuckles. "Let's get training."

Chapter 30: My One Best Friend's a Traitor and My Other Best Friend Keeps Attacking Me with Wolves

I hug the oak tree I'm nestled in as tight as possible. That doesn't really help with my nerves. But I think the real reason my vision's blurry and my knees are weak is because of the flock of wolves barking at the end of the tree I'm climbing.

"This is not training Jorge, it's torture!" He doesn't even look up from his loaded bow. Instead, he shoots his arrow at the tree. Ugh, why does he keep ignoring me! "At least Val gave me useful advice! She actually taught me how to deal with different fighting situations…Somewhat."

Jorge rolls his eyes, pulling his arrow out of the tree. "Well, Val's not here right now, is she? Apparently Miss Perfect Evin girl thinks she's too good for training." Wolves continue snarling at my feet. They scrap at the pine tree's base, snarling viciously. I know they're not supposed to hurt me but it really feels like they will if they get the chance.

"She's off getting supplies for her potions!" I shriek as one jumps up and almost grabs my dress in a fistful of claws. "Trust me, her potions work really well. We're going to need them before we try sneaking in and rescuing those kids. She's not going to train until she gets back." I can't wait for her to get back. Jorge's training has been nothing but me running away from his wolves and failing to fight them off.

I sigh. What would Val tell me if she were here? I furrow my brows. Doesn't she always say to think outside the box? But I'm in a tree, that doesn't really help—Wait, I need to think outside the tree, that's it!

I narrow my eyes at the long dragon bones next to me, which curl around the grass. They probably used to be his tail. After fighting Val here, Jorge thought it would be best to train near the dragon bones. Now, I get why. I crouch on the extended branch, leaning over the tail, and leap.

The bones rattle under my sandals as I balance on top of them. Good thing they are as hard as rocks. Confused, the wolves turn their heads around. I race across the bones, leaping from tail to leg to wing. Then Phemus shouts, "Good job, Leda!" Immediately, all the wolves turn their heads towards me. Seriously, Phemus!

"Phemus, you're supposed to be a bandit." Jorge sighs.

The leafer's ears perk up. "Oh, right!" He grabs a stick next to him. Then with a jolt, lurches himself on top of the dragon bones. He rushes straight towards me. "I'm a big bad bandit and I'm coming to get you Leeeddaaaa!!" I unsheathe my sword.

The bones rattle beneath me as Phemus roars. My feet slip and I start tipping over. The wolves yap underneath the tall dragon bones. Shoot, I can't lose my grip! I drop to my knees, holding onto the bones and my sword.

"Sorry Leda!" Phemus raises his stick toward my head. I block his blow with my sword. Then use my other hand

CHAPTER 30: MY ONE BEST FRIEND'S A TRAITOR AND MY OTHER BEST...

to hold me onto the bones. Fortunately, that blow alone is enough to make Phemus go wide eyed and stumble backward.

I quickly get to my feet and launch at Phemus. He barely blocks. Then his body shudders and he almost topples off the bones. That's it! Phemus is big. The kind of big that makes you trip over your feet and marvel at your own hands. The kind of big that makes it difficult to stop, to move where you want to go. I know that kind of big because I'm the same way. At least I was, compared to Jorge and Val and my younger siblings. There was even a time when I was bigger than my older siblings. But compared to Phemus I'm basically a mouse. And I can use that to my advantage.

Grinning, I slash at Phemus' legs this time. I move slowly enough so he can dodge the blow, but even that is difficult for the leafer. He stumbles back and I slash again. Then he tries to whack his branch at me again. As fast as I can, I deflect the blow. Sure enough, it sends his log scattering onto the snow.

"Oh no!" Phemus shrieks, only to slip off the bone and into the pile of rabid wolves. Except as soon as they see him they lick his face, matting his fluffy black hair with spit. A few even nudge his eye-extender.

Jorge narrows his eyes. "That was too easy for you. I'm coming up." He drops his bow and quiver onto a bunch of flowers. Then grabs the dragon rib and hoists himself onto the bony structure.

I laugh. "You're gonna fight me. You were terrible when we were kids."

Jorge smirks. "I know. I was going easy." My gut sickens. He has to be bluffing. Right?

Then he unsheathes two daggers from his belt. How many weapons does this boy carry!? Both are hooked like my blade and decorated with patterns. One contains a carved image of a village. It must be Walend. I'd recognize those rocky shores, quaint stony houses, and wildflowers anywhere. The other has a picture of the Solian woods: wolves, cliffs, and pine trees. The usual.

Jorge lunges. It's the complete opposite of Phemus' blow. Sharp, quick, and focused. It hits me and I stagger backward, heaving. I stare at my dress. It tore neatly into my shoulder, sinking just enough into the fabric to cut it, but not enough to rip into my skin. I narrow my eyes. He did just enough to scare me but not enough to hurt me. That was precise. Like really precise. "S-since when were you this good at fighting?"

Jorge keeps a fighting stance but doesn't charge. Neither do I. He's too unpredictable right now. "Since I was the only heir to the family dedicated to protecting Walend. They made me do this instead of read books."

I wish my parents had taught me to fight. But Jorge and I are very different people. "No way, you're an awesome fighter like Val!" Phemus cheers and Jorge's eyes drift towards him. Now's my chance!

I lunge when Jorge isn't looking. He turns and blocks my blow anyways. He only slips a few inches backward. Then he easily pushes back against my hold. His eyes darken. "I was trained to do this sort of stuff. To fight or make animals fight for me. To spot danger. To know when something or someone is bad news. And Val is bad news." He breaks my hold, sending one of his daggers flying into the air.

I leap up and grab it. My feet slip and I barely land back on the dragon's bony tail. Jorge takes the opportunity to knock my sword onto the ground. I grit my teeth. He did that on purpose! "Val is not bad news."

CHAPTER 30: MY ONE BEST FRIEND'S A TRAITOR AND MY OTHER BEST...

"She talks like someone who barely understands our language even though she attends one of the best boarding schools in the country." Jorge slashes at me with his dagger. I duck backward to avoid him, stumbling onto the dragon's skull. We circle around its pointy teeth. "She can't use moonstars, can she?" I avoid his gaze. "I knew it. And she uses weird potions I've never seen before."

I jab back at him. "She just has an accent. Different people from different parts of Solia have different accents. And using moonstars has to do with having magic in your blood. Plus her potions are probably something specially taught in Evin."

He deflects. We keep slashing at each other and deflecting the blows, dancing around the dragon's skull. He raises his eyebrow. "I'm not talking about her accent. I'm talking about the fact that she can't even understand basic grammar structure. It's harder for you to tell because you don't read but you have to notice how it sounds...wrong when she talks." I gulp. Because I don't want to admit it, but I know he's right. I know exactly what he's talking about. I barely deflect his next blow.

"And as for using moonstars, their magic isn't some special substance only certain people have, like Kore's abilities. It comes from being part of the order. Every Solian's ancestry dates back hundreds of years in this land so every Solian is naturally a part of the order and can use moonstars. You just need to be trained in it, which I guarantee they do at Evin. So, if she's not from Evin, then why does she really want this phoenix?" With one swift move, he jolts the dagger out of my hand and pins his to my neck. It depicts Walend on its glossy surface. I lost again.

"Val!" Phemus calls, rushing up to the end of the clearing.

Sure enough, there rests Val. A faithful Pine darts behind her. Someone had to keep the girl company. Val's hair is matted and streaks of mud plaster her face. Jorge and I exchange glances as I hand him his dagger.

"We needta prep the kids now." Her accent and clumsy words pierce my ears.

I tilt my head. "Why?" My voice cracks but thankfully she ignores it.

"I saw the bandits. They're talkin' about making the ceremony sooner."

"Why would they do that?" Jorge hisses.

"Cause they caught the phoenix."

Chapter 31: Phemus Carries Planks Around. Well, Sorta.

"Are you sure the bandits don't use this river too?" Jorge tilts his head as I scan our glowing map for nearby bandits. Mud squelches under our feet.

In front of us rests a river with glass-like water. Ice and rocks line its edges. According to Val and Phemus, this was the river they used to sneak into the bandits' base to rescue me. We should be able to sneak inside their cave system, rescue the kids, and work with them to ruin the ceremony. But I have to agree with Jorge. If Val is lying about Evin, she could be tricking us about this too. Phemus wouldn't go along with her though, right?

I narrow my eyes on the map.

"Course no—"

"There doesn't look to be anything on this map," I cut off Val. The girl glares at me but I keep my eyes trained on Jorge. Her face falls. "But there are a few boats docked ahead with bones carved into them. I'm guessing the bandits use them to get around this river, so we'll have to make sure no one else sees us when using it."

Jorge nods. "Thanks, Leda." Then he stares ahead while Phemus splashes around in the river. I don't know how he does it. River water in Solia is super cold. "We're going to borrow one of their boats, right?" I nod. "I'm just worried they'll notice we took it."

"A boat..." Phemus sighs, shoulders sagging. Pine stops splashing next to him then looks at me. "I guess my plank won't work."

"You have a plank!" I shout. "Phemus, that'd work perfectly!"

"Hooray!" He dives into the mud. His large meaty hands easily race through the slime and dirt until his hand thunks into a piece of wood. He grabs a giant plank from the middle of the ground and drags it over to the river "Ta da!"

"Where did you get a giant plank from?" I gawk.

"Oh! Another leafer put it there, we put lots of things underneath the ground. Clothing, food, planks!" He shrugs, dropping the plank into the deep blue river. "Anything another leafer would need if they're in trouble."

"That's actually really cool." I smile. I wish humans did that.

Meanwhile, Val snaps a branch off a tree to use as a paddle. Then she pulls the plank into the water. Sure enough, it begins floating over the rocky waves. Val, however, almost loses the plank to the jolting waves. Jorge snorts. I wade into the water, holding the plank still on the rocky shore.

My hand nearly slides off the damp wood. Saltwater stings the tiny scars swarming them. Already the plank sinks a little. "I don't think this is going to hold more than two people."

"I'll go," Val says. Jorge and I both stare at her only for her face to flush. "I know how to navigate the river."

"Right." I cough. "I'll go too." I need to interrogate her anyway. Jorge bites his lip then nods. I smile. He trusts me. Val and I board the plank while Phemus lowers his head. Pine nudges the leafer.

CHAPTER 31: PHEMUS CARRIES PLANKS AROUND. WELL, SORTA.

"I guess you don't want me to use my other plank then…"

"You have another plank!" Phemus nods. Leafers are awesome! "That's even more perfect, quick, get it!" Next to me, Pine whimpers.

"Sorry bud, you're gonna have to sit this one out." I pat his neck before Val and I push off. He snorts, rolling his eyes before scurrying back into the bushes. "Thanks for understanding!"

Phemus scatters over and digs up another plank. A few seconds later, Jorge and him are on the plank a few paces behind us. "So. Why'd ya wanna come?" Oh no. Does she know I'm trying to interrogate her? Is she suspicious? What if she's already leading us straight to the bandits' grasp—

"Well…" Val starts.

"Oh! Um I just wanted to really make sure I saw Penelope." It's not technically a lie. I definitely want to make sure she's okay.

She narrows her eyes. Then keeps rowing ahead. I do the same, trying not like her gaze unnerve me. "Yeah. I'm worried about her too. I'm worried about everythin'. A lot more than I thought I'd be." She laughs. I bristle. What does that mean? I gulp, inching slightly away from her on our plank.

I laugh nervously as she shoots me a weird look, then rows our plank faster. "This water's tough. Really have to work at rowing past it, dontcha?" I nod as she digs into the water like a madwoman. "Makes me wanna just crush it all." My gut tightens. Was she always this violent?

"So, what are you going to use the phoenix for in your exam thingie? At Evin. Yup. For your great Evin exam!" I squeak.

"What'd Jorge tell ya about me while I was gone?" I stiffen. She knew this whole time! "You're acting real funny. He told you some lie, didn't he?"

I focus on the bobbing waves ahead of us and the emerging cave system. How was my cover blown so easily!? Ugh, I guess I'm bad at spying.

"Well?" Val pushes us around a rock. "What? He say I was a jerk for wantin' to get supplies on my own? Or make fun of my eyes being different colors?" I still don't respond. "Leda, if ya don't tell me I can't explain to you what's really going on. For some reason Jorge doesn't like me, I guarantee what he said 'bout me only comes from him not liking me."

She does have a point. Jorge is biased against her. But what he said made sense. Then again, it could be good to hear her side of the story. Plus, Val's been nothing but nice to me so far. "Jorge, um, he can read. And he says you speak Solian worse than I do despite you supposedly being from Evin." Val freezes, still bent over the plank. "Plus, he found it weird that you couldn't use a moonstar and had strange potions, since at Evin you would've learned about moonstars. Not potions."

Val's voice wavers. "So ya think I'm lying about Evin."

"I'm sorry, Val." I lean over and pat her shoulder. "I didn't want to believe it, but there's no other logical explanation…"

Val locks eyes with me. "There is." She pauses, her eyes still locked with mine as her voice slows. "Potions are a type of moonstar, you have to be trained differently for each different type. I was never trained on Kore's translator in Evin because I didn't specialize in navigation. Potion making was my specialty." That actually makes a lot of sense. "And I don't speak Solian well because it isn't my first language. In Evin…in Evin they taught us another language first, a language that the people beyond the mountains speak. We were only allowed to speak that there. That's why I can't speak our own

CHAPTER 31: PHEMUS CARRIES PLANKS AROUND. WELL, SORTA.

language." Her voice breaks.

My eyes widen. Of course, how could I have been so stupid! The bandits may hate the outsiders and love Solia but most of the country, especially the people in Evin, believe the outsiders are better than us. It makes perfect sense that they'd prefer speaking their language instead!

"Val..." I place my branch on the plank and scoop her up into a hug. She stiffens for a moment then her body relaxes, a smile forming on her face. "I'm so sorry. I completely forgot how the people in Evin think the outsiders and their language is better than ours."

"Yeah." She laughs. "They do."

"I shouldn't have doubted you. You've helped me try and find this phoenix since the beginning. I—"

She drops her log and hugs me back, smiling. "It's alright. Jorge has it out for me. I got no idea what that pipsqueak's problem is with me."

I shove her shoulder then return to rowing. "Hey! Don't call him that!"

"It's true, though. He's tiny and got a high voice."

I roll my eyes, laughing. "Val! He's my best friend, don't say things like that about him!"

"Right, sorry." Val tries to maintain a straight face. Only to burst into giggles. I can't help but join.

After a few minutes, we both recollect our thoughts. "In all seriousness. I know why he doesn't like you." I pause as she leans in, tilting her head. Should I tell her why? I think so. Maybe if she can understand him better, she'll get into less fights with him. "Evin was his dream."

"What?"

I stare ahead at the gray rocks marking the bandits' base,

which draw closer and closer. "Jorge and I became friends because we were both dreamers. We had these crazy, impossible dreams, but we dreamed them anyway. Mine was to be chosen as the Sun. His was to attend a boarding school in Evin. We both got rejected. I wasn't chosen and he wasn't accepted into the school."

"I see." Val sighs. "Ya know, the things you dream of, sometimes they're not as good as you think." I tilt my head. Is she talking about Evin or my dream? It has to be Evin, right? Sure, I did listen to my dad's advice once. But it can't be a bad thing to be the Sun. To be the hero who saves the day. Who everybody loves.

A sharp laugh interrupts our conversation. Val and I freeze, glancing ahead. Bandits.

Chapter 32: Bandits Give Even Worse Love Advice Than I Do

There are two bandits rowing in the middle of the river. Their dorky boat rocks on the bumpy waves. I narrow my eyes. Mateo and Barak. I can tell by the men's equally crazy hairstyles. You don't forget those hairstyles.

Fortunately, Mateo and Barak fixate on the cave system ahead as they chat with each other. At least, Mateo watches the caves ahead. Barak's busy furiously rowing the boat.

I glance at Val and then at Jorge and Phemus. How do we avoid them seeing us!? Val slows the boat and I nod, following her lead. The best we can do is not talk, follow them from a really long distance away, and hope.

"Hey, Mateo," Barak says in between rowing the boat. "Do you, um, ever think Phoebe and Bone and all of them, that they're maybe going a bit too far?"

"Uh. No. Those losers deserved it." The man wipes his dirty hands on his pants. "Only thing Phoebe did wrong was send us to fetch her stupid fancy boots for Bone's meeting today. Seriously, we had to chase after that phoenix in the woods all day. And now go back to the base for Phoebe's boots before going right back for Bone's little announcement he's hosting tonight. Why's it in the middle of the woods anyway?"

They're meeting in the middle of the woods tonight? What could Bone possibly want to meet with everyone about? My eyes widen. What if Val was right and he wants to move the ceremony date to earlier? I'm going to have to go to that announcement if I want to know what's going on.

Mateo grunts, leaning over the edge of the boat. Barak furrows his brows. "It's because Bone doesn't want the phoenix to get wet, so he's taking him by foot back to the base, which is a day's trip away. But Mateo, are you really sure about all this?"

"Shut up, Barak!" he hollers and Barak sulks in the boat's back, head hanging low. Mateo sighs. "You know what your problem is?"

"My problem?"

"Yeah, the reason Phoebe will never like you." Barak gulps, whimpering. I glance back at Jorge desperately trying to get Phemus to stop rowing so fast. He looks up, clearly hearing the conversation with the rest of us. "You don't have guts. Or a backbone." Jorge stiffens, I glance back at Barak who freezes in nearly the exact same way. "Girls like guys with backbones. Guys who know what they're doing."

Why am I sitting here, listening to bandits give advice on picking up girls!? Phemus giggles when he sees my face.

"Did you hear that?" Barak sniffles. "It sounded like a giggle."

Val facepalms next to me as I shoot a death glare at the leafer. His ears droop downwards.

"A giggle." Mateo laughs and glances behind him for a second. Oh no. "You!?" His eyes flicker from me to Jorge. They go livid. "And you!!" He nearly shoves Barak into the water as he races to the back of the boat, shaking his fist at Jorge. Then he dives into his satchel. "Oh, you brats are going

CHAPTER 32: BANDITS GIVE EVEN WORSE LOVE ADVICE THAN I DO

to pay for spying!" He retrieves a small glittering white crystal.

Barak's eyes widen. "Mateo, that could hurt them—"

"I don't care!" He twists the crystal, bending its tips. Then he tosses it in the rolling waves. Nothing happens.

"I'm so scared!" I roll my eyes, chuckling. Val snickers too. But I cast a glance at Jorge, whose face is pale. Oh no. What is he worried—

A huge wave stretches out of the river, immediately separating us from the bandits. Then it comes crashing straight towards us. Seawater sprays on my sides as I scream. It's going to kill us! I grit my teeth. I need to focus on getting us out of here. I glance to my right. There's a long twig. I wonder...I unsheathe my sword and hook onto the twig, pulling us closer to land and out of the wave's grasp.

"Jorge!" I call and look back. He nods before I can say anything, grabs their log, and uses it to hook onto another root, pulling them away from the wave. Only for Phemus to fall forward, knocking the log out of Jorge's hands and straight into the river. Shoot!

Before I can say anything, Val dips her hand into the raging river, grinning. "Don't worry. I got an idea." She twists open a vial of foamy white liquid. She lets a drop of it slither into the river. Steam and foam rise up, expanding to create a fluffy cloud-like white bubble.

"Val, what is that!?" Jorge growls. His chest heaves as the wave draws closer and closer. Already its ripples have pushed us far away from the bandits' base.

"It's awesome!" I cheer.

The bubble rises as Jorge shakes. "Y-you can't do that. It's not in order. You can't disrupt the order!"

"Order? Whatcha talkin' about?" Val asks. Wait a minute, is

he talking about the animal thing? The thing that lets Solians use moonstars? Why would that matter now? "Get in the bubble, quick!"

Val steps into the foamy bubble. I jump in as well, Phemus and a reluctant Jorge following my lead. The gooey foam wall brushes against my shoulders as I struggle through it. With a sucking sound, it flaps open and we all fall inside. The clear surface bounces underneath my legs while its hazy veil cloaks everything outside the bubble in gray and white. The wave crashes straight into use, but not a single drop of water passes into the bubble. It's actually quite beautiful to watch the water and fish that got swept in it fly past us.

Val pokes the bubble, smirking, once the wave passes. "See, Jorge—"

A deep scream, one that mirrors the roaring of a waterfall mixed with the screech of a dozen hawks, knocks Val off her feet. The bubble pops with a hiss, evaporating into smoke. All four of us land on the scaly back of a serpent, which rises out of the water. Blue, gray, and green scales flake across its winding tail. The scales are dull and slippery, the kind that could easily hide beneath a river.

The monster jabs its face in front of Val, roaring again. Its eyes are closed, protected by green eyelids, but its nostrils flare. Meanwhile, its head is coated in seaweed and it has two spiky gray horns jutting out of its skull. Its mouth is filled with rosy pink gums which lack teeth. It spits on Val, narrowing in on her. My eyes widen. How does it know? The sea serpent has to be targeting only her because she disrupted Jorge's "order." Is the order really that powerful?

"Jorge," I grunt as my head throbs from its loud screech. "Can you communicate with it?" I turn to the boy but he's

CHAPTER 32: BANDITS GIVE EVEN WORSE LOVE ADVICE THAN I DO

frozen in place.

The serpent leans over and gulps up Val in one swoop.

"Val!" Phemus and I yell. Then it flicks us off into the woods with its shaking tail. It dives through the river and down the waterfall.

Chapter 33: Sea Serpents Are Possessive of Water. It's Rude.

A monster just ate Val. A giant sea monster. Well, it's Solia so I guess that was bound to happen at some point. Time to go get her out of its stomach. I get to my feet, ignoring my dizziness from being whacked onto the grass by a giant sea monster. Then I dust the snow off my dress and tread down the hill, following the winding river. Pine races over, screeching as his antlers point towards the end of the river, towards a raging waterfall and the lake it feeds into. Good. He knows what we have to do too.

"Val got eaten!" Phemus whimpers, his eye watering up in its eye-extender. "Sh-she's gone."

My fists clench around the hilt of my sword. "Not yet she isn't." Jorge still lays on the snowy ground, shaking. "Come on guys, we've gotta get her before it digests her."

"How do you know it hasn't already!?" Phemus follows me down the hill. He grabs Jorge and slings him over his shoulder. The boy yelps in alarm.

I stop, sighing. I don't know that it hasn't already eaten her. My fists clench. But I can't give up. The least I can do is try to save her. "We have to try."

"Okay! I'll try too!" Phemus jogs down the hill with me. We

CHAPTER 33: SEA SERPENTS ARE POSSESSIVE OF WATER. IT'S RUDE.

both race towards the waterfall's bottom, which is a big blue lake. Pine scampers down with us.

Phemus pulls out his eye-extender, fixating on the river. "I don't see—hey wait, look!" He points at the lake we run towards. A flash of silver glimmers inside it. That has to be Val! She must be using her crazy potions. I grin and rush towards the lake as quickly as I can.

Phemus, Jorge, and I finally reach the lake. Based on where the bolt of light came from, the serpent isn't too deep. I should be able to swim to it.

"Alright. Here goes nothing." I stretch my arms, bracing myself to swim. Fortunately, the lake is still and calm. Should be an easy swim.

"Leda!" Jorge squirms in Phemus' grip. I turn to face him but the worry drains from his face. "Never mind. Go get her."

I beam, then dive into the water, my legs kicking me deep inside it. Unlike the other river I swam through, this river is lighter and easier to see. Bits of seaweed sway underneath me while the sea serpent curls its long body. Its chest glows silver again, right at the center. My arms begin throbbing but I push on, swimming deeper and deeper. Finally, I reach the sea serpent which swims further into the lake, trying to reach the water's sandy floor.

My arms ache again while my chest starts to hurt. The pain makes me wince and float backward. The serpent continues swimming downwards. If I don't stab it now, I'll lose my chance to save Val. I need to keep going even if it hurts like crazy. I swim after it, latching onto some of its scales nearby where Val made that serpent glow. The massive serpent doesn't notice my movements.

With shaky hands, I unsheathe my sword and jam it into the

serpent's body, ripping open its chest. Blood curls through the water while the serpent screeches. Unfortunately, my blade doesn't make a big enough gash for Val to escape out of. I slash again, only for my slash to be followed by a glow. Val's inside there! Helping me! The serpent wiggles back and forth, trying to buck me off it. My head spins and I grab onto the serpent's scales then bring my sword up and slash at it again. My third slice bursts a hole through the serpent's body. It screeches and its head whips toward me, mouth opening.

A pale hand bursts out of the serpent's body. I grab the hand and pull Val out of the serpent's body. Her blonde hair spirals all around the water as she grins. She holds her tiny purple vial, the one which shot a silver bolt at Jorge.

She's alive! Yes! Oh wait, a giant serpent head is now heading right towards me... Wonderful. I brace myself to slash the serpent's head. Only for Val to open her vial and let out a drop of purple liquid. She closes it then, pulls me backward, and we both swim away from the floating drop. It immediately reacts with the water, exploding into a silver bolt that rushes straight towards the serpent. The water makes it expand further and further, frying the serpent's face. It screeches in alarm as the bolt hits it, before swimming down to the lake's bottom.

My lungs, arms, and entire body ache but I keep going, pulling Val up with me to the surface of the lake. We gasp when we reach it, breathing in the brittle air.

"Val! Leda! You made it!" Phemus shouts at the other side of the lake, waving his arms happily. Jorge teeters on the lake's edge next to him, glaring at the blue water.

Val coughs, bringing her cauldron to the surface as well. "That monster was awesome!"

CHAPTER 33: SEA SERPENTS ARE POSSESSIVE OF WATER. IT'S RUDE.

I wheeze, laughing. "That's what you're thinking right now?" She joins in on my laughter as we swim towards the shore together. Then I grin. "Hey, looks like you're interested in something besides your exam, Miss I Don't Care About Anyone." Jorge bristles on the lake's edge, tilting his head in confusion. I'll have to tell him the truth about Val later.

Her face flushes. "I always cared." Then she bites her lip as I glare at her. "Okay. I learned to care."

Jorge grabs my hand and pulls me out of the water as I reach the edge while Phemus does the same with Val. We both collapse onto solid ground, chests heaving up and down. My arm finally stops aching. Hooray! Oh great, now I'm starting to sound like Phemus.

Speaking of which, Phemus scoops us up into a big hug. Almost killing us after he put us in a near death experience.

"Phemus. Can ya let us rest?" Val chuckles.

"Oh sorry!" Phemus drops us both and we settle onto the muddy ground, sighing. I rub my head, water dribbling off my thick braid and saggy clothing. Pine nuzzles me, warming my body.

Jorge hugs me too. Unlike Phemus, his hug doesn't nearly squeeze me to death. It's soft and warm and kinda cool since I can't remember the last time he hugged me like this. He releases me. "Guess my training worked well."

I grin. "It did."

He smiles, turning to face Val. His eyes tighten. "Val, next time don't interrupt the order."

Val's face flushes, tracing the edges of her purple potion. It's indented with a lightning bolt that zigzags around the vial. Awesome.

"Hey Jorge, what did she do that interrupted the order?

Actually, what does the order even have to do with that sea serpent and river in the first place? I thought it was about understanding that every animal has a role in the forest."

"Oh, there's a lot more to the order than that. I used that comparison because it's easiest to help beginners understand the concept. My parents told me it when I was five." He leans on a tree trunk, glancing at Phemus.

"You explained it to me like I was a five-year-old!?"

"It worked, didn't it?" He laughs as I scowl. "Anyways, Val's potion interfered with the flow of the river by creating a bubble out of its foamy waves. Like a hawk's job is to watch the skies, a sea serpent's job is to protect the river from losing water. The bubble violates that. I'd expect someone from Evin to know that."

She sighs, hugging her knees and dragging her fingers through the mud.

"But the serpent's a monster, there are probably billions of different monsters in these woods, does your book cover all of them?" I tilt my head.

Jorge taps his satchel. "No, only the major ones my family knows about. Sea serpents living in rivers and attacking people for disturbing their water was a pretty major grievance for my family. I guess it wouldn't technically be in Evin since there are no rivers there but—"

"What's a grievance?" I blurt out. Jorge groans. Then I grit my teeth, sighing. Now that the bandits saw us, they're going to keep their base guarded for the rest of the day. That means we're not going to be able to free those kids until tomorrow. Great. I've just got to hope that at Bone's meeting tonight he doesn't change the ceremony's date to too soon. Otherwise, I'm going to be in trouble. "Never mind. Let's go back to our

CHAPTER 33: SEA SERPENTS ARE POSSESSIVE OF WATER. IT'S RUDE.

camp and regroup."

Chapter 34: I Actually Feel Bad About Kore

Tonight is the night. The night Bone is going to meet with all his little bandits to reschedule his ceremony. I know it not just because I have a map showing me exactly where they are, but because I can also hear it. Well, I can hear the phoenix. Its screams and wails pierce the air, lapping over my ears like ocean waves. So, the map was right. The bandits are meeting surprisingly close to us.

The phoenix's shrieks rip into me. Every muscle in my body tenses, willing me to follow and save it. I don't know how the others are able to sleep comfortably. Even Jorge is nestled among his wolves, eyes firmly shut. I didn't bother waking them up because I figured it would be better if they got their sleep. Besides, I'll only quickly visit the bandits, then leave.

I rush up, following the sound as fast as I can. Pearly white dragon bones and dull flowers pass by me. A few leaves stick to my hair. Tree after tree passes by me until I finally come across a bony, shivering girl.

"K-kore," I gasp. The girl's slumped under a pine tree, shivering in the cold. Goosebumps rise across her tan arms. Her eyes are hazy, focused on nothing but the two purple flowers in front of her. And her hair is completely black.

CHAPTER 34: I ACTUALLY FEEL BAD ABOUT KORE

"What are you doing—Woah, your blue streak, it's gone!"

Kore sighs, looking up at me with sullen eyes. "I never had a blue streak."

"What? But your hair, part of it's blue. It's always been," I stammer.

"It's not naturally that way. My grandma just dyed it," she murmurs. Dyed it? "Like how you dye wool."

Her hair was fake? My eyes widen, then I shake my head. Wait, why am I worrying about this right now? It's not even important. I clear my throat. "Oh, well, I've got to go. Y-you're not going to spy on the bandits' meeting tonight too, are you?" I don't need her spraying water on me again.

She laughs. Oh great, she's going to lecture me on how great she is because she's the Sun again, isn't she? Maybe I should've taken up the bandits' offer. Just to see the look on her face. We'd finally be on equal terms. "No, you're better off doing it without me," her voice cracks, eyes watering. Okay...that's weird. She's never acted that way before.

"Are you sick, Kore?" She laughs again. A dull, bitter laugh that reminds me of when I vomited sea flower petals up after accidentally eating them as a kid. Then she shakes her head.

She points to her right. At the edge of the right is a tiny, fiery dot. "The phoenix is there. Why don't you go chase the fire like you always do, Leda?"

I back away from her. My entire body shudders at the sight of her tiny, trembling figure. Why do I feel even weirder now that she's like this than how I did when she made fun of me? I always hated her, I couldn't understand why she thought she was better than me or why she didn't want to be the Sun. But now...She looks so broken. I never wanted to see her this broken. "I-I think I will."

I scurry off into the woods, but instead of going straight to the bandits, I go back to our campsite. Suddenly, I don't want to do this alone anymore.

* * *

I grab Pine first. He keeps whining too. His eyes are petrified, his ears flattened as the phoenix's cries ring out. The phoenix being in danger must scare him as much as it does me. The noise wakes up Phemus, which of course wakes up the whole team. Jorge is immediately up, Val closely follows, while Phemus is still rubbing his eyes.

"What's going on…" he murmurs. Jorge stiffens beside him and whistles for his wolves. Val secures her potions. Then I leap onto Pine.

"The bandits are meeting tonight," I whisper. "We're going to spy on them and figure out when they're moving the ceremony to." Then Pine kicks up before we take off into the woods. Jorge's wolves follow close by, forming a sea of blue and gray fur under Pine's hooves.

"Ya should've told us earlier," Val grumbles, still rubbing sleep from her eyes. But she dutifully follows me anyway.

"Wait for me!?" Phemus screeches in the background. His voice fades into the background as I focus on the fire ahead of us. It swarms and glistens as I rush forward. My heart pounds. The dark trees. The fire. The phoenix shrieks. All of it. Not again. I can't take it happening again.

Pine skids to a halt behind a few trees. So do the wolves beside us. Heat presses on my face, swarming under my clothes. I look up. Beyond the trees which hide us, rests a giant burning pine tree. Just below it is a swarm of bandits. I

CHAPTER 34: I ACTUALLY FEEL BAD ABOUT KORE

recognize Phoebe, Barak, and a rather proud Mateo. It's only when I squint that I realize why.

He's holding the phoenix.

Well, he got to hold the cage trapping the phoenix. In his hands is a contraption made of goo-rimmed wood, which encases the poor bird. Its eyes are wild; the red slits have become so narrow they remind me of goat eyes. And not in a cute way. It paces around the cage, screeching and jamming into the bars. My fists clench while Pine tenses underneath me. This has to stop.

I jump off Pine and nearly unsheathe my sword. Only to inhale. I can't charge in immediately. We're going to fix this soon. We're going to help that phoenix and those kids in the bandits' base.

So, instead of charging in, I focus my eyes on a tall man. He wears the skull of an elk over his face and a long black cloak filled with grizzly bear fur. Mateo bows then hands the cage over to the taller man. Bone. That has to be him. But what's with the skull?

"Friends!" He hoists the phoenix above the cluster of bandits. It twinkles like a fallen star. "Tonight is a night of celebration. Tonight is the final night where we have a wretched, useless Sun!" His voice reminds me of a crackling warm fire. Why does an evil bandit mastermind have such a nice voice?

The bandits hiss and boo as Bone gestures to a shorter bandit. He pushes an even shorter figure to the ground. Soft black hair surrounds her head while her dull eyes stare ahead. Ropes bind her wrists and she shudders under the heat. Kore! I gulp. Why are they after her too? They were supposed to at least leave her alone!

"This Sun here can't even control her own magic. She

couldn't use it to rescue our children or defend herself from the one bandit it took to defeat her! Imagine! Being blessed with powers and being so incompetent that you can't even use them correctly." The bandits laugh, hissing and spitting in Kore's face. Okay, they're really getting on my nerves.

"But fortunately for us, friends, by tomorrow night we won't have to worry about having a useless Sun." Kore's eyes widen. Tomorrow night? No, they can't be moving the ceremony that soon. We're not ready! "Because tomorrow night I will choose our own Sun. A Solian Sun chosen by a real Solian! Not some freak from outside the mountains. With the help of this phoenix, we will create a Sun more powerful than anything we've ever seen before. A Sun capable of not only protecting Solia but deciding what's best for it. Because if Evin has already lied to us about the Skycharter being the best chooser of our Sun, then what else are they lying about?"

Cheers erupt throughout the crowd. My stomach sickens. Replacing Evin? That would basically make them the rulers of our country. I scowl. I knew it. I knew they were going to use this Sun for more than just defending our country. They're going to force all of us to be under their reign of terror. They're going to hurt more people just like they hurt my dad.

Slowly their cheering morphs into shouts. "Tomorrow night! Tomorrow night!" My heart pounds. We haven't even had a chance to sneak in and alert those kids. I've barely trained. Are Val's potions even ready? There's no way we'll be ready to stop the ceremony by then. There has to be some way we can buy time. Something we can do. My eyes sharpen on the phoenix. What if…?

I grip my sword's hilt then I glance at our group. Val, Jorge, me, and Phemus. Along with Jorge's sea of animals. He

CHAPTER 34: I ACTUALLY FEEL BAD ABOUT KORE

whistles again, drawing in more and more hawks. If it were just the four of us, I'd say we wouldn't have a chance. But now we have practically the entire wildlife of Solia on our side. Jorge nods at me. He's thinking what I am. We need to free the phoenix. Sure, the bandits will be able to find it again but it should buy us time.

I raise my sword and charge. "Leave that phoenix alone!" At first, the bandits laugh but then their faces pale when they see the sea of animals charging behind me. Jorge loads his bow. Val pops the cork of her potion off. Even Phemus raises a giant stick and growls (it's still not scary at all).

Mateo's face pales. Hah! I knew I'd show him. Then the phoenix screeches, its eyes going further into slits. All of the animals whine and wince in pain. The wolves flatten their ears, the elks paw the ground, the hawks flutter their wings nervously. They all back away slowly. The phoenix shrieks again. And then they scatter off into the woods.

Jorge whistles. Once. Twice. A third time. None of them come back. The twenty-something bandits break into laughter.

"Let's slit their throats. Starting with the girlie first." A large, bulky bandit lumbers towards us. I quiver, trying not to back away. This can't be happening! I can't lose to them again, not in front of the fire, not when there's so much to lose if I don't win this. I can't really be this bad at fighting them. At protecting Solia.

"Leave them be," Bone laughs in his smooth voice. It sounds like chiming bells. "These kids are nobodies, they're not a threat to us." The other bandits relax, chuckling at their leader's words. "Come on, we have a ceremony to prepare for."

One of the bandits hoists Kore onto his shoulder and the group rushes through the forest. I grit my teeth. I'm not letting them leave again! Not when they've kidnapped Kore and the phoenix. I chase after the bandits as they dive into the fiery trees. Heat smothers my body. All I can taste and smell is smoke.

"Come back!" I yell, squinting through the fire. I can barely make out one bandit's wavering figure. But I chase after them as fast as I can. "I have to stop you! I have to!"

A sudden cough followed by a looming figure bumping into me knocks me onto the ground. My sword scatters away and the bandit disappears into the woods.

"Sorry, Leda!" Phemus coughs again, spitting all over me.

"What is wrong with you!?" I snap and Phemus' little ears droop down. "I lost the bandits! Do you know what this means!? We're not ready to stop the ceremony because you alerted the bandits this morning that we were following them! And now they're going to hold that ceremony tomorrow night and we're going to fail. We're going to fail to save Solia because of you!"

Phemus' eye widens in horror as he backs up. I huff. Wait, what did I just say to him? His lip quivers. "Thanks for showing me that all humans are meanies!" he huffs and rushes off into the woods.

"Wait, Phemus, come back!" I rush after him. "I didn't mean—" My sandal slips on a gnarled root and I slam into the ground.

Chapter 35: Giant Creepy Black Mountains Are Oddly Inspiring

"Beautiful view isn't it?" My dad cocks his head towards the sky. Dark black mountains jut up, blocking bits and pieces of it. Blue waves push gray sand onto our sandals. "In an odd sort of way. It gets your blood pumping and heart racing, doesn't it? Pity everyone wants them destroyed."

He smiles, taking his meaty hands out of his pockets. Then he claps my back with them. The impact sends me stumbling into the water. Its icy grip chills my sandals, sending shivers down my spine.

"Why are you so happy? Aren't you cold?" I point at his feet, which are also drenched in water.

He chuckles. "Typical Leda. Always worried." He gestures to a little girl swimming through the waves. Eventually, she emerges from it, a drenched rabbit in her hands. She turns to me. Her face looks exactly like mine. Of course it does, I remember saving that rabbit. "You were worried even back then. Back when you had nothing to worry about. Well, you still have nothing to worry about." He laughs. "After all, you finally listened to my advice."

"But—" I stare at the water. A bucket floats inside it,

eventually stumbling onto the shore. My dad bends over to pick it up. Glossy blue liquid swirls in it. I back away. The little girl version of me stands still.

"You're so close." He dips his hand in the blue liquid, it dribbles down his arm. He approaches me as I tremble. "So very close. You just need to keep listening." I scamper away as he paints the liquid on the little girl's face.

"I can't do that again." My eyes water. "Kore's been kidnapped and no one else is left. I have to help those kids and the phoenix. I have to save Solia…"

He chuckles. "I thought we were done with the excuses, Leda?" He sets the bucket down. "Stop pretending this is about anything else besides your desires. You were able to sacrifice them before. Why won't you do it again?"

"I just…" My hands shake as my voice breaks. "I just don't want to be ignored again."

He tilts his head. "Ignored? I never ignored you. Do Jorge or Val or Phemus ever ignore you? Or Kore and Belen, for that matter?"

I furrow my brows, waves lapping at my feet. "I-I never thought about it like that."

"You didn't?" He strokes his fluffy beard, kicking at bits of sand. "Well, in that case… Maybe you're thinking about everything wrong. Maybe you were never seeing clearly in the first place." W-what is he talking about?

My dad takes my shoulders in his big hands. I'm close enough to smell the furnace he uses to make glass. Or used to use to make glass.

He shakes me and for a second my vision turns red. Burning ashes flicker through the air while the sky is orange instead of blue. Everything smells like fire. A phoenix shrieks, causing

CHAPTER 35: GIANT CREEPY BLACK MOUNTAINS ARE ODDLY INSPIRING

me to pinch my ears. I turn to my dad for help, but he's gone. The only thing remaining is the Aurorian Mountains, standing tall in the distance.

With another shake, I jolt back to the sea with my dad. He smiles. "Do you see it now?"

"Dad, that's what I'm fighting against." My head throbs. The phoenix and fire, its destruction. "That's what the bandits are going to do to this country if I don't step in."

He shakes his head. "Bandits? No, Leda, you've got it all wrong." He points to the younger version of myself, who still stands there with a grin on her blue face, holding a rabbit. In a flash, flames engulf her and she turns into ashes. "That's what needs to happen. All of it needs to disappear. Her."

He clenches the remaining bits of ashes spewing from my old self, then points to the water. A girl rises out of it made of glistening water. Kore. "And Kore too. She needs to disappear," he explains, and she too burns into black ashes. I block the remains with my hands. He kicks the water. "This sea, too. But you understand, only heat can evaporate water."

A sudden, thick heat presses against my chest. Orange rims my vision again. I gasp. In front of me, the entire ocean burns.

"It all needs to burn." My dad touches my shoulder. "You have to remember. I need to disappear, too."

"What?" I reach out to his arm as it turns to ashes. "Dad, wait! No!" Tears well in my eyes. "I don't understand this. I don't get what you mean with this fire and disappearing and none of it makes sense. I need you to explain it to me. Please!" I try holding onto his shoulders, but they too disappear. "Please, I need you!"

He just smiles.

***

I wake up to ashes. Seriously, they're everywhere. In my hair. On my arms, basically turning me gray. And in my mouth (they taste disgusting). What's even more disgusting is the slurping sound I keep hearing.

I narrow my eyes. In front of me is the same pine tree as last night, except this time, it's charred. The same black snake-like monsters that Kore saved me from slurp the tiny bits of fire and ash left on the pine tree. Wait a minute, when that monster first attacked me I'd been touching ash, hadn't I? I wonder if that's their job? To get rid of the ash?

A morning chill whizzes through my hair. That doesn't matter, does it? The bandits got away with the phoenix and Kore. And now they're going to make one of the most powerful Suns ever. I couldn't even stop them.

"You got knocked out too?" Val's voice rings out behind me. Jorge groans beside her, rubbing his head. I look between both of them. They each sport red foreheads and angry eyes.

"Did you two knock each other out last night?" Their faces turn red. They look at each other then back at me. "You've got to be kidding me—"

"It was your fault!" they both holler. "No, yours!"

"Stop with the fighting!" I snap, then slump back onto the cool grass, groaning. "Jorge, Val isn't a spy. They taught people in Evin a language beyond the mountains instead of Solian. And Val, Jorge isn't a bad guy, he's just worried about me. So, can you two both stop fighting? There are so many other, bigger problems we need to deal with right now."

Jorge and Val glance at each other. Then both of them look down at the ground. "We're sorry," they murmur. Their faces

CHAPTER 35: GIANT CREEPY BLACK MOUNTAINS ARE ODDLY INSPIRING

both flush as they realize they talked at the same time.

After a few awkward moments of silence, Jorge clears his throat. "Where's Phemus?"

And that's one more problem to add to the huge stack of ones I currently have. "He's gone," my voice cracks. Why did I have to mess that up too? "It's my fault. He stopped me from chasing the bandits and I got mad and said some really stupid stuff. I should never have lashed out at him."

"Where'd he go?" Val asks.

I peer off into the woods. Pine's there and a few straggled wolves, who cast guilty looks at Jorge. At least Pine came back. "I don't know. He ran off. He could be anywhere."

We all three sigh. Val and Jorge plop onto the ground next to me. My gut tightens. Look at us, sitting in front of a dead pine tree while the bandits are preparing for tonight's little ceremony. The ceremony where they're going to change the world.

"It's over, isn't it?" Jorge sighs. "I don't even know why my wolves left. I can barely control them anymore."

I glance at the edges of the forest. At the sky and the gray mountains rimming their edges. They remind me of when I was little and used to sit here with Dad, claiming I'd figure out a way to get us out of them. I frown. That was before everything. Before Kore and before I cared about being chosen. Dad used to ask me why I said that. Why I thought I could destroy those seemingly unmovable mountains. I always told him that if no one else was going to save the world that I'd have to be the one to do it. Because I didn't want to see everybody suffer anymore.

I clench my fists, getting to my feet. Maybe little me was smarter than I thought. "We're not giving up. There may be only three of us, but that's enough to break into their base and stop that ceremony."

"What about the kids?" Val fiddles with a blade of grass.

"We can still free them and get them to cause chaos during the ceremony. We just need to find another way into the bandits' base before this evening. A way where they won't see us."

Jorge tilts his head. "But none of us know how to unenchant the map and Phemus was the only one magical enough to figure it out without being taught."

I nod. "Then we'll have to sneak in the good old-fashioned way."

Chapter 36: Don't Mess with Crale Children. They Are Scary.

The woods are quiet for once. No one talks. Not Jorge. Not Val. No one. Even the bugs and animals seem to have disappeared. I miss Phemus already. I hope he's okay and not off crying somewhere.

The thumping of boots interrupts my thoughts. Loud talking follows the rumbling sound. "Why are we picking so many orange flowers for Bone's Choosing Ceremony again?"

Bandits. Jorge, Val, and I all dive into the bushes, leaves bristling against our bare arms. Pine shuffles behind me.

"Because the Sun is orange," a second bandit responds. He has shaggy black hair and wears a thick leather jacket. "Idiot."

"Well, I think the Sun is yellow so I'm going to pick some yellow flowers," the first bandit responds.

"Go ahead. If he yells at us, I'm telling him it was your fault," the second bandit grumbles, folding his arms.

"Crale Kids," a voice yells from the other side of the forest. The bandits stroll in between us and where the sound came from. "Attack!"

Teams of children spill out of the trees, all wearing long black leather coats. Leading them is Belen, who unsheathes his curved sword and charges towards the bandits. He easily disarms one while a pair of twins disarms the other.

"What am I watching?" Jorge mumbles.

"I have no idea." A kid leaps from a tree and pounces right on my back, pulling at my braid. His long leather coat scratches my face. "Hey!" I yelp and tumble out of the bushes. Jorge and Val jump out to help me. Pine is too busy running away from a kid trying to pet him.

"Hey!" a voice snaps. "Stand down! She's not a bandit. Even though she's super annoying."

The kid leaps off of me, grinning as I grovel in the dirt. I look up and lock eyes with Belen.

"Leda," he growls.

"Belen."

"We meet again." He bends over, offering me a hand. I take it. It's a lot softer than I would've imagined. "I should've known you would be after the bandits too." Then he glances at Jorge. "And of course he'd be with you."

"How do you know them, Captain Belen?" Captain Belen? I snicker. The boy who asked the question scratches his head, peering at us. He can't be older than nine.

One of the kids grabs Jorge's hand and gasps. This one doesn't look over seven. Belen recruited young, didn't he? "Look, look! They're from Walend! They have those hand gloves that don't even have fingers!"

"Those gloves!?" another kid squeaks. I glance at my hands, which sure enough have fingerless leather gloves on them. They're very fashionable in Walend right now. "Ha! People in Walend dress funny!"

"Can we beat them up?"

"Please, Captain Belen. Can we? Can we?"

"Silence!" Belen snaps, running his fingers through his inky

CHAPTER 36: DON'T MESS WITH CRALE CHILDREN. THEY ARE SCARY.

hair. "The bandits were jerks to Walend too."

A little girl folds her arms. "Now, we have to pay them back! Only we get to be jerks to Walend." I roll my eyes. Please, Walend is the village being a jerk to Crale. We make them cower behind that stupid wall!

"Alright. What's with the name, Captain?" Val snickers.

"And why are you here?" I add.

Belen rolls his eyes, leaning in so that only we can hear him. "The bandits raided Crale, and kidnapped Penelope along with a few other kids. The adults wouldn't go after them since they believed it was Kore's job. The only people who would listen were kids. And I had to use some tactics to keep them entertained. Hence them calling me Captain." A kid puts berries in front of his eyes, causing the rest of the group to crack up. "It's not ideal. But I'll do anything to save her."

I nod, smiling. Of course, Belen would come to help Penelope. "Okay, well, Jorge, Val, and I have been trying to stop the bandits too. We were actually on our way to help save the other kids. So maybe we can work together." Woah, did those words just come out of my mouth? Belen looks surprised about it too, but what I think surprises him more is the fact that he's nodding.

"Y-yeah, that makes sense," he stammers. "But before we go, we need to interrogate these guys and figure out where they're keeping the kids." Belen gestures to the bandits who lay dazed on the ground. Kids jump on top of them, laughing.

"Oh. Val, Jorge, and I already know where it is. But it could be useful to bring them along. We don't have the layout of the entire base memorized since we were using Kore's map."

"Y-you already know..." Belen gawks.

"We've been training to disrupt Bone's choosing ceremony,"

Jorge explains as we begin trudging through the forest. "Unfortunately, they found the phoenix earlier than we expected. Which means we need to hurry before they infuse someone with its magic."

"Infuse someone with phoenix magic!?"

I pat his back. "Don't worry, we'll fill you in."

* * *

We race through a gloomy tunnel, which is filled with our footsteps' echoes. Or maybe that's the footsteps of the bandits racing above us. They shake the ceiling, spilling dirt into our hair. What are they doing up there!?

"This better take us straight to the cells." Belen jabs at the bandit's back. I do the same for the other one. They both nod nervously. Turns out these bandits were useful for something. We were able to get them to reveal a tunnel the bandits barely use which leads straight to their cells.

All the children turn to stare at Belen, who clears his throat. Their overwhelming number of little eyes unnerves me. Val and Jorge fidget beside me. They must feel the same. And Pine definitely doesn't like them poking his antlers.

"Everyone listen up!" Belen whisper-shouts. The children nod, turning, what seems like millions of little eyes straight to him. "Alright, us four are going to free the kidnapped kids right now and scout out the area. So, for now, wait here. We'll be back with plans about how we're going to sneak into and ruin the ceremony later."

"Yes, Captain Belen!" The kids whisper-cheer (I didn't know that was a thing until now).

Val, Jorge, Belen, and I all ascend the staircase, grinning.

CHAPTER 36: DON'T MESS WITH CRALE CHILDREN. THEY ARE SCARY.

Pine waits behind with the kids. Just like the bandits said, very few people use this staircase and tunnel, meaning we don't run into anyone on our way up. Plus, when we do reach the top, we stand right in a hallway filled with cells.

All four of us narrow our eyes, squinting at the cells. There are three bandits standing guard. The rest must be busy preparing the ceremony. Kids inside the cells whimper, leaning on the bars. One of them has a familiar frizzy bun. Belen stiffens. "Penelope," he whispers.

I clench my fists. Only three guards? This should be simple; all we have to do is avoid them and sneak into those cells. Plus, it helps that the guards are all leaning over a hole in the cave to peer into a larger room. What are they looking at? I shake my head. It doesn't matter right now, what matters is not letting them see us. I crouch behind the cave wall, its mossy slime tickling my thighs. The others follow my lead.

Slowly, we creep towards the padlock. Val grabs a needle from her cauldron, prepping to pick the lock. I glance up at the bandits once more and finally see what they're looking at. They're staring into a large cavern lined with yellow and orange flowers. Bandits dart about inside, setting up a podium, chairs, and tables. Some even hang ribbons from the ceiling. They're setting up for the ceremony.

"Guys!" a voice calls behind us. No. We all spin around. A taller, twig-like bandit scampers up the stairs, bursting through us. He's one of the bandits we captured in the woods. "There are intruders! The same ones that tried to steal the phoenix!" he yells. That jerk!

I unsheathe my sword and leave the staircase, entering the main area of the cave where they guard the children. The others follow me.

One of the bandits tosses a spare weapon to the stick bandit (yes, that's what I'm calling him now). "They're trying to disrupt the ceremony," he hisses.

"What!?" The other bandits growl, unsheathing their weapons.

"Well, we can't let that happen, can we?" says a female bandit. She grins.

Chapter 37: Behind the Mask

I charge at the stick bandit. Maybe if I overwhelm him first, I can beat him. Beside me, Val opens one of her vials and Jorge loads his bow. Belen unsheathes his sword as well.

Stick Bandit wields a curved sword identical to mine, which he jabs at me. I dodge and it clangs into the bars of a cell. The children inside shriek and scatter backward in fear. That blow was hard! These bandits must be scared of us disrupting the ceremony. I grin. Well, too bad.

Then I slash at his legs. He jumps backward, yelping. I slash once again and he blocks my blow this time, almost ripping the sword out my hands. I clench onto the sword's hilt, just barely stopping it from leaving my grip. While I'm weak, he slashes at my chest. I dodge out of its way.

I inhale. Stay calm. I've trained with Jorge and Val. I can do this. Then I clench my fist around the hilt of my sword. Use your environment. As he charges at me, I dodge his blows, letting them clank into the cells and hit the stalactites. A rock tumbles off one of them. I bend down and grab it. Then I hurl it at his head. He dodges, laughing.

I grit my teeth. I need that rock. I scamper out of his way as he slashes at me again. It clanks into the cave floors. Finally, I grab the rock again and hurl it at his leg. He yelps and stumbles. *Disarm your opponent.* I slash at his sword. It spins onto the ground, and I pin mine to his throat. Yes!

He laughs. "Why are you laughing!?" I hiss. Then he points to the right at a swarm of bandits, all fully armed. Oh great.

Val readies her potions. She stands atop a bandit stuck in a hard orange substance. Meanwhile, Jorge loads his bow. He's already pinned a bandit by arrow to the wall. He must not be able to call animals inside the cave. They actually have to hear his whistles after all. Belen slashes his sword just like I do.

We fight our way through the bandits as hard as we can. But their overwhelming numbers and strength soon take out each one of us. I growl as a bandit pins me to the ground, kicking as hard as I can, only for him to slap me. I whimper and sag under his grip. The bandit laughs and pulls me upwards. Belen makes eye contact with me, then glances at the staircase. The first bandit may've escaped and we may have been captured, but there are still some Crale kids left with the second bandit. We've just gotta hope he doesn't rat them out too.

The stick bandit gets to his feet, dusting off his pants. "These kids tried to steal the phoenix last night. They know about our plans."

"Which is exactly why Bone wants to see them. This one specifically." Phoebe emerges from the crowd. She points to me, then folds her arms. "She's the one who orchestrated all of this." A new scar zigzags across her cheek.

"Her?" twig bandit growls. "Are you sure the blonde didn't do it? She has a lotta fancy potions."

"Or maybe the boy with the cloak and bow. He looks deadly," another bandit suggests.

"What about the tall one, he has to be the oldest and

CHAPTER 37: BEHIND THE MASK

strongest," one finishes.

"Appearances can be deceiving," Phoebe growls, glaring at me. Then she grabs me from the bandit, lugging me away from my friends. No!

She drags me up another staircase as bandits rush by us, preparing for their ceremony. I struggle in her grip, but without my weapon I'm defenseless. She lugs me up another staircase. "You've made my life quite difficult," she hisses. "Bone gave me a new scar 'cause I told you about everything and you went and did all this."

I fidget again. There must be a way to escape her. "That's your own fault," I growl. "You chose to tell me."

"And you chose to disobey me." She tightens her grip around my arm. "What did we ever do to make you hate us so much?"

"Y-you took something from me. And besides." I remember the way she snapped at Barak. "I don't like people who treat their friends like dirt."

"Friends?" She laughs, shaking her head. "Those unprincipled fools are not my friends. Barak, the lovesick moron, does whatever I say. And Mateo just likes destroying things. Both have no long-term goals and are nothing but idiots." She sighs. "But that's beside the point. You—" She stops in front of a heavy locked door. "We're here." She shudders. "You should've joined us when you had the chance." My gut churns. Is she right? Did I pass down an opportunity I'll never get again?

Then she opens the door and shoves me inside. I find myself in a room similar to Kore's house. It's filled with exotic items found throughout Solia. A pot of steaming eyeballs bubbles in the corner, making my eyes water while glowing phoenix feathers flood the room. Above all are the numerous animal and monster bones. Tiny rat skulls hang from the ceiling, twigs jutting out of their eye sockets.

Meanwhile, there are countless bones rearranged to form different, odd shapes. Wing's bones are used to form legs while claws are wedged into tails. Caged animals rattle on the desk flanking the room's end, one of which contains a phoenix. I meet its slitted eyes and my gut churns. They must've given the poor bird something to put it to sleep. I have to help it.

I struggle against my bonds. I'm so close to the phoenix if I can just—Phoebe shoves me to the ground, the rug scratching my knees. Then a sword is pinned to my neck. I look up. A tall man with a shaggy beard and mask made of bones. I shiver. That's him. That's Bone.

He surveys me with surprised eyes, as though he expected someone else. "This is the girl you told our entire plans to." His voice shakes with rage. Phoebe flinches and nods her head, practically bowing to him.

"Y-yes sir," she murmurs.

He snorts. "You seriously thought this nobody had a chance of being our next Sun." That hurts. I don't know why. He's a bandit, after all. He was the one who hurt my village. But for some insanely stupid reason, it still hurts. Phoebe lowers her head and doesn't say anything back. He continues on in his warm, fire-like voice. "Well, since she's the leader, I suppose we can throw her in with Kore. There might be some hope for the rest of the kids who helped her, so, you can put them with everyone else."

Phoebe's eyes widen. "But sir, she's too weak. Those roots were only meant to hold Kore! Not someone ordinary like her. Without magic, she won't be able to fend them off. They'll kill her!"

CHAPTER 37: BEHIND THE MASK

Bone snorts and the large skull on his head rattles back and forth. "So?" His simple response sends shivers down my spine. Phoebe's lip quivers, but she grabs my arm and jolts me back anyways. No! It can't end like this. I can't just let him win. There has to be something I can do, something I can say.

"The Skycharter will come back! He made a mistake with Milos the Arrogant too and he came back. He came back to choose Thea instead. You don't have to do this!" I plead. "You just need to wait and he'll choose someone better. I know he will!"

Bone freezes, staring deep into my soul with soulless brown eyes. His long bony fingers twitch, rubbing at the edges of his wolf-fur coat. In a quiet voice that mimics a chair squeaking, he asks, "Do you think he will come back and choose you? Is that why you're trying to defeat us?"

Phoebe tenses behind me. I stare at the ground, my face reddening. I wanted to avenge my dad. I wanted to help my country. I wanted…"Y-yeah."

The tall man tilts his head, his mask rattling again. The pale bones jut out against the bits of tan skin I can glimpse. Finally, he says, "Phoebe, drop her and leave." I go tumbling to the floor. Cold stone scrapes against my bare knees, sending shivers through my body. Why did I think telling him that would do anything except get me in more trouble!?

Phoebe glances at me, fear smothering her eyes, then she leaves. I'm left alone, staring up at the bandits' deadly leader.

Bone sighs. "I've waited a long time to tell anyone this and you'll be dead soon." He touches his mask. "It's not like telling you will make any difference." I clench my fists. Then he rips off the skull, resting it on his desk. My entire body freezes. No.

The Skycharter.

Bone is the Skycharter. "No," I whisper. Not today. Not now, not this.

He narrows his dark brown eyes. Identical to mine. How could he be here? How could he be the leader of a group of bandits? How could he look like every other Solian I've seen? With the same matted brown hair and brown eyes and hooked nose. My eyes water. "Your precious little Skycharter will never come back from across the mountains ever again. Because I never traveled across them in the first place. We have been trapped here for over a thousand years, and not a single foreigner has contacted us." He drums the edges of his skull, watching my face fall with glee.

"Why would you lie to us?" I try to hiss. I try to make it sound threatening or scary or make him feel as terrible as I do. All it comes out as is a croak. "Why would you lie to Solia? Do you not care about us at all?"

He chuckles, grabbing a large clay pot. "Of course not. I needed power." He glances at the phoenix. "It is a pity only young people are able to handle the phoenix's power. Nevertheless, I've already picked my new Sun, he's a weak-minded boy, who'll be perfectly under my control. It will be the same as if I had absorbed this phoenix myself."

"Power? That's it." He killed my dad for power! I shake on the ground.

"What?" He takes the pot off of the table. "Were you expecting a grand scheme like one of those fairy tales you love?" I grit my teeth, shivering. He chuckles and walks over, patting my head. "You're so optimistic. So young. Exactly why I chose to infuse the phoenix's power into a kid, it's so easy to fill their heads with lies."

CHAPTER 37: BEHIND THE MASK

"They're not lies!" My vision blurs. It can't mean nothing. It can't.

"Yes, they are. No matter how much you deny it." He sets the pot on the ground next to me. "Would you like to know the dark truth of your little fairy tale?" I avoid his gaze, instead choosing to meet the poor phoenix's eyes.

"The Lords and Ladies of Evin stole me from my family and they killed all of them. Every last person who knew I was born. Then I was raised in isolation for forty years, preparing to be the perfect Skycharter. I told myself it had to mean something. That all of this would result in power. But it was only one moment. One single moment where I chose a spoiled girl. I didn't even have the power to choose her myself, it was all decided beforehand. They always want to choose the child with the strongest magical abilities but can't risk taking that child to Evin with the rest of the magical kids. Otherwise, everyone will get suspicious of why the Sun only comes from Evin. So, they have to pick ten years in advance. They didn't bother telling me that, of course," he hisses.

I shudder. Decided beforehand? Like some fake show? Was that why Kore was never taken to Evin as a baby? To make sure no one suspected anything. To fool us. My stomach sickens. There was no way I could have been chosen. Ever.

He smiles. "You and I aren't that different. We both can't stand being ordinary and powerless. The difference is that I soon will become the most powerful person in all of Solia. And you…" He dips his hand in the pot, and blue liquid dribbles down it. That can't be. He bends down to my level.

Then he smears the liquid over my face. It's just as cold as before. As when I put it on myself, the day I wasn't chosen. "You are a nobody," he hisses. "You were a nobody back then.

And you are still a nobody today. You are the first to have their face painted blue, the first to be marked ordinary. The first to not be chosen. The Girl Who Wasn't Chosen." He laughs at his little nickname. Then he gets up and puts on his mask. There are only two slits in it, revealing his slimy eyes. "Get her out!" he yells, his voice thundering. Two bandits burst through the room. "And take her to the roots."

Chapter 38: Make Do With What You Have

The bandits throw me in a small cavern. Thick black roots coil around its slimy walls. The stench of smelly animals steams off the roots' bodies as they wrap around a quivering figure on the floor. Is that person okay? I stumble over to them, only for the sickening creak of wood to interrupt me.

A root jolts out of the dark, latching onto my arm. I screech and writhe as it yanks me forward, towards an area covered entirely by roots. Then another one latches onto my other arm. It easily tears apart the rope binding them together. With my newly freed hands, I push against the thick roots. Ew! It feels like wood but somehow soggy and sweaty. The roots simply tighten their grip. Purple light flickers through them as they drag me further.

No! This can't be happening! I have to fight this. But with Bone being the Skycharter... what's the point anymore? My shoulders sag and the roots drag me into their hissing pit.

Then the cavern explodes.

Light fills every corner of the room as the roots drag me out of the cavern and into a village. Then they shrivel up, disappearing in the sun's rays.

A chill runs through my spine as I gaze at the village. Its buildings are an odd mashup of Crale and Walend. Some have stony walls with Crale flags. Others have flowers growing out of reddish wood. A few are completely split between wood and stone. Where am I?

I creep forward. But no sound occurs under my feet. My sandals don't even touch the cobblestone. I furrow my brows, passing by a woman trying to eat a sandwich. She's frozen, midbite. This has to be a nightmare. Does that mean the roots put me in some sort of weird dream state? Like the figure I saw earlier wrapped head to toe in roots, shaking like a madman. My head droops. Does it even matter anymore? Everything I thought was true was wrong. The Skycharter. The Sun. Even Evin. Believing they were kind and good when all they did was lie to us. All they did was breed a monster. So, what's the point of fighting at all?

For some stupid reason I keep walking.

This time I pass people I recognize. Penelope's bent over, about to pluck a berry from a bush. Belen smiles by her side. Phemus is in the middle of sniffing a flower. Val is about to brew a potion. Jorge is loading his bow. Even Pine rears up on his hind legs about to buck at some invisible enemy. My dad's at the end, smiling, arms extended like he wants to hug someone. Somehow, I know it's me.

My eyes water. I've pushed him away for so long, choosing to focus on my adventure and saving the world instead. It was all a distraction, wasn't it? A silly way for me to not face him. I thought playing hero would make up for everything. Me not listening to his advice. Me not being there. Not saving him. But it was wrong. I was so wrong. And I have to tell him that.

"D-dad," I whimper. "I'm sorry. I was so selfish. I thought

CHAPTER 38: MAKE DO WITH WHAT YOU HAVE

all I wanted was to be the stupid Sun. I thought—" A roar interrupts me before I can hug him. I spin around. There's one creature that isn't frozen. A sea monster. The same one Val and I fought. In midair, it swims through the town straight towards me, barring its gnarly teeth.

I dodge straight out of its way. Bits of seaweed flop against my bare arms. I glance at my dad, to see if he's okay. Warm blue light dances across his face. His eyes are now white while water surrounds me. I'm in the river. I blink and I'm back in the village. His eyes are brown again and the sea monster is gone.

I inhale sharply. Then, with a grunt, I get to my feet. I'm going to finish saying what I wanted to tell him. Even if it's not the real him. Maybe he can somehow, somewhere hear this. Hear what I wish I had told him all along. With clenched fists, I finally grab his shirt, pulling him into a tight hug. He feels light this time. Airy, as though he's already gone. "I thought you wouldn't ignore me then. I thought all of it, the cheers and the titles and the people who never forgot my name. That it would finally make me happy."

I shake my head. A roar pounds through the air. I have to do this quickly. "But I was wrong. I was so wrong, I don't need the cheers or the fancy titles or the people glorifying my name. I already had what I wanted all along: Jorge and Phemus and Val and Belen and Penelope. And you. I always had you. And now you're gone and I can't save you. I can't bring you back." I sob. "I can't change anything. I can't change that I wasn't chosen. I can't change that you're gone…"

My words echo through the forest. Then they repeat over and over, bouncing off houses like they're cave walls. Ha. Very funny, nightmare universe. Or wherever I am. Repeating my words to make a mockery of me—I shriek. Except this time, my voice is muffled. Icy water prickles my sides as the sea monster swims straight towards me again. Somehow I'm back in the river.

I try to swim out of its way. But this time I can't move. I glance down. Dad. He's now below me, and his hand is the one gripping my ankle, tugging me down into the sea. His eyes are milky white, his mouth agape, sending tiny streams of spit into the water. I kick upwards again but he yanks me even further into the water. Of course, that didn't work in the last dream either. I have to try something new. But what?

The sea monster screeches again, rushing towards me. *Y-you can't do that. It's not in order. You can't disrupt the order!* Jorge's voice pummels into my head. Right! The sea serpent chased after Val last time when she disrupted the order by messing with water. But what am I doing right now to disrupt the order?

This time, a thicker and much stronger voice than Jorge's rings through my ears. Dad. Little snippets of his voice peek through my mind.

Only heat can evaporate water.
It all needs to burn.
You have to remember. I need to disappear too.

I peer down at him, but the man trapping me in this water isn't saying a word. This time the voice becomes softer yet firmer. The kind of voice I remember my dad actually having.

Make do with what you have.

That's it. That's what I was missing. That's how I disrupted the order. My dad was never telling me not to be a hero. He was just telling me I was never going to be the Sun. And he was right. After all, the Skycharter didn't choose me. Twice!

CHAPTER 38: MAKE DO WITH WHAT YOU HAVE

I bite my lip as his phrase echoes through my head again. Then I glance at the man holding onto me, sighing. This man isn't my dad. As much as I wanted to hug him again. To laugh with him. To have him kiss me goodnight. I can't. Because my dad, my real dad, died that night. And I can't go back in time and save him. Just like I can't force the Skycharter to choose me.

But I can save what's right in front of me. My friends. The people who've never ignored me. And my country. My beautiful, super dangerous, and somewhat weird country. All I need to do is make do with what I have. With who I am. A regular girl from a village nobody's heard of. The Girl Who Wasn't Chosen.

I smile. Time for this nobody to save the world. I glance back down at my dream dad. But he's gone. I guess we both finally let go. Then I dodge out of the sea serpent's way, swimming deeper and deeper into the river. The serpent shrieks in alarm while water pushes back on me.

Tiny fish weave their way past me, scampering upwards. As if they want me to go that way instead. I frown. If I'm right, this is all an illusion created by those roots. So, those roots would probably do everything in their power to convince me to stay in their nightmare land. They'd try to trick me into wasting my time fighting a sea monster I know I'll never be able to beat. Or encourage me with tiny little fish to swim upwards.

They'd make their escape route the place a person is the least likely to naturally swim to. Especially if a giant sea monster is trying to kill them. Deeper into the river. Water whips my hair, sticking to my body. But for some reason, my lungs never ache. Hah! Take that, roots, your dream world doesn't even make sense. Well, I guess my dreams don't make sense either.

Ouch. A tiny white crab pinches me. The tips of its legs glow purple. Wait a minute, that's what color the roots glowed earlier too! I grab the crab. Sure enough, it casts a purple hue on my cupped hands. I glance down at the sandy bottom of the ocean. Dozens more purple crabs crawl across its surface. Perfect. If these crabs really are the roots, maybe destroying them in this dream will destroy the roots.

The sea monster roars above me and dives straight for me. I barely dodge again and bits of its teeth slice into my arms. Blood curls up in the water like clouds of smoke. My arms feel as though they're on fire. The sea serpent can do a lot of damage. I wonder...

I swim right towards the sandy bottom, balancing lightly on its surface. A few crabs start pinching me, but I don't pay attention to them. Fortunately, the sea serpent pays a lot of attention to me. I grin as he dives again. Three. He swims closer. Two. His mouth widens. One! I roll to my right in the sand, smushing a handful of crabs. The sea serpent slams straight into the wall of glowing crabs, killing them instantly.

Immediately, the river shakes. Bits of fire jolt out from underneath the serpent's snout, where he smashed the crabs. Then a thick, ugly hissing sound that reminds me of a screaming toddler mixed with a dying rat pierces the air. Yes! I smash the crab in my hands. Fire seeps out of it and the shaking continues. I ram my knuckles into as many white crabs as I can. Sand blows into my face and fire brushes at my fingertips, melting away the sand and crabs and water. The crabs scream, trying to swim away, but I keep going.

Until all that's left is that hissing sound. The crabs are gone,

CHAPTER 38: MAKE DO WITH WHAT YOU HAVE

and so is the water and the sea serpent and the bits of seaweed floating around me. Everything's turned red. And then with a flicker, it's black.

I gasp and jolt up. I'm back in the cave. All around my feet are shriveled gray roots. Steam rises off of them. I killed them. I actually killed them. I stumble to my feet, my ears buzzing. Then I survey my surroundings and screech. I didn't kill all of the roots. Because a few are coming straight for me.

Chapter 39: Kore's Grandmother Tries to Shut Me Up

I dodge out of the grasp of a black root, the scent of sweat and dirt stinging my nose. Then I twist my body, grabbing a sharp stone beneath me, and stabbing its back. It screams. Bits of purple light seep out of its sides as it shrivels up into a gnarled root. Awesome.

Another root slams into my chest, smashing me straight into a cave wall. I heave and try to regain the breath the blow took out of me. A giggle pierces the air. I glimpse shadows of people. Figures and places I recognize. No. I'm going through those nightmares again! I grunt, then bite into the root. It screeches and lets me go. I tumble to the ground, groaning, but somehow manage to hold onto my stone. With a roar, I raise the jagged stone up and slice into the root. Finally, it shrivels up too. But not before nearly blinding me with purple light.

I pinch my eyes shut as bandits cheer above me. No, the ceremony! Shoot, how much time have I lost here? Jorge, Val, and the others were captured too. Which means they'll be powerless to stop the ceremony. I'm the only one who's escaped. I have to get up there and help them!

My heart pounds. I glance around the room. More and

CHAPTER 39: KORE'S GRANDMOTHER TRIES TO SHUT ME UP

more hissing roots slither towards me. Their twisted black bodies darken the floor. There's no way I can possibly fight them all on my own. I need someone—

A muffled scream interrupts my panicking. Of course! I completely forgot about the figure I'd first seen when tossed in here. They struggle against the thick vines, thrashing back and forth. My heart tightens. I have to help them.

I race towards the figure, dodging slimy black roots that whack me from all directions. My lungs burn and legs ache. But finally, I reach them. I raise my stone and first aim for the roots wrapped around their head. It must be suffocating them! I slash once. Twice. But it barely does anything except free the person's mouth and nose. I narrow my eyes. Kore. It has to be. After all, I recognize her soft jaw and olive skin.

Except this Kore has bright yellow paint plastered over her cheeks. Just like the paint they used when first choosing her. I have paint on my face too, don't I? The smeared handprint marking me as a nobody.

A root jolts up towards me. It grabs my wrist, chilling and rattling my whole body. I scream, trying to wiggle out of its grasp. Then I hear it. A faint whisper. Like a voice from someone else's dream. But somehow, I recognize that voice. Kore's grandmother.

"You let this happen!" she whispers. Tears streak down Kore's face as I struggle to shake the root off me. I freeze. Wait, the roots died when I broke out of my dream. If I can get Kore to break out of hers, maybe she'll kill them. "It was supposed to be your job, your duty to save our country and a village girl did it better than you!" the mean woman cackles.

A village girl did it better? Your duty? I never thought about it, but it must've been horrible for Kore. I must've been horrible to Kore. I blamed her for everything when she's a kid just like me. This whole time she had to live with the weight of the entire country on her shoulders. Every time she read or laughed or played, she had to worry that somewhere, someone else needed her help. She could never relax. Never have fun. Never be a kid.

"Look at her, that villager," Kore's grandmother continues.

"Leda…" Kore whispers. My face flushes. Me? Why is she dreaming about me? I thought she looked down on me! "She's probably defeating the bandits as we speak. You always knew she was a better Sun than you. Imagine that, a village girl better than our own Sun."

"I tried to be better. I tried to show her," Kore murmurs, voice cracking.

My eyes widen as I peer at the whimpering girl. She always made fun of me. Was that why? She was scared I was a better Sun than her? "Kore, I'm so sorry," I whisper, shaking her shoulders. "I should never have lashed out at you. Put all that pressure and blame onto you. You're only twelve, it's completely unfair to expect you to save Solia all by yourself."

The roots weaken around my wrist as Kore's frown starts to twitch.

"What was that voice?" Kore's grandma growls through the roots. Bits of flickering purple light pop out. "Don't listen to it, you fool! You're just like your mother, ruining the family name and forcing me to move to this stinky village to look after you. We used to live in Evin in a big house with riches and wealth beyond compare. Your mother had the opportunity to marry a Lord of Evin. An actual descendant of Evin herself. But instead, she had to have you, and of course, you had to be born the most powerful girl in the land and chosen as the Sun.

CHAPTER 39: KORE'S GRANDMOTHER TRIES TO SHUT ME UP

Which means they practically banned the two of us from ever visiting Evin again."

The roots grow stronger and stronger. Now, they snake down my arm and onto my waist. They do the same for Kore, suffocating us both with their slimy hides and sweaty stench. No! I have to stop her. I open my mouth, only for a root to wrap around it.

"And now, you won't even be the Sun! You're going to be known as a Sun worse than Milos the Arrogant. You'll be Kore the Useless. Because you're so—ARRGGGHHH!" I sink my teeth into the roots. Ew. It tastes like cow poo. Don't ask how I know that.

I spit out the root's guck, groaning. "Kore, you're not useless! You're human, and your grandmother and me and everyone else are asking you to do what no person can do. You can make mistakes- mmph!" I groan as the root wraps around my mouth again. It squeezes my chest. Then it pins me to the wall, swarming me with ugly vines. Glowing golden figures appear in front of me. No, I'm not letting them get to me!

The roots hiss as the glowing figures evaporate. Then they squeeze me even harder. As if they're angrier that I won't go back into their nightmare world. Slowly, they start to shake. A soft voice rings through the cavern.

"I am not useless," Kore murmurs. The roots hiss, bouncing off the walls. "And I'm not perfect. I'm only a person. No mere person can save the whole world by themselves. But I'm going to try my hardest to do the best I can."

The roots shake and wither, dropping me to the ground. Then they shrivel up around Kore and me, leaving us in a sea of withered gray shreds. Purple light colors our faces while Kore slowly opens her eyes.

"Leda?" Kore asks.

"Uh, hey. Guess we both got on Bone's nerves." I laugh. For once, her eyes twinkle.

Suddenly, light blows onto the room. Kore and I glance at the end of the cave. A bandit's eyes widen as he opens the door to the cave. I look at Kore again, wielding my rock. She grins as water drips down her arm.

Chapter 40: I Jump into Fire. Literally.

The bandit is tied up in a matter of seconds. He quivers as I grab his sword then pin it to his neck. "Did the ceremony finish?" I grunt. Please, let it not be true. Please, let us still have time. The bandit growls at me, exposing rows of gnarled black teeth.

"I ain't telling you anything!" He struggles in the shriveled gray roots we used to tie him up. Kore places a hand on my shoulder, stopping me from pressing my blade further into his neck.

"They painted this on my face for their ceremony." Kore gestures to the sun on her face. "Bone said he wanted to weaken me and then wipe this symbol off my face before choosing the next Sun." She shivers. It must be to symbolize that she's lost the title. Bone wants to put on a show, even if doesn't care about the Sun at all. "Which means if this bandit has come to get me, they haven't chosen the new Sun and infused him with the phoenix's power. Yet."

"So we still have time." Yes! I crouch down and tighten the bonds around the bandit.

"B-but there's only two of us."

"Then we'll work with what we got." I get up and rush out of the cave. Kore groans, but follows me anyway. The hallway we enter is empty. All the bandits have already left to watch the ceremony. They're all so excited that none bother guarding the long caverns lined with cobwebs and stalactites.

Together, Kore and I pass through hall after hall. None of them contain any clues as to where we are. I furrow my brows, panic setting into my chest. How close are we? If we don't get to this ceremony in time—

Laughter and shrieks rumble above. Bits of dust scatter onto our hair. Are they above us? Kore whimpers, touching her bouncy thin bob.

"My face is already hideous, and now this?"

"Kore!" I grab the girl's arm, yanking her with me through the tunnels. "We need to find a staircase. I think we're directly below them."

"Gee, I couldn't tell." She runs her fingers through her hair to shake off the bits of dust.

A thunderous voice followed by more cheers sounds above us. Even more dust scatters directly onto our hair. Kore slumps in my grip before trudging forward. Finally, we reach a staircase coated with thick moss. Voices start to leak out of the top of it. I can only pick out half the words.

"Before…pick… newest Sun … rid…current …." Bone's voice rings out as Kore and I clamber up the stairs. Heat sticks to our shoulders. Of course this is the only place in Solia that is actually hot.

"Sacrificed …to dream roots…consumed …by nightmares." Come on Bone, keep talking! I rush up the stairs, ignoring the stone at my knees. We're so close!

"All that remains of her is…" Bone's voice smothers my ears. Kore points ahead. Sure enough, we're next to a small hole in

CHAPTER 40: I JUMP INTO FIRE. LITERALLY.

the cave wall, which peeps into a larger room. A huge cavern, to be specific.

Thick stalactites hang from the ceiling while orange and yellow flowers drape from one to the other, linked in tiny little chains. They'd actually be cute if they weren't being used as decoration for the ceremony that's going to destroy Solia. Below it is a sea of bandits. All of them sport scars and daggers which glint in the sunlight.

They pin these to the backs of the poor children gathered in the center of the room. Their wrists are bound together while their ankles graze across the monster skins decorating the floor. One of which I recognize as a sea serpent's scales. That's not the only thing I recognize. Belen and Penelope are at the crowd's back, holding hands. Belen scowls while Penelope presses her face into his chest. I can't find Jorge or Val anywhere.

But I can see the giant hole filling up the entirety of the cave's right wall. It displays the beautiful Solian woods, with their evergreen pine trees and lush vegetation. You can even see the Aurorian Mountains' tips. It drapes sunlight over the whole room, dowsing even Bone's miserable skull in cheery light.

Bone, the jerk, stands on a stage covered in wolf hides (I'm sure Jorge would be disgusted) and animal skulls. The dark wood perfectly complements his leather coat, making his pale skull stand out like a shining star. But the whole thing's so poorly put together that it reminds me exactly of the same makeshift stage Walend's Lord made for our choosing ceremony. Except this time Bone is going to do something much, much worse.

A shorter bandit whispers something and both of them

glance at the outskirts of the cavern as if they're waiting for someone to burst in with Kore Vasil. When nothing happens, the bandit's face pales and uncertainty flickers in Bone's eyes. The shorter bandit then hands him a pale object before darting away.

I fixate on the pale object. It's a skull. A human skull. Bone tosses it onto the cave floor. The pale object scratches against the sea serpent's glittering green scales. Children scream, scampering away. "This skull is the last of Kore Vasil. The last of our old Sun. So now I will pick a new, better Sun. One fit to protect Solia!" The man begins contorting his body. The same way I saw the Skycharter move all those years ago. No, I can't let him do it again!

I glance at Kore, hissing, "What do we do?"

"I don't know, there's no way the two of us can defeat all those bandits all by ourselves!" By ourselves. That's it! Val and Jorge are already in there. If I can just f—

"The heavens have decided, it will be you, young boy!" Bone points to a boy with spiky brown hair. His eyes barely widen as the bandits cut off his ropes. Kore steps away from the hole, her legs shaking. I, however, lean into it, nearly falling into the room.

I search everywhere for my friends as the boy steps closer and closer to Bone. Where are they? He descends onto the stage. Wait, I think I just spotted blonde hair. Then he slumps to his knees. That's them, next to Barak! Bone dips his hands in yellow paint, drawing a sun over the boy's face in slow strokes. How do I get their attention? Cheers erupt then Bone strolls over to phoenix's cage.

Barak, however, continues standing next to my best friends, guarding a glowering Val and petrified Jorge. Suddenly, the

CHAPTER 40: I JUMP INTO FIRE. LITERALLY.

man meets my eyes, staring directly at me. I freeze. No! Instead of saying anything, Barak prods Jorge. His eyes flicker to me and Jorge follows his gaze. They both smile, but Jorge still looks petrified.

I grin back. Barak has no principles, huh Phoebe? You're in for a shock. Slowly, Barak cuts through Jorge's ropes then he goes for Val's, placing a stolen key to the phoenix's cage in her hands. None of the other bandits notice as he continues doing the same for more and more kids. They're all fixated on the ceremony.

Now, Bone has set the phoenix's cage on the ground and surrounded it with ash. With one final shake of his fist, the last of his ashes fall into the ring. Then the phoenix cage starts to rise. The phoenix screeches in pain, its voice echoing through the cave. Blazing firelight bounces off the walls while a stream of golden flames starts exiting the cage. Its fiery ends plunge straight into the boy's heart. His whole body convulses and he screams. Fire starts brewing in his fingertips.

Barak freeing a few kids isn't going to be enough now. I have to go in there and do something now! But what? *Make do with what you have.* I glance at Kore then at the hole in the wall and the stage. Okay, I've got an idea.

I grab Kore's shoulders. "You can control your magic now, right?"

"Um, no," she squeaks, sagging under my grip.

I shake her. "Well, you're going to have to use it to break down this wall and send me right into that phoenix."

"I told you I don't have that much control!" Her hands shake. "I can't—"

"What did you tell those roots?" I demand.

Kore bites her lip then her eyes sharpen. "Okay. I'll do it."

She extends her arm and intricate patterns of water weave all over it. Slowly, a bubble of water forms in front of her, expanding larger and larger. I grin. This is what the girl born with so much magic in her blood she can create water at will can do. Wow, it's oddly beautif—

Water slams into me, cracking the cave's stone walls. With me, it's oddly gentle, guiding me right onto the stage. Suddenly it picks up speed and intensity. The salt water stings my hands and swarms my mouth.

It slams me straight into the phoenix cage. The heat makes me want to vomit and the goo practically melts onto my skin. But with one kick, I sever the ring of ash. The tendrils of flames lurch out of the boy's body and back into the phoenix. Yes! Then the cage goes toppling to the ground, taking me with it.

Screams, cheers, and boos erupt all around me. It's so loud. And distracting. How could I have ever wanted this much attention!? Somehow through all the crazy commotion, I manage to hear Bone say, "You useless brat!"

He unsheathes a sword from his side, raising it above my head. But before he can deliver the deadly blow a whistle pierces the air. Three—no, five—no, ten! Ten hawks pummel straight towards his skull. I race backward, stumbling to my feet. Then I fiddle with the phoenix's cage. I need to free it! But there's a giant padlock, locking it inside. Shoot! I need a key.

"Leda!" A voice calls. Val! She jumps onto a table and tosses me a silver key. I leap off the stage, my arm jutting out. Just as my fingertips graze its cool surface another bandit jumps up, snatching it straight from my hand. Phoebe. I race after her, but a million other bandits are swarming towards me, trying

CHAPTER 40: I JUMP INTO FIRE. LITERALLY.

to get the phoenix. I'm surrounded and she's already so far ahead of me. What can I do? I grit my teeth, tightening my fingers around my sword's hilt. I'll have to f—

"Charge!" a voice yells across the room. Belen! He's free! Dozens of previously captured kids race behind him, using any weapons they can find to attack bandits. Even Penelope wields a giant metal rod. She's surprisingly good at whacking bandits on the head with it.

Kore joins the fray too, spraying water into dozens of bandits. Between her, the captured kids, Jorge, and Val (Barak smuggled in her cauldron), most of the bandits are occupied. I'm able to dodge the few who still come after me and somehow stumble over to Phoebe. She's all the way at the right side of the cave.

"We meet again Leda Roubis." She draws a dagger, backing me away from the key. I teeter on the cave's edge, almost falling into the woods below. The phoenix shrieks inside the cage I hold. I grit my teeth. I have to win this.

"Give that back, now," I growl.

She clicks her tongue. "That's all you've got? What a disappointment. I was a fool to think a child would be able to understand the complexity of this situation, to—"

"You killed my dad." The words tumble out for some reason. Maybe it's the fact that she's trying to lecture me or that I need to let her know what she did to me or simply because I want to distract her. All I know is that it tumbles out.

Her hand shakes as her eyes water. "W-what?" She begins lowering her dagger. A breeze flaps against my back. I'm so close to that key! Maybe I can convince her. I have to try something.

"You, Barak, and Mateo. I saw you go into our house back

in Walend. When I got back he was dead." Phoebe shudders, stepping back. "You used his blood to summon the phoenix. His innocent blood to fuel your ceremony. I will never join someone who thinks that's okay."

Phoebe continues shaking, frozen by some emotion I don't understand. "Leda…" she murmurs. I'm done with her excuses and her lectures! Fury pulses through me. I slam my foot into hers and she shrieks, dropping the key. Then I grab it, trying to use it to free the phoenix.

Phoebe swings her dagger at me. "I can't let you!" she shrieks, her voice hoarse. "I can't let it go to waste!"

I block her blow, but she easily breaks her hold. I'm not going to be able to fight her one-handed like this! I glance at the exposed woods behind me. There's only one way out of this.

I jump.

Chapter 41: The Phoenix

The wind roars in my face as I shove the key into the cage. Come on! There isn't a river beneath me right now. Inside, the phoenix shrieks and flaps, rattling the cage. My heart rams in my chest. I'm going to slam into the ground at this crazy speed. There's no way I'm making it out of this alive and my body knows it. But I have to save the phoenix, I have to do what little I can while there's still time!

"Stop moving!" I scream, shoving the key inside the lock. The phoenix keeps thrashing. But then slowly, bit by bit its feathery body stops twitching. Finally, it quiets as I fiddle with the key again. Then I yank the door. It stays firmly shut.

What!? Did I twist it the wrong way? I try plucking the key out of the lock but it's already jammed inside. I yank it once. Twice. The third time the phoenix rams into the padlock too and the key slips free. Finally, I shove it back into the cage and twist. With a click, the door swings open.

Yes, it's free! The phoenix soars out. Its heat and fluffy feathers tickle my face, like a sunny day's warm embrace. Then it jolts up into the sky becoming a speck of beautiful red in the sea of blue. I did it! Wait, now I'm going to fall to my doom! I scream again as my body nears the jagged rocks and trees beneath me. The cage slips out of my hands, shattering into pieces on the hard ground. I shut my eyes. I guess I'll be joining Dad n—

Talons sink into my shirt, prickling my back with their fiery touch. I open my eyes. A wildflower tickles my nose. I'm a few inches from the forest floor. I sneeze and the phoenix caws as if he's laughing at me. He. How do I know he's a he? I peer up at the phoenix's slitted eyes. A whistle, a sound I never thought I could make, presses at the back of my throat. I don't dare utter it, not now, but I can't help but wonder if this is how it feels to Jorge too. This weird, yet natural feeling. I'll have to ask him later.

The phoenix lurches me upwards. Leaves and pine needles whack at my face as we head straight towards the sky. The trees become nothing more than dots beneath us while creamy white clouds soothe my fingertips. The phoenix roars, his echoing cry bouncing through the entire woods. Its huge wings seem to take up the entire sky as he leans back then darts straight forward. A small cave comes into my view. It grows and grows like a disgusting spot in our way until finally, I'm able to fit through the same hole I jumped out of.

The phoenix sets me down inside with such a force that I tumble over. Then it roars again, its burning wings stretching far out behind me. Bandits and children alike skid out of my way. I get to my feet, grinning, and extend my arm. Then, with another shriek, the phoenix lands on it, glaring at the crowd. Gasps erupt.

"She tamed a phoenix!" a bandit shrieks.

"She's the real Sun," another one murmurs.

"Who are you?"

I shake my head. The dried and caked blue liquid smeared on me by Bone tickles my cheeks. I make eye contact with

CHAPTER 41: THE PHOENIX

Bone, all the way from across the room. There's panic in his dull eyes. He still grips the sword he wanted to kill me with. No one else has dared try to fight him. I grin at him. "I'm the Girl Who Wasn't Chosen."

Bone stomps his foot on the stage. "Get her! Now!" After a few confused glances, the bandits charge at me. The phoenix caws and soars into the sky, spewing fire at the bandits. They scream and scramble backward. A few of them drop their weapons. This is awesome!

I grip my sword, weaving my way through the crowd. The phoenix continues blowing fire at any bandits who challenge me. Perfect! If I can get through this crowd and beat Bone, all of this can stop.

Ahead of me, Val uses her potions to electrocute a few bandits. Meanwhile, Belen and Penelope fight side by side. Kore splashes bandits with icy water. Jorge whistles, attacking people with various animals. A trail of angry bugs follows him, buzzing at anyone in their way.

Finally, I reach the stage, only to be greeted by nothing but soggy wood and shredded flowers. Bone's gone. But bits of his leather cloak cling to a tunnel a few feet ahead. He must've gone in there. Just as I'm about to follow him, Mateo rushes in front of me. The wild bandit hisses, slashing at me. I block his blow and glance up. The phoenix is busy blowing fire at some other bandits. Looks like I'm going to have to deal with this myself.

Mateo unsheathes another dagger, slicing at my legs. I jump backward. Then slash at his arm. He blocks my blow. We keep sparring. But with each blow, he knocks me further and further from the edges of the cave.

Laughing, he bellows, "You may have weirded out Phoebe

but you'll never defeat me!" Then he knocks my sword out of my hand, sending it clattering across wooden boards. He pins his blade to my neck.

All around me children fall down, bandits pinning swords to their necks. The phoenix is a significant advantage, it sets fire to numerous bandits, but even it's not enough to fight swarms of them. We're going to lose!

The walls next to the hole I leaped out from, crack, and a giant monster emerges, carrying two leafers, followed by an army of kids in Crale coats and a familiar elk.

"Crale Kids: Leafer Addition, Attack!!" Phemus shouts on top of his pet monster. "But don't be mean! Only nice fighting is allowed!" Nice fighting, is that even a thing? I laugh as the kids pour through the hole, charging the bandits. Who cares? Phemus came back! And Pine's with him, too!

Chapter 42: Bone is a Moron

Mateo falters and I roll to my right. I grin as kids cheer when Phemus charges the bandits. They immediately let go of the kids they were defeating, stumbling backward. Meanwhile, I grab my sword and race to my feet. Mateo finally rushes towards me again. But this time a swarm of bugs whams into his face.

"I'll take care of him," Jorge calls. He whistles again and hawks fly towards Mateo's head. The man screeches.

"Thanks!" I yell. Then I rush into the cave tunnels after Bone.

By now the tunnels are empty, and the cheering grows fainter as I rush further and further away. Slabs of black stone fly under my sandals. Cold water sprinkles over my toes. They drip off blue-tinted stalactites. Familiar stalactites. My eyes widen. I know where Bone went.

I race down through the tunnels, lowering myself into a small staircase smothered with moss. All the way back to the same waterfall where Phoebe first told me the bandits' plans. Its blue hue flashes across my arms and sand scratches at my ankles. A looming figure cloaked in dark leather races towards the roaring waterfall, tipping back and forth in the gray sand. Bone!

"Stop!" I yell, pinning my sword's tip to his leathery back. He freezes then slowly spins towards me, chuckling. The screams of bandits and the splash of water rumbles above us. "What are you laughing about?"

Through gnarled teeth he grins. Then kicks my stomach. I grunt, doubling over in pain as my sword slips out of his way. He draws another long sword from under his cloak and swings at me. I barely block the blow. "Nobody will remember you after all of this, even if you defeat me."

He swings again and this time I dodge. I slip on the sand, crashing into a wall. I manage to hold onto a rock jutting out of it and prevent myself from tumbling to the ground. He raises his sword again and swings. I dodge again. It clangs right by my head. "The Lords and Ladies of Evin will do everything to make sure Kore is framed as the one who's behind it. If they even acknowledge that it happened. You'll get nothing!" He rams his sword again into the wall. I drop to the ground. Then crawl over sand and rocks to avoid him.

"They control our history!" He rams it right above me. The blade nearly chops off my braid. "They control our stories, our legends." This time a blow grazes across my shoulder. I shriek in pain. Drops of blood dribble down my shoulder and into the sand. "They control exactly how we think and they will never let you, a poor little village girl, go down in history as a hero."

I spit out bits of sand and wiggle desperately forward. Finally, I manage to dodge another blow and stumble to my feet. My back faces the waterfall. He swings again. I barely manage to block this blow. Then I stumble into the water, trying to avoid him.

I emerge on the other side, where dizzy sunlight and crisp

CHAPTER 42: BONE IS A MORON

air greet me. I shiver in my wet clothes. Thick water pulses across my feet and fish fins wiggle across my toes. The entirety of the Solian woods border the river behind me while wolves bark at its edges.

Bone emerges from the waterfall. Clear water dribbles down his skull and onto his damp cloak. He laughs again, swinging his sword. I block his blows, but with my bloody shoulder, my reaction becomes slower and slower. "I, however, will surpass this. I'll form another group, make another name, another mask. Solians are fools. So easily convinced. I'll do it all over and this time I'll make sure no brats get in my way." He whacks my sword. It goes flying out of my hand and into the water. Oh great.

Bone pins his sword to my neck as I heave. He forces me onto my knees. My hands trace a stone in the cool water. Seaweed flickers across my fingertips. The man heaves and laughs again.

"You look so defeated," he sneers as blue paint dribbles down my face. "I bet your parents told you something stupid when I didn't choose you. Like that everyone's special in their own way or that you'll always be a hero."

I grit my teeth as he raises his sword and swings towards me. "No," I growl.

He stops, mid-motion. "What?"

"My dad didn't tell me that." My hand grips the rock underneath the water. "He told me to make do with what I have!" I hurl the rock straight at Bone's skull. The thunk of the rock slamming into his skull rings out through the forest and he stumbles backward. Then I get to my feet and step on one of his. He yelps in pain, dropping the sword. I grab its hilt and slash at Bone. He unsheathes a dagger, barely blocking me. "He was right. I don't care if people forget about me."

I take a step forward in the water, delivering another blow. He stumbles back as he tries to block this one too. "I don't care if they all cheer for Kore or someone else. I'm not fighting for glory or fame!" I slash again. This time it knocks his dagger out of his hand. It disappears into the murky water.

"I'm fighting for Solia. For the thousands of people whose lives your selfish actions would destroy. Because you're right. I'm never going to be the Sun. I'm never going to be able to go back and save the people I wish I could have saved." My dad's smile flickers in front of me. I pin my sword to his neck. "But I can still save them."

Bone's chest heaves. Uncertainty flickers in his black eyes. "Really? You're telling me that you don't mind being ignored. Being another one of Evin's sheep. Having nobody know your own name, nobody care about you. Nobody recognize you for who you are?"

I laugh. It sounds a little shriveled like those roots Kore and I defeated. Then I glance up at the top of the bandits' cave. Inside the hole, Kore gathers at the center. Kids cheer for her as the bandits lay defeated at their feet. Phemus swings Jorge through the air, grinning while Val laughs nearby. I smile. "Sometimes there are more important things than being called special." Then I grin. "It's over, Bone."

Chapter 43: Val Just Blew My Mind

The scent of pine trees, wildflowers, and open air bristle against my nose. Below me, children scamper back and forth in the Solian woods, prodding the bandits we defeated and laughing as they fight with spare twigs.

I, however, swing my legs over the edge of the bandits' cave. Dried flowers shake above me in the wind. Their once linked chains are broken, now falling to the ground in a straight line. Petals float off them and onto my shoulders and hair.

I already know what the cavern looks like behind me. I saw it when I first walked up here. After I defeated Bone and dragged him through the tunnels to show the remaining bandits that their battle was over. There's bits of leather, animal fur, and feathers scattered across the floor. The stage is a mess. Floorboards upturned, yellow paint splattered everywhere, purple curtains practically torn to shreds by dagger slices. The only real difference is that now it's empty. For once, I like the quiet. It's easier to think.

"Hey, why are you up here? Jorge is looking everywhere for you in the woods." I spin around to see Belen. He bends over, grabbing a few remnants of the phoenix's cage. Some of the dream root Kore and I killed already lies in his arms.

I turn back around to continue staring at the Solian woods. *They control exactly how we think.* Bone's words echo through my head. I haven't told anyone what I saw. What this means not just for me but for all of Solia. Evin lied to us. Which means Val lied to me too. *They will never let you, a poor little village girl go down as a hero.*

I glance at Kore and the numerous kids bowing to her. Now, her face flushes, her arms hang out at awkward angles. She's told me countless times how sorry she was that all the kids looked to her instead of me. I don't care about that anymore. But doesn't she have a right to know that everything was a lie? Doesn't all of Solia have a right?

I spent my whole life agonizing over being chosen as something that was already predetermined before I was born. Something that turned out to be fake in the end. How many other people are living like this? How many other kids are being told that because they're a nobody they should wait for a fake Sun to save them instead of saving themselves?

"Well?" Belen coughs. My eyes sharpen.

"S-sorry. I just needed some clean air. Why'd you come?"

He strolls over to me, not bothering to sit so that he can still look down on me. "To gather evidence."

"Evidence." I chuckle. "We're taking these bandits to Crale. They arrest basically everyone and everything for no reason."

"Spoken like a true Walender. Your village doesn't even have a jail, does it?" I roll my eyes, then the tall fourteen year old clears his throat. "Crale always sends its worst prisoners, the ones that are a threat to the whole country, to the Evin jail cells. They require an actual trial and evidence up there."

So the bandits are going to be sent straight to Evin? Bone will probably be locked away, never to see sunlight again. No

CHAPTER 43: VAL JUST BLEW MY MIND

one will even know who he really is…My gut churns. No one except me. Belen stares at me, his light brown eyes sinking into my soul.

He tilts his head then coughs. "Well, I should get going, come down when you're ready."

I nod. "Alright." The sickening feeling in my stomach only grows. He has no idea either. They all have no idea that our entire history, our entire culture was one big fat lie. And now we're going to give the only evidence exposing it to the liars themselves. Should I stop it myself? But what if by doing that, I ruin everything? What if Evin is right and Solia really does need a hero to boost our morale?

"Hey." Val taps my shoulder, staring at the phoenix perching in the trees beneath us. Somehow the phoenix meets my eye, gazing at me through nervous slits. Val plops right next to me. Does she still want to take him to Evin? He saved my life and if Evin's anything like what Bone said…then I'm not sure I'm okay with it anymore. Val chuckles. "That was crazy what you did today. Defeating Bone. Saving the phoenix. Everyone's talkin' about it."

Now it's my turn to laugh. "I doubt that. They've already forgotten about the ordinary village girl." Then I grit my teeth as my worries flutter back into my stomach. "You lied to me."

Her icy eyes don't meet mine. "I had to protect myself."

My face flushes. "Protect yourself? What does telling me the truth, that the Skycharter and the Sun and basically our entire tradition of choosing heroes was all just a scheme you and your little Evin friends made up, have anything to do with protecting yourself!?"

Val shifts beside me. I can practically see her neck hairs stand on their edges. "Oh. I don't what you're talkin' about. I thought ya figured it out."

"Figured what out?" Evin's lying even more?

"I'm not from Evin." She stares ahead. Her eyes water. What? But her hair and her eyes, where else could a person like her live? "I'm not from here at all. The place I come from is just beyond the mountains." She glances at the mountains' snowy peaks as my head spins. "It's not like here. There aren't monsters in the woods or glowing wolves or elks the size of horses. We don't even have books." She laughs. "We use scrolls instead."

I scoot away. She lied this entire time.

She inhales, her voice stammering for the first time as she sniffles. "M-my best friend. He died because of me. I couldn't live with it. So I learned everythin' about magic. But there was nothing in my land strong enough to bring someone back from the dead. The only place, the only creature with that kinda power was the Solian phoenix. That's why I used a spell to cross the mountains."

My eyes water. "How long have your people been out there? Why didn't you help us earlier?"

She sighs. "I was told Solia was dead. That the monsters killed ya. When I came here I was shocked to find people alive. But maybe that's what they…" She shakes her head. "That's not important. When I came here I thought the Sun and the Skycharter, all of it was foolish. I knew it had to be fake. There's no way someone from my land would risk coming here. Plus, I thought, why rescue a bunch of strangers? All I did was come here to save my friend."

She kicks at some rocks. "But then I fell in love with it. Everythin'. The woods, the country, my friends…" Her eyes flicker towards me. "And I realized this would be what

CHAPTER 43: VAL JUST BLEW MY MIND

he wanted. He always said there was a greater meaning to everythin'. And there has to be. There has to be a reason I crossed those mountains and met you."

"Val, I don't understand." I think my mind has been blown twenty times at this point. It's too much information at once.

"Don't you see..." She takes my hands. "The Skycharter is the person who crossed the mountains. I crossed the mountains. I'm the real Skycharter." She smiles at me. My face flushes. "Which means my job is to choose the Sun. It's you. You're the person I choose."

My heart instinctively flutters. She's the real deal. The real Skycharter is choosing me. "W-why?"

"You're a hero." She taps my chest. "You have been ever since you first rescued me from bandits. Then you fought Belen, and I didn't have any real sword fighting advice. But you took what I said and beat him. You saved Phemus, you rescued me from that sea monster. You even saved Solia and tamed a phoenix in the process! It's you. It's always been you." My heart jumps again then I glance at the phoenix, who continues watching me and Val with wary eyes.

There's one question that burns at the back of my throat. "Why are you doing this now? What's the point of choosing a Sun anyway?"

"Because. I figured it out. There's a way to save Solia. To stop all of this." She gestures to the woods and the Aurorian Mountains. "You need to absorb the phoenix and use its powers to burn down those mountains." She grabs my shoulders. "You can do it. You can finally save Solia."

Save Solia? My gut churns. This is what I've always wanted but...it doesn't feel right. I glance at the phoenix, whose fiery glow pulses like a beating heart. A forest's heart. "No."

"What?"

"I'm not the Sun." I smile. "I was never supposed to be, and that's okay. I don't need a fancy title or magic powers. I don't even want those things after seeing how they affected Kore."

"Then don't be the Sun! You can be somethin' else. It doesn't matter, let's save Solia. That phoenix loves you, it'll bond with you easily."

Now it's my turn to grab Val's shoulders. "The forest has an order. Everything has a purpose. Do you understand what would happen if we destroyed the phoenix?" I remember how the phoenix ordered Jorge's animals away. How it made them bow. How it destroyed the bandits like they were nothing. "The phoenix is a protector. Our forest's heart and its ruler. You saw how that sea serpent reacted when we destroyed its order. Imagine what'll happen if we destroy the heart of the forest!"

"Then whatta we do?" She scratches her head. "I used magic to cross the mountains and only have enough for a one-way trip back home."

"Go home," I tell her. "Cross the mountains and figure out a way to destroy them from the outside. Using magic that doesn't hurt people."

"Me!?"

"Yes you, I'm sure you can do it." The outside is rumored to have much stronger magic than we do and after seeing Val...I don't doubt it. There must be something there that can peacefully free Solia.

Val's shoulders slump. "O-okay. I'll go." Her eyes water. "But don't tell anyone who I am. I don't want to give Jorge any more ammunition to make fun of me."

I laugh as she stumbles to her feet. "A-aren't you going to

CHAPTER 43: VAL JUST BLEW MY MIND

say goodbye? To Phemus and Jorge and me?"

She stiffens, keeping her back to me. "I don't wanna attract attention. Plus, I don't like Jorge. Stay away from him while I'm gone."

"Hey!" I rush up to the girl and hug her. She stiffens. "Thanks for caring. About Solia and my quest. And for being there. You're an amazing friend. And at least say goodbye to Phemus before you go! Get him away from the crowd!"

"Will do," Val's voice cracks as she steps forward. "Hey, Leda?"

"Y-yeah?" Great, now my voice is cracking too.

"I think you know what to tell everybody." My eyes widen. How did she know that was what I was worried about?

Before I can ask, she disappears into the caves. My eyes water. I've just gotta remember that she'll be back. She has to come back.

Chapter 44: I Make the Biggest Decision Of My Life

Val was gone by the time I arrived in the woods. Everyone else was already packing up. Jorge had used his whistling to call in a few elks to help carry everybody to Crale. So now Penelope, Kore, and Belen are all forcing the bandits on top of them. Each makes sure to share an elk with a bandit so that they don't try to get away by riding away on one.

Meanwhile, Phemus crunches on a rock. Yes, a real rock, as he leans on the monster he rode to get here. It looks like a large black panther with a starry blue back and fish fins instead of regular black fur. Next to him is another leafer, who keeps feeding him darkened stones. I'm assuming they're baked. Baked stones. Wait a minute...

"Leda, why are you laughing? Are the wildflowers you've been standing on for a super long time funny? Oh! Can you hear them talking to you?" Phemus squeals and rushes over to the wildflowers, leaving his friend. I laugh.

"No, I was just thinking about something funny." I hug the leafer. "I'm glad you came back and I'm so sorry about yelling at you. I never should've said those things about you. You've been nothing but kind and helpful this whole time."

CHAPTER 44: I MAKE THE BIGGEST DECISION OF MY LIFE

"It's okay." He chuckles. "I was thinking about it and I realized I've been the one acting like a meanie too. I expect humans to be these super perfect awesome creatures when nobody's perfect. Everybody makes mistakes, even you!"

I nod, glancing back at Bone, who remains tied up to a tree. "I've definitely made a lot of mistakes before." My voice trails off.

"What are you worried about?" Phemus whimpers, his wiggly ears tilted back. He glances at Bone again. "All the bad guys are tied up. Are you sad we won't get to see each other anymore? Because I won't let that happen! I'm going to show you and Jorge and Val all the tunnels. It's going to be great, you'll meet my parents and everything. They'll love you!"

I grin. "I'm not worried about that, Phemus. I know we're going to stay friends no matter what and I'm definitely going to visit your, um, tunnels. It's just…there's something I know that nobody else does. And I'm scared that if I tell everybody it, they'll all freak out, but I'm also scared of keeping this secret instead of giving everybody what they deserve. The truth."

"Hmmmmmm." Phemus' eye widens in his eye-extender. His ears flap up and down before they abruptly stop. "Well, sometimes it's worth telling the truth, even if it's easier to keep the secret and lie. Plus, what you said was right, everybody deserves to know the truth and make up their own minds on something."

That actually makes me feel a lot better. Phemus has a way of making complicated things seem simple. "I think you're right. Thanks for the help."

"No problem!" the leafer says as I head towards Bone. Wildflowers brush against me. Their smooth flower petals are oddly soothing against my beat-up feet.

"Hey."

"Jorge!" I spin around. The boy leans on a tree. I laugh, biting my cheek. "I didn't see you there."

"Sorry about surprising you." He laughs too as the phoenix flies towards us. He happily chirps, shuffling along the branch. "So, you can whistle to him, can't you?"

My face flushes. "Y-yeah." Great, now I can no longer make fun of him for whistling to animals anymore. "But the sound I have to make to do it is super weird."

"Perfect. Now you can be even weirder than me."

"Jorge!" I rush over to the pine tree he leans on. Then I playfully shove him before shuffling my feet. "So, are you going to drag me back to Walend now that this is all done?"

"Oh." His face flushes. "I hadn't thought about it, but I guess we'll have to go back, won't we? Your mother's worried sick. And my parents." He shudders. "I don't even want to think about what they'll do when they realize that I actually helped you defeat the bandits instead of protecting you like I'm supposed to be." Right, I forgot his family was trained to be protectors of Walend. Jorge must've broken a lot of rules when he helped me instead of protecting me. "But I was thinking..." He fiddles with a curl. "I saw some of your blows in the fight and they could've been executed a bit better."

"Excuse me? Did you defeat Bone?"

He crosses his arms. "No. But that's mostly because I was preoccupied with that Mateo jerk." He shakes his head. "That's beside the point. What I'm trying to say is that you're definitely going to need some fighting lessons when we get back to Walend. We'll start with sword fighting, then archery, then maybe I'll teach you how to call a few animals."

CHAPTER 44: I MAKE THE BIGGEST DECISION OF MY LIFE

My face lights up. No way. He isn't actually offering... "You want to train with me in the woods again!" Have our evening talks under the stars. "B-but I thought you'd given up on Evin and adventures."

"Oh, I've given up on Evin. If the people there are anything like Val, I want nothing to do with them." I roll my eyes, trying to hide the guilt brewing in my gut. "What? I'm only joking. I just think it wasn't the right place for me. Just like you realized being the Sun wasn't for you?"

I tilt my head. "How did you know that?"

He raises an eyebrow. "You called yourself The Girl Who Wasn't Chosen and you're acting surprised when I comment on the fact that you clearly got over not being the Sun."

"Fine, fine. I guess you have a point."

Jorge smiles. "What I was trying to say is that maybe it's time for both of us to get a new dream. Because I don't think I'm the only one who loved going on this adventure." I beam. Took him long enough to get his head screwed back on correctly.

Then I hug the boy, only to furrow my brows. Guilt seeps back into my chest. "Jorge?"

"Yeah?"

"Before we go on our adventures, there's something I need to show you. Something I need to show everyone." He tilts his head, confusion setting into his eyes.

I grab his hand, leading him to the crowd of children. The phoenix shrieks above me, darting from branch to branch. I smile. No matter what happens he'll be here with me. His warm presence does help calm some of my many nerves. Enough to let me approach a now beaten-up Bone.

His dark eyes loom ahead, matching the emptiness of the skull surrounding them. Bound to the tree, his trembling figure looks no different than the ordinary kids we rescued. No different than me. I take one final glance at the kids behind us. They're laughing, playing with flowers and jabbing sticks at each other. They beg for Kore to join them. For her to show them her fabled blue hair. Their mouths twitch into wide grins, cheeks lifting. Can I really do this to them?

I turn back to Bone and crouch down to his level, gazing back at his regular brown eyes. My hands shake, sweat rolling off my palms. Already kids are crowding around us, bending down to watch me with tilted heads and fixated eyes. I have to show this to them. Because they deserve the truth. Even if it's hard. In the long run, it will be worth it for them to understand the lies. To understand that it doesn't take a made-up Skycharter or being called a Sun to be a hero. All it takes is a little courage.

I turn to Jorge, my hands latching onto Bone's skull mask.

"Look." I rip it off.

Acknowledgments

Okay, where do I even begin? To put it simply, God has blessed me in a manner that words can't even describe. There is no way that if you sat nine-year-old me down and told her she would've published a book before graduating high school she would have believed you. But for some reason, I was blessed with a lot of luck and a lot of amazing people in my life that made this book possible. So, this is for the people who took a chance on the shy, weird girl. She really appreciates it.

First, I should probably mention my little sister, Natalie. My whole family thinks I'm being nice for dedicating this book to her, but the truth is she deserves it and so much more. In addition to being the most genuine and thoughtful person I know, she has been my number one supporter since day one of this book. From reading multiple drafts to coming up with the name Crale to listening to my crazy rants. Thank you for not only being the best little sister I could ever ask for but also my best friend.

Next, I want to thank my parents for supporting me in everything I do. You taught me to believe in myself and pushed me to be the best person I could be. Thank you for always doing what's best for me and supporting me in this whacky publishing journey.

I also want to thank the rest of my family. I have a big one, so there are far too many names to mention in this short acknowledgments section, but I wanted to thank each and every one of you for being incredibly supportive of all my writing and a joy to spend time with. Specifically, I wanted to thank all my grandparents: Grandma Linda for reading an early copy of my book, Grandma Hanna for giving me an awesome paperweight with my pen name on it, and Papal for always boasting about my writing. Of course, I also have to give a quick shout-out to my cousins (as annoying as you all are).

Along with my family, I definitely need to mention my friends and teachers. I was absolutely terrified to tell anyone at school I was an author since I'd heard horror stories about teen authors getting bullied. But instead, I was met with more support and love than I could ever possibly deserve, so thank you for showing me what amazing people I have in my life.

If there's one thing I've learned from writing this book, it's the importance of connecting with the writing community. I've had the fortune of meeting some amazingly talented writers and having them offer feedback on my work. Thank you to Alexander Thomas, you were one of my first critique partners and your feedback made my side characters a lot more interesting than they used to be. To Kayla Martinez Foster, for your detailed feedback and making me excited to edit my book. To Sage Mullins, for critiquing my novel and helping me nail my blurb.

Of course, there are far too many other writers and readers

ACKNOWLEDGMENTS

who have critiqued my book, first chapter, or blurb to mention here, but I wanted to thank all of you as well for your feedback. Your work has helped grow this teenager's crazy writing into a real novel, and I can't thank you enough for that.

On the artistic side, I wanted to give a huge thank you to Wickard for designing this book's cover. I fell in love with your drawing style as soon as I saw your detailed character designs and beautiful fantasy scenes. You definitely didn't disappoint and were incredibly patient and kind throughout the entire process. If anyone reading this is looking for a wonderful cover designer, I highly recommend him!

Additionally, I wanted to thank my editor Alexandra Ott for your detailed edit letter and proofreader McKenna for your eagle eyes in spotting typos. Alexandra's comparisons of my book's plot structure to T.V. shows and movies helped me think of novel plots in a completely different light. Plus, her willingness to respond to my extra questions about future revisions helped ensure that I made the correct edits to my novel. As for McKenna, she definitely saved me from using the British spelling of gray on multiple occasions and caught a lot of typos. I'm incredibly grateful for both of these women's work to make my book the best it could be.

Lastly, I have to thank God for giving me this incredible opportunity to share my writing with the world and being there for me in my darkest times. And to you reader for taking a chance on my book, I hope you liked reading it as much as I did writing it.

About the Author

A.y. Johlin is a Christian teen author currently living in Baltimore, Maryland. When not writing she loves spending time with her little sister, building robots, and, of course, reading books.

You can connect with me on:
🌐 https://ayjohlin.wixsite.com/mysite

Made in the USA
Las Vegas, NV
13 December 2022